"Her Unexpected Gift"

Bulbs, Blossoms and Bouquets #10

By Laura Ann

This is a work of fiction. Similarities to real people, places, or events are entirely coincidental.

HER UNEXPECTED GIFT

First edition. January 31, 2022.

Copyright © 2022 Laura Ann.

Written by Laura Ann.

DEDICATION

To my Oldest Sister.
Thank you for being so dedicated.
Your help with my work is immeasurable.
I'm so glad we're family.

ACKNOWLEDGEMENTS

No author works alone. Thank you, Tami.
You make it Christmas every time
I get a new cover. And thank you to my Beta Team.
Truly, your help with my stories is immeasurable.

NEWSLETTER

You can get a FREE book by joining my Reading Family!
Every week we share stories, sales and good old fun.
Join us at lauraannbooks.com

PROLOGUE
NOVEMBER

Jude sucked down the last of his protein shake and set the glass on the counter a little harder than was absolutely necessary. He winced at the sound and forced himself to carefully let go. The last thing he needed was a broken glass at the moment.

Grumbling to himself, he picked up the mail off his small breakfast bar and walked to the couch, dropping onto it as he thumbed through the collection of bills and advertisements. Just as he found a card shaped one that looked interesting, his phone buzzed.

Are you ever going to forgive me? I've got a seat at Thanksgiving with your name on it.

Jude dropped the phone as if it had burned him, then snorted in disgust at himself. Why was he still letting Elania get to him? He'd known her for years. They'd been in the same physical therapy program at college and to his current frustration, it had taken no time at all for Jude to fall head over heels in love with her.

Too bad she never felt the same.

After two dates that Jude thought had gone well, Elania had stated that he was a wonderful friend, but could never be anything more.

Not willing to accept defeat, Jude had tortured himself by sticking around, being the exact friend she needed, all until four months ago when she married someone else. He convinced himself that he probably could have handled the situation, moved on, if she hadn't gone about it by lying to him. Lying was something he couldn't forget and struggled to forgive.

He knew it was time to move on, but it had been harder than he'd expected, especially since Elania still called on him as if nothing had ever passed between them, as shown in her Thanksgiving invitation just now. As if he could just forget being treated as less than dirt.

Jude blew out a breath and scrubbed his hands down his face. He was tired. Tired of fighting to hold onto his righteous indignation, tired of being a third wheel with all his friends, and tired of being alone.

His eye caught the envelope he'd seen before Elania's text. Grabbing it, he tore it open. "You've got to be kidding me." He groaned.

Where Elania had been his best female friend, Jude was also close with Grayson Cordova. World renowned actor and director. Jude had been lucky enough several years ago to get the job of being Gray's personal physical therapist. Gray was an action movie star and Jude had helped keep the actor's body in tip top shape.

During that time, they had become close and Jude had been with Gray when he'd gotten hurt on set, and spent time up in Oregon recovering. Jude had also been there as Gray fell in love with a beautiful woman who lived up in Seaside Bay and the two had eventually gotten married.

Jude was happy for his friends, he really was! He couldn't even begrudge Elania her happiness. But where Elania had driven a wedge between them with her deceit, Grayson was quickly putting one between them by allowing his wife Brook to use every excuse in the book to set Jude up with single women. He was lonely, but he wasn't *that* lonely.

Jude's phone rang and he almost let it go to voicemail, but at the last minute he grabbed it. "Hey man," Jude answered.

"Jude the Dude," Carson, Grayson's younger brother, quipped. "What's up?"

Jude sighed. He knew that Carson only called him that to get a reaction. The lawyer enjoyed poking his friends a little too much.

"Really? You're over thirty years old now. Don't you think the dumb nicknames have gotten a little old?"

Carson chuckled. "Ticking you off never gets old," he responded.

"You're impossible," Jude grumbled. "Did you have a point for this call?"

"Did you get today's mail?"

"You too, huh?" Jude said. "I was just looking at the invite and deciding how to politely decline."

"What?" Carson cried. "You can't decline!"

"Why not?"

"Because then I'll be left without a wingman!" Carson explained.

"You're a grown man," Jude said. "I have no doubt you can handle it. Besides, aren't you friends with a lot of Brook's buddies up in Seaside Bay?"

"Aren't you?" Carson shot back.

"I really only got to know Brook while I was there," Jude said. "Though I met the rest once at a bonfire...and at the wedding. They're all nice."

"They are, but they're also all very married."

"Why do you think I was trying to get out of it?" Jude said with a laugh that held little humor. "Like I want to walk around Gray's coastal mansion for a week being a third wheel to every person I meet. Or giving Brook a chance to set me up."

"Which is exactly why you need to come." Carson groaned. "Otherwise, I'm the one walking around like that."

"Yeah, but you're family."

"Which is why *I* can't say no. Gray won't let me," Carson argued.

Jude sighed. "Car, I really don't want to go."

"Me either," Carson grumbled. "Please...I'm begging. Don't leave me alone like this."

"I have to work..." Jude hedged. He could feel himself starting to cave and he didn't like it. He really didn't think he could handle being around so many happy couples while his own heart refused to mend. Call it girly, call it wimpy, but every man went through a rough patch once in a while, and this was Jude's.

"I'll pay you twice your normal salary."

Jude perked up. "Really?"

"Yep. Scout's honor."

"I didn't even know you were a Scout, but I just might take you up on that. I might need to get a new car, so if you richy lawyer types are passing out money just for spending time with friends, then that might be a good deal. Torture. But a good deal." The words were said in a teasing way, but they were also true. Jude wasn't starving, but he wasn't rolling in it like most of the Cordovas. A boost in his paycheck just might be enough to make up for any emotional turmoil he'd experience while in Oregon.

"And people say money doesn't talk."

"It doesn't," Jude replied. "We just let it lead us by the nose." He huffed. "All right. I'll come, but you have to promise not to throw me under the bus."

"Scout's honor," Carson said for the second time.

"Again, I have no idea if you were a Scout."

"I plead the fifth," Carson answered and Jude could hear the smile on his face.

"You would." Jude took a deep breath. "Fine. I'll confirm. But if I regret this, then next time you ask me to work on your back, I'm totally going to throw something out of alignment."

"So noted." There was a slight pause. "We've only got three weeks. Better let your boss know."

"Yeah, yeah. I'll make sure things are fine on my end. You just worry about getting your own butt there." Jude had a lot of vacation time owed him. It sounded like now was the time to use it.

"Yes sir!" Carson barked like a military sergeant. "I owe you one!"

"You owe me a new car!" Jude called out before the line went dead. He dropped the phone and shook his head with a long sigh. "What have I gotten myself into now?"

CHAPTER 1

Ruth stiffened her spine, bit her lip, clenched her nails against her fist...anything to hold back the tears, but there was nothing for it. They poured down her cheeks, causing her throat to close up and making speaking nearly impossible.

"Thank you," she said hoarsely. "Thank you, thank you, thank you."

"We're so happy for you, Ruth," the deep voice on the other end of the line said. "The whole office has been rooting for you! Congratulations!"

Ruth nodded, her trembling hand covering her mouth. "I know," she said. "You've all been so wonderful!" A sob broke through and she bent over, trying to breathe.

"I'm going to let you go," the doctor said. "But feel free to come back and visit any time."

Laughter bubbled through the tears. "I think I've seen more of you and your staff in the last few years than I have my own family," Ruth joked.

"I wish I could argue, but that's probably the truth," Dr. Stanley said with another laugh. "Anyway. Again, congrats. I'll see you again in six months for a follow up, but otherwise, go. Enjoy! Do something fun!"

Ruth ended the conversation and slowly set her phone down on the coffee table. It was a good thing she was already on the couch, or her knees might have given out. After years of diagnoses, treatments, illness and tests...she was finally free.

Ruth was officially a breast cancer survivor.

She wiped her tears and slid a hand along her bald head. She might have come out the victor, but looking in the mirror was a stark reminder that cancer had left a large amount of damage in its wake. Ruth studied the back of her hands, noting the sallow skin and blue veins that could be easily seen. She had lost so much weight during her treatments, she struggled to find clothes that fit.

"But I won," she whispered, hiccuping another sob. "We did it!" Her smile shook and she finally covered her face with her hands, letting the emotions take their toll. There was nothing for it but to ride the wave.

For years Ruth had pretended it didn't matter. She'd had down moments, like all people, but for the most part, she had been determined to take control where she could. She couldn't control the cells in her body, but she could control her attitude.

Cancer had stolen her hair, her health, and her carefree college years, but it hadn't taken her smile.

She needed to share this. Grandma Nan would be wondering what was going on. It had been on the calendar for days that this was when the results would get back and Ruth knew if she didn't call her closest living relative, Grandma would hunt her down.

Her fingers still shook as she picked her cell back up and punched in the name she wanted. One ring was all it took for Grandma to get on the line.

"Well?"

"Hello to you too," Ruth said, her voice still slightly hoarse from her crying.

"Don't you hello me," Grandma Nan snapped. "I'm too old for these shenanigans! Give it to me straight. We can handle it."

Ruth smiled and chuckled lightly at the use of "we". In Grandma's case, she was referring to herself and her quilting club. Grandma lived in a small town on the Oregon coast called Seaside Bay and nothing went on in anyone's family that everyone else didn't know about, largely due to the elderly population of women just like Grandma Nan.

Still, Ruth couldn't be upset. She'd received enough lap quilts, afghans, and homemade cookies during her sick time that no one could be mad about a group of bored older women using her as the focus of their time and energy.

"It's gone."

There was silence on the other side of the line.

"Grandma? Did you hear me?"

"Praise be," came the murmured reply. "Are they sure? Really sure? They're not going to come back and say they misread the numbers?"

Ruth shook her head, then cleared her throat. "No. It was triple checked, according to Dr. Stanley. It's not a mistake." She swallowed hard. "I'm cancer free."

Grandma Nan wasn't usually a very emotional person, but when Ruth could hear crying on the other end of the line, she knew her grandmother had been holding it back for Ruth's sake. "They aren't going to believe this," Grandma Nan said. "They just aren't going to believe it."

Ruth wiped her own eyes again and settled more comfortably on the couch. "Our hard work paid off."

"It's a miracle and don't you forget it," Grandma Nan argued, getting herself back under control. "Now...when are you coming back?"

Ruth opened her mouth then shut it. "Coming back?"

"If you think I'm going to let you continue to live in the dirty city now that you don't have to, you better think again," Grandma retorted. "What you need is good clean air and enough homemade bread to put some meat back on those bones." Her voice dropped and the love that Ruth had experienced during the last five years was clearly audible. "Come home, Sweet Pea. Let us take care of you until you get back on your feet, huh?"

Ruth took a deep breath. Her light blue eyes moved around her stark apartment. Really, she had nothing holding her back. No job, no friends that weren't ones she had met during her time in and out of treatment centers and hospitals, and no family.

Grandma Nan was the closest relative, being a few hours south of the Oregon border. Ruth's parents had already passed away, her only sibling didn't even live in the country, and her three cousins were spread all the way from Colorado to Maine.

"I don't want to be a burden," Ruth argued lamely. Truth was, she had no idea what she was going to do. Grandma Nan had already been taking care of her financially since Ruth had been too sick to keep working. The meager inheritance she had received from her parents' deaths was enough to keep Ruth off the street, but not enough to take care of all the bills that came along with fighting for one's life.

"Don't even start," Grandma Nan said bluntly. "It's a privilege to take care of family and while the rest of my grandkids find it fine to gallivant around the country and only say hi once in a blue moon, I won't let you do the same. If it makes you feel any better, you can work at the motel to earn your keep. And when you feel good and ready to spread your wings, we'll figure out just where you want to settle."

Ruth pulled at a string on her pants. "Okay."

"Good girl." Grandma Nan cleared her throat. "You stay tight and I'll send Cooper or someone to come get you."

"No. No way, Grandma," Ruth argued. "I can get myself there."

"Not unless you've put on twenty pounds of muscle since I last visited," Grandma Nan pressed.

"I'll have you know I've gained five pounds in the last two weeks," Ruth said proudly. Now that the treatments had ended, her appetite was slowly coming back and Ruth was excited to look like a normal person again. Maybe by Christmas she wouldn't be quite so sickly.

"Cooper and Captain Ken will come," Grandma Nan said with confidence. "You just focus on getting better."

Ruth sighed, knowing there was no point in arguing. "Make sure they know I'll pay them for their time."

Ignoring the comment, Grandma Nan went on to make a few more arrangements, and then the phone call ended.

Ruth took a minute to sit and just meditate on everything that had happened in the last half-hour. She was free. Free from cancer, free from hospitals, and soon, she'd be free from any reminders as well. Grandma Nan was right. Getting out of Seattle would do wonders for Ruth's spirits and would be a great boost to her health. And with the holidays coming up quickly, there was no better time to be with family.

A COLD WIND SLAPPED Jude in the face as he and Carson exited the airport. Pulling up his collar, he ducked his head and hurried toward the parking lot number they'd been given.

As they got closer, Jude whistled low. "This thing is sleek," Jude said, walking around the car.

"Yeah. Merry Christmas to me," Carson said with a grin.

It only took a few minutes for the men to get on the road. A couple of hours of driving lay in their future and Jude wasn't in a hurry. Arriving in Seaside Bay would only bring on the inevitable Third Wheel Syndrome, and despite the paycheck he would be collecting at the end of this, it wasn't something Jude was looking forward to.

An hour into their trip, Carson's phone buzzed.

"Don't you dare look at that," Jude warned. "No texting and driving."

"Then you see who it is," Carson retorted.

"Aren't you afraid I'll see something from a case I shouldn't?" Jude asked, picking up Carson's phone. With Carson being a lawyer, Jude was semi-afraid he'd read something he couldn't forget.

Carson scoffed. "Uh, no. We don't just leave messages like that out in the open. If there's something dire, they'll ask me to call. But just see if it's Gray or Brook. I'd hate for them to change plans just as we were getting into town."

Jude grinned. "Oh, ho! Not a case at all." Apparently, Carson had been keeping secrets! Jude smiled, but the revelation was just another stab in his already bruised heart.

Carson frowned. "What? Who was it?"

"You never said you were dating anyone," Jude pressed.

Carson gave him a look. "I'm not."

Jude's smile fell. "Really? You're not dating her?" That's not what it looked like according to the text.

"Who in the world are you talking about?" Carson demanded.

"And I quote," Jude said, holding up the phone, "Car. I miss you already. Be sure and let me know when you land."

"What the—?" Carson shook his head. "Who wrote that?"

"Emme?" Jude responded. It came out as more of a question than a response.

Carson rolled his eyes. "You've got to be kidding me," he grumbled.

"So, not a girlfriend then."

Carson shook his head and rested his elbow against the door. "Definitely not. She's my neighbor and only interested in me as a means to an end."

"Let me guess," Jude said wryly. "You can get her closer to Grayson." Since he worked for Grayson, Jude absolutely knew what Carson was complaining about, though he assumed Gray's brother received that kind of attention much more than Jude did. The fact that Jude was Gray's physical therapist wasn't as widely known.

Carson tapped the side of his nose. "Exactly."

Jude sighed and shook his head. "Women are crazy."

"That one is," Carson grumbled. "I barely even speak to her. I'm not sure how she even knew I was leaving." He pointed to a sign for Seaside. "Winner, winner, chicken dinner!"

"Speaking of...I'm starving," Jude said. His stomach felt as if it was going to eat itself. Apparently, he should have prepped himself with more than a small bag of airplane pretzels.

"Me too, but Brook'll probably skin us alive if we eat first."

"What she doesn't know won't hurt her," Jude said in an enticing manner.

Carso glanced over and raised an eyebrow. "Are you thinking what I'm thinking?"

"They can't be closed yet, right?" Jude let a slow smile creep across his face.

Carson pursed his lips and shook his head. "I wouldn't think so."

Jude rubbed his hands together. "I haven't had one of Jack's cookies since last year." Just the thought of the sugar, vanilla, and chocolate was enough to make Jude salivate. Jack made the best cookies on the planet and Brook was friends with Jack and his wife, so Jude had easy access whenever he was in Oregon.

"And Brook can't blame us if we accidentally filled up on airplane pretzels, right?"

Jude laughed. "Nope. And she wouldn't anyways. She's too nice."

"Which we are going to take full advantage of," Carson said as he took the off ramp. "Cookies Up! Here we come!"

It took another forty-five minutes for the men to arrive in front of a pink and white striped awning. As if on cue, Jude's stomach growled.

"Looks like we got here just in time," Carson said with a laugh.

Jude grumbled but got out of the car and hurried inside. The air was wet and windy and a stark change from his California roots.

Once inside, Jude shook himself like a dog before sucking in a deep breath of sweet baked goods.

"Well, look what the cat dragged in," a feminine voice with a Southern accent drawled.

Jude turned and smiled at the petite blonde. Her grin was a welcome sight, and her large stomach was a reminder of everything Jude was missing in life. "Caro, Caro, Caro," Jude teased. He shook his head. "It looks like you're eating for two these days."

Caro's smirk fell. "I don't understand." She blinked her large blue eyes.

"Uh…" Jude's jaw dropped and he turned to Carson for help. "I mean, you're…" Jude motioned around his stomach. "You know…"

"I know…what?" Caro tilted her head to the side. "I don't get it." She paused, then gasped, one hand going to her stomach. "Are you saying I'm fat?"

Jude put his hands in the air and backed up. "Carson said it first."

Carson barked out a laugh. "Smooth. Real smooth." He turned to Caro. "You're as beautiful as always, Caro. There's just more of you to love."

Caro laughed so hard her stomach shook. "You should see your face," she said to Jude.

Jude shook his head. "You're mean." Even with her teasing, however, he couldn't help but smile. Caro wasn't shy, that was for sure, and anyone was fair game to her sassy attitude. "Just for that I think you owe me a cookie."

Caro fluffed her hair. "That's Jack's department."

"Speaking of…" Jack said, obviously having heard his wife's last statement as he came into the storefront from the kitchen area. Jack came around the counter, hand out. "Carson! Jude! Good to see you both!"

Jude shook the cookie maker's hand. "I've been going through withdrawals," he joked. "Think you can help with that?"

Jack laughed. "I'm pretty sure we can handle it." He moved back behind the counter, kissing Caro's temple as he went. "Just last month I came out with one called Death by Chocolate," Jack continued. "Wanna give it a whirl?"

"I won't even ask why you needed so much chocolate," Carson snickered.

"Watch it," Caro said, pointing a manicured finger at him. "Jack does the baking, but I still wear the pants around here."

Jack looked at Caro's skirt and raised an eyebrow.

Caro rolled her eyes. "Get them their cookies and then get outta here," she snapped.

Jude watched the interaction with a mixture of humor and longing. His mind immediately went back to Elania. He'd once had that kind of relationship with her...minus the kissing, of course.

NO! he shouted in his mind. It was time to let her go. Elania was a married woman, had been for four months, and she was happy as a clam and didn't think him worthy of speaking the truth to. She'd used him. Their friendship was over.

Slapping a silly smile on his face, he stepped up to the counter and joined the conversation. It wasn't a perfect solution, but right now it was all he had.

CHAPTER 2

"I think you're all set," Ruth said with a smile. She handed the room key to the couple. "Thanks for choosing us and be sure to let me know if I can make your stay any more comfortable."

The man nodded and ushered his wife away, heading down the hall to their room.

"You're a natural," Grandma Nan said from behind her.

Ruth spun. "Grandma! You startled me!"

Grandma Nan waved away the exclamation. "You're too young to be startled."

"No...I'm too young to *die* from being startled," Ruth argued. "But I can definitely be startled."

Grandma Nan snorted and settled onto a stool. "I was saying that you're a natural with the customers."

Ruth smiled and relaxed against the counter. "I have to admit, I like it. I never thought I would say that, but it's so nice to be able to talk to people, find out where they're from, what they came to Seaside for... It's all really interesting."

"Sounds like you're going to write a book," Grandma Nan muttered with a grin.

"No, but if I did, this kind of job would be perfect for giving me character ideas." Ruth straightened the desk, setting it up just the way she liked it. She was feeling so much better since she'd arrived a month ago. In fact, she had eaten her weight in pie on Thanksgiving just a few days ago and had fallen asleep in a food coma. It was an experience Ruth had missed, and she didn't regret the caloric intake at all.

"So you're just going to come in here and take over...is that it?" Grandma Nan pursed her lips in a pout. "After all I've done..."

Ruth laughed, knowing her grandmother was teasing. "No one can take over for you," she said, walking over to hug her elderly relative. "The world wouldn't be the same if Grandma Nan wasn't running it."

Grandma huffed, but gave into the hug. Ruth knew her grandmother enjoyed playing the role of crotchety, old woman, but the truth was, she had a heart of gold. The entire town knew it. "Oh, here we go."

Ruth leaned back with a frown. "What?"

Grandma Nan pointed to the glass doorway. "Every year that old geezer comes," she said in a whisper.

Grandma Nan was pointing to an older gentleman, who was wearing a collared shirt tucked into slacks. A fedora was on his head and he was driving a pristine Cadillac in baby blue.

Ruth whistled. "Wow. That car is gorgeous."

"The car is, but the man is not," Grandma Nan snapped. "I don't even know why he comes, but he does it every year. And every year he spends the entire time complaining about everything and everybody."

Ruth's frown deepened. "What a sad life," she said softly. "I wonder why."

Grandma Nan rolled her eyes. "Who cares. With you here, this time I won't have to deal with him." She stood and patted Ruth on the shoulder. "Good luck." Without another word, Grandma Nan disappeared into the back room.

Ruth watched the man as he locked the car and rolled the suitcase to the door. His movements were precise, if a little stiff. Grandma Nan's description wasn't very flattering and it made Ruth curious if he was difficult as her grandmother said.

The bell jangled as the man pulled it open and came inside. He grumbled as he approached the desk. "Your bills would be better if you turned down this infernal heat."

Ruth bit back a laugh. Yep. Grandma Nan was right on. "Thanks for the suggestion," Ruth said politely. "We'll keep it in mind next time I work with the thermostat."

The small man glared and slapped his wallet on the counter and waited.

Ruth kept her smile and waited as well.

The man's eyes narrowed even further. "Aren't you going to check me in?"

"I'm afraid I don't know your name," Ruth said cheerfully.

"Harry Portman."

"Nice to meet you, Mr. Portman," Ruth said as she turned to the computer. "I can see your reservation right here." She glanced back at his scowling face. He was a fairly handsome man, or at least he would be if he wasn't glaring at her so hard. His hair was mostly white, but had been combed nicely under his hat, which had been set on the counter after he stepped inside. His clothes were neat and clean and pressed well. He obviously groomed himself immaculately and Ruth couldn't help but think that if he would simply smile a little, he would be surrounded by women his age looking for companionship.

He didn't budge.

Turning back to the computer, Ruth went through all the details. "I can see that you're staying in the same room you were in last year," she said, ignoring his grunt. "Do you need a reminder of how to get there?"

Mr. Portman snatched his wallet off the counter, grabbed the key and his hat, then pulled his luggage across the room. "I'm perfectly capable," he ground out.

"Enjoy your stay," Ruth called after him. "Please let me know if there's anything I can do to help make it better." Her smile widened as she heard him mutter under his breath again. The man was a true curmudgeon. Ruth had only ever read about those in books, but now she was seeing one in real life.

Her mind was whirling as she watched his back disappear. Why was he so angry all the time? Did he enjoy being rude? Had he ever been married? Was he left with a broken heart after his wife died? Or did they divorce? Why did he come stay at the motel every year?

"Figure it out yet?"

Ruth spun, her breath leaving her chest yet again at Granda Nan's reappearance. "You're going to take ten years off my life if you don't stop that," Ruth scolded, patting her wig to make sure it had stayed in place.

She knew she shouldn't be ashamed of her bald head. Being a survivor was a mark of pride, but at only twenty-five years old, Ruth found that deep down, she still had a little vanity inside her. And she couldn't quite bring herself to meet the public without a wig on. The wig was the one thing Ruth had splurged on after leaving Seattle. It had been custom made for her and was fitted to her head in a way that only someone who knew what to look for could see it wasn't her own hair. Only a hard yank or hurricane-style winds could pull it from her head, but Ruth found herself constantly checking on it anyway.

Grandma Nan's eyes darted to Ruth's hair, then away, as if wanting to say something, but letting it go instead. Ruth was grateful.

"Have you figured out his story yet?" Grandma Nan pressed.

Ruth shook her head. "No. Should I have?"

"Well, the way you were staring at his back made me think you could read his mind."

Ruth laughed. "I was just curious. If he hates it so much, why does he come here? I also noticed he has an open reservation. Just how long does he stay?"

Grandma Nan shrugged and tugged on her ear lobe. "No saying. I've had him here until just after New Year's, and as long as Valentine's Day."

"Wow. And he never visits anyone? Just stays here?"

Grandma Nan nodded. "No one in town seems to know why. We all know his face, but no one can get close enough to the pit bull to know the man."

Ruth looked at the hallway again. "Huh. You know...I feel sorry for him."

Grandma Nan patted her shoulder again. "Feel sorry all you want, but if I were you, I'd steer clear. Mr. Portman seems determined to blacken everything in his path."

JUDE WATCHED ALL THE smiling faces as he shoveled pancakes in his mouth. He was starving this morning, which was funny considering how much food he had been consuming since arriving two days ago. Brook made sure there was a buffet available at all hours of the day and Jude had enjoyed every bit of it, but it would be smart to have a little more self-control or he'd go home twenty pounds heavier than he arrived.

The biggest problem was the fact that every time they sat down to eat, he was surrounded by happy, smiling couples. While that shouldn't be a big deal, Jude was quickly realizing it was possible to be surrounded by people and yet be utterly alone.

Instead of coming just for the week of the party, Carson had convinced Jude to join him a week early, so they could enjoy time with Gray and Brook without the pressure of all the activities.

The plan wasn't working out quite as well as Carson had hoped, however, since there seemed to be friends at every single meal. Brook hadn't been in Seaside for quite a while and her friends were dropping by constantly in order to spend time with her before she and Grayson left after the New Year.

Next week would be the official start of the week-long party and Jude knew all the chaos would only double.

He wasn't sure if he could handle it.

"I'm heading out to go fishing," Carson announced from Jude's left. "Did you want to come?"

Jude's eyes widened. "It's freezing out there. Are you serious?"

Carson shrugged and took a swallow of orange juice. "It's better than sitting around here with all the newlyweds."

Jude went back to eating, considering the comment. It was true. Sitting around the house with all the couples stunk. But did he really want to go out on the water and turn himself into frozen chum? Jude shook his head. "I'll figure something else out. It's too cold out there."

"Careful, your Cali is showing again," Carson teased.

Jude nodded. "I know, but seriously. How do people live in this kind of weather? It's wet and cold. All. The. Time."

Carson snickered. "I guess they get used to it. Just like you got used to being warm."

Jude gave a dramatic shiver. "Have fun. Just leave me out of it."

Carson grinned. "What are you going to do, then?"

Jude chewed on a bite and thought about it. He really wasn't sure. "I'll figure it out," he finally responded.

"If you say so," Carson said doubtfully.

Jude nodded. "Yeah. Maybe I'll see if Gray wants to play hooky or something, but still...you're not going to get me on that boat."

"The boat will be worth it if it keeps Brook off my back," Carson grumbled.

Jude frowned. "What?"

Carson glanced sideways. "She's playing matchmaker."

"Oooh." Jude winced. "Sorry." Shoot. Brook had done that to Jude a few times back in California. Was she going to meddle during his visit now? Jude hoped not.

"I mean, I guess on one hand that means she loves me, but on the other, I really, *really*, don't want to take some Grayson hand-me-downs just because Brook thinks they're nice."

"Maybe they aren't all hand-me-downs," Jude offered weakly. He had to admit that he felt the same way as Carson. Jude wanted nothing to do with being set up, no matter how sweet the girl. Brook was a wonderful woman and was perfect for Grayson, but that didn't mean she knew the kind of person that Jude wanted...or needed.

Carson shook his head. "You don't really believe that, do you?"

Jude made a face. "No," he admitted.

"Exactly." Carson took another large bite. "I want to find someone on my own terms. No one else's."

Jude poked at his sausage, feeling worse than ever. Even Carson, who had dragged Jude along to be a wingman, was ditching him. True, Jude could go fishing with them, but there was nothing about that that sounded enjoyable. Cold, wet, and rocking boats? No, thanks.

He sighed, his appetite gone. Why couldn't he seem to catch a break? He wasn't such a bad guy...was he? He tried to be nice, gave to charity when he could, volunteered in his community, supported best friends who left him in the dust...

Nope. Once again, Jude had to forcefully push thoughts of Elania out of his head. She was no longer in his life. That was all that mattered. He needed to stop mourning something that was over.

"You never did say what you're going to do," Carson pressed.

Jude shook his head. "I don't know. Maybe I'll walk down Main and do some window shopping."

Carson chuckled. "You sound like a woman."

"Would it be better if I said I was people-watching?" Jude asked with a sarcastic grin.

"No. That only makes it worse."

Jude punched Carson's shoulder. "So, I like to relax differently than you. Can you blame me? You go get wet and frozen. I'll walk around where I can grab hot chocolate any time I feel like it."

"You do you," Carson joked. He wiped his mouth. "And on that note, I'm off."

"What?" Brook called from farther down the table. "You're leaving already?"

Carson nodded. "Yeah. I've got a date with a ship captain."

Grayson snorted and nearly blew his orange juice across the table.

Brook frowned as she slapped her husband on the back. "You're going out with Felix?"

Carson stood and grabbed his plate. "Yeah. We're gonna see what we can catch."

"In this weather?" Brook argued. "Don't you want to stick around?" She smiled enticingly. "I'm sure I'll have some friends stop by. You can meet them."

"I know all the important ones," Carson said breezily, moving past the table and into the kitchen. He poked his head back in. "Have a good day, folks!"

Jude stiffened when Brook's gaze turned his way.

"Are you ditching us too?" she asked.

Jude swallowed, the pancakes suddenly feeling like lead in his stomach. "I don't know. Should I?"

Once again, Grayson nearly lost what was in his mouth. "Could you two keep the jokes to a minimum?" the actor grumbled, wiping his face. "Or at least wait until I've swallowed?"

Brook folded her arms over her chest and huffed. "I thought you two came up early so you could hang around with us?"

Jude toyed with his fork. "What did you have in mind?"

Brook beamed. "Maybe we could invite a few people over for lunch?"

"And how many single women are you planning to invite to this?"

Brook's smile fell and she glared. "Why does that matter?"

Jude pursed his lips and shrugged. "Because that might make a difference as to whether or not I can make it."

Grayson chuckled. "Give up, hon. No one wants to be set up."

Brook rolled her eyes. "You men are impossible. It's no wonder you're not married yet."

The teasing stung Jude harder than it should have. If he'd had his way, he would be married, but no one knew that and he planned to keep it that way.

"I have a meeting with the caterer anyway," Brook said on a sigh. "So if you don't mind entertaining yourself, maybe we can just chill today."

"Sounds good." Jude stood. "And thank you for the breakfast." He put his dishes in the sink and went to grab his coat. Maybe he would take that walk down Main. It couldn't hurt and if he managed to find something to occupy his time, then that would only be in his favor.

Time to work off those calories he'd been consuming.

CHAPTER 3

"Bye, Mr. Portman!" Ruth said, waving as he walked out the front door. "Enjoy your walk!"

The older man grunted and didn't bother turning back. Every couple of hours, Mr. Portman would walk out the front door, ignoring Ruth's calls. Each time, Ruth would make sure she was smiling her best and chuckle when the door closed. She was probably driving him crazy, but the more Ruth saw him, the more she was determined to bring a little light into the old man's life.

He walked around with a dour look all day and that couldn't be good for anyone's health. Ruth was positive that part of the reason she was actually able to beat cancer was because she never let herself let go of hope, and it seemed like Mr. Portman could use a good shot of it.

"He's going to turn around one of these times and let you have it," Grandma Nan said as she came in from the back room.

Ruth laughed. "Wouldn't that be something?" She leaned onto the counter, her chin in her hand. "I wonder if he bites his tongue as he leaves in order to keep from snapping at me."

It was Grandma Nan's turn to laugh. "If he does, I'll bet he's bitten the tip clean off by now."

The bell went off and Ruth looked to the door, smiling when she recognized one of her grandmother's friends. "Mrs. Swallows! How nice to see you today."

The older woman shuffled in, carrying a cloth-covered tray. "Ruth! You're just as radiant as ever!"

Ruth hurried around the counter, not bothering to argue with the sweet fib. "Let me take that for you."

Mrs. Swallows patted Ruth's cheek. "Always so helpful. Bless your heart." They finished walking to the counter together and Ruth set the tray down. "It's for you," Mrs. Swallows said, pointing to the tray.

Ruth's drawn-on eyebrows shot up. "What?"

Mrs. Swallows looked her up and down, tsking her tongue. "You're still too skinny," she scolded. With a secretive grin, the visitor pulled back the cloth. "I brought you something to put a little meat on those bones." She beamed as she presented a pie that smelled of pumpkin, spice, and heaven.

"Mrs. Swallows," Ruth said softly. "You shouldn't have!"

Mrs. Swallows waved away her objections. "I had one in the freezer from Thanksgiving and I was thinking to myself this morning that you could use a little sweetness."

"If we could find her a man, she'd have enough sweetness in her life," Grandma Nan quipped.

Ruth rolled her eyes. "Grandma, I don't need a man." The key word being *need*. Want? Now that was a totally different matter. Ruth had settled in well in Seaside Bay. She was happy, she was getting healthier, and her body recovered a little more each day. There was very little she could ask for, but if she did, she had to admit her grandmother was right. Ruth would love to meet a companion.

She adored her grandmother and all her quilting club buddies, but sometimes it would be nice to spend time with someone who was younger than sixty-five.

"Well, until she finds a man, she can make do with a pie," Mrs. Swallows stated firmly. "Now." She lifted the tray and gave it to Ruth again. "Take this in the back and fill up that tiny stomach of yours."

Ruth grinned. "I don't think I can eat this whole thing, Mrs. Swallows. Won't you join me?"

Mrs. Swallows shook her head. "No, thank you. I'm going to sit next to your grandmother and catch up for a while."

Ruth could read between the lines. The women were planning a gossip session and Ruth wasn't invited. In fact, Ruth was probably one of the main topics. With a beleaguered sigh, Ruth playfully shook her head. "If I must, I must," she teased. Walking back around the counter, she stepped up to her grandmother. "I'll see you in a bit. Thanks for the break."

"Don't take too long," Grandma Nan huffed. "Matilda might want to catch up, but I've got work to do."

Ruth held back her laugh. Gossiping was one of Grandma Nan's favorite things. There was no way either of those women were budging from their spots for at least an hour, whether Ruth came back or not.

Snickering quietly under her breath, she headed to the back room and set the tray on the table. The break space was small, but efficient. There was a place to eat, a place to work, and a small set up with a sink and a few dishes. They didn't need much and Grandma Nan had never bothered to update it to something more.

Grabbing one of the plates and a knife, Ruth sat down to enjoy her treat. She knew eventually, she'd have to watch what she was eating, but not yet! Besides, pumpkin was a squash, which meant it was healthy.

Standing up to grab a fork, Ruth hurried back and took a big bite, humming in pleasure. The only thing missing was a big dollop of whipped cream. Cinnamon and nutmeg danced on Ruth's tongue, only to be followed by buttery flakiness from the crust.

"How is it?"

Ruth's head jerked up and she swallowed quickly, smiling at Mrs. Swallows. "Perfection, as always."

The white head bobbed in delight. "Don't be afraid to eat a second piece," she said with a wink.

Ruth gave her a playful salute. "I just might do that."

Laughing, Mrs. Swallows ducked back out to the front.

Ruth polished off the piece she had and was just dishing up another one, when she heard the bell over the door ring. She stood and listened, trying to figure out if Mrs. Swallows had left or if a visitor had arrived.

When she heard a low, masculine voice, Ruth knew they had a visitor. She slowly pushed the door open, trying to see if Grandma needed her help or not. At first, she could only see Grandma Nan standing and talking to whoever had arrived, but Ruth pushed the door a little farther.

There was just something about the voice...

She held in a gasp. Standing on the other side of the counter was a man who appeared to be only a few years older than Ruth. His hair was dark blond, a very similar color to the wig she was wearing, in fact. The hair was windblown and Ruth's fingers twitched. For a reason she couldn't explain, she wanted to straighten it for him.

His skin was smooth, though there was a slight stubble along his jawline that kept drawing her eye.

Ruth blinked when her grandmother said something and the man smiled. It was like the clouds parted and a ray of sunshine came out of the heavens. His smile was glorious and Ruth felt her heart respond.

His eyes darted to the side, catching hers for just a second before he turned and walked down the hall, disappearing to the rooms. Ruth stood still as a statue, completely star-struck. There were only two things on her mind.

Who was that man and when could she see him again?

JUDE WAS BREATHING heavily by the time he got to his room. He unlocked the door and walked inside without ever bothering to turn on the light, before sitting on the edge of the bed.

Blue eyes. The woman had blue eyes that were the color of a bright Caribbean sea.

He'd barely seen her, just a glimpse really before Grandma Nan had handed him his key, but those eyes were imprinted on Jude's mind.

"Who was she?" he mumbled into the dark. He put a hand to his chest. His heart was thumping heavily against his rib cage and Jude could feel it against his fingers. It had been a long time since his body had reacted so dramatically to another person.

Elania had had his attention for so long that Jude had almost forgotten what it was like to feel those first stirrings of attraction. There was nothing subtle about this reaction, however. Instead of a gentle reaction, however, Jude felt as if he'd been smashed over the head with a two by four.

He had come to the Motel on Main to rent a room so he had somewhere to escape when things got too crazy at Gray's. Somewhere he could recharge and not worry about being interrupted. But now, Jude was afraid that every time he showed up, he wouldn't get any rest at all. Those blue eyes...

He shook his head. This was crazy. While he had no idea who that woman was, there was no way Jude would allow himself to go gaga over a stranger. Whoever had been in Grandma Nan's backroom had been lovely, but that was it. Maybe during his time here he would be able to figure out who she was, but it wasn't like Jude was staying in Seaside Bay permanently. There really would be no point in getting to know her.

In just a couple of weeks, he'd head back to the sunny skies of Hollywood and forget all about those wide, soulful eyes that seemed to suck him in like a...

Jude threw himself back on the bed, the mattress squeaking under his weight. "You're an idiot, Jude Lisbon," he grumbled to himself. Throwing an arm over his face, he forced his breathing to slow down.

He wasn't some young teenager seeing a pretty girl for the first time. This was stupid. Maybe what he needed was a run.

Jude jerked upright. That was it. A good, hearty run would work out all that excess energy and help him rid his body of dumb overactive hormones. How could he not have thought of this before?

He stood and turned on a light, grabbed the backpack he had dropped, and pulled out his running gear. It was a good thing he'd thought to bring just a few clothes with him. His plan had been to have something comfortable to wear when he needed to escape, but now it would be helpful for something else.

Stashing his key in the zippered pocket at his hip, Jude headed back outside. Instead of walking through the front way though, he forced his legs to leave via the side entrance.

"It's closer," he told himself, all while a small voice in the back of his head snickered that he was a coward.

The wind bit at his skin and Jude shivered, then shook it off. *I'm not a coward,* he told himself. *Just good at self preservation.*

Putting one foot in front of the other, Jude began to move down the sidewalk. It only took a few minutes for him to find his rhythm. His breath evened out and his feet pounded steadily on the concrete sidewalk.

With every yard he put between him and the motel, he found himself feeling better and better. His reaction to that woman had just been a result of his recent heartache. That was all. It was nothing a good cardio-driven activity couldn't cure. By the time he'd broken a decent sweat, he'd feel much better.

Jude ran from one end of town to the other and even though he was exhausted by the time he arrived back at Grayson's, his head and heart were feeling much improved.

"Dude," Carson exclaimed when Jude came in the door.

Jude wiped his forehead on his shirt sleeve. "How was the fishing?'

Carson shrugged. "Cold."

Jude grinned. "Told ya."

Carson pointed at Jude. "It looks like you found a way to keep warm." He wrinkled his nose. "Just how far did you run?"

Jude thought about it. "I don't know. Probably close to ten miles total."

Carson's eyebrows jumped up his forehead. "What's wrong with you?"

Jude laughed. "Less than there was before the run."

Carson shook his head. "You're nuts. Why in the world would you run that far?"

Jude walked by his friend, slapping his shoulder on the way. "Sometimes you just need to run."

"The question is...from what?" grumbled Carson.

From blue-eyed sirens. "Could be anything," Jude responded. "And in this case, it might be from newlywed happiness."

Carson stilled. "Maybe I'll join you next time."

Jude chuckled and headed toward his room. "I think I'll go take a shower."

"Yeah...everyone thanks you in advance."

Jude chuckled as he walked up the stairs. Considering how soaked his sweatshirt was, Jude would probably thank himself for showering by the time he was done.

The cool water was like heaven on his heated skin and he stayed in a little extra, just enjoying the pressure against his back. When he finally got out and dried off, he was feeling like a new man.

Miss Blue Eyes wasn't going to stop him from enjoying his vacation and spending time with friends. And Elania's disappearing act wasn't going to keep him from moving forward.

Jude opened his door and headed downstairs toward the laughter that echoed through the marble halls. He had friends, he had a good career, Christmas was on its way, and there was an abundance of good food at his fingertips.

Matchmaking attempts aside, who needed anything else?

"Jude!" Grayson called out from his seat on a couch. "Heard you looked like a drowned rat!"

"Hardy, har, har," Jude said sarcastically, giving Carson the stink eye. "Better watch it, Car. One of these days I'll challenge you to a race and take your man card when you lose."

"Oh, ho!" Carson crowed, sitting up straight. "You really think you can take me?"

"You really doubt it?" Jude challenged.

Grayson slapped his knees. "You're on!"

"Wait...what?" Carson asked.

"Shove that table over here," Grayson directed, pulling on a coffee table.

"Why are we doing this?" Jude asked, putting his hands on his hips.

"We're going to see who's the manliest," Grayson said with a grin. He leaned forward and put his elbow on the table, hand up and ready for an arm wrestling partner. "Who's first?"

CHAPTER 4

Ruth reshaped the stack of maps on the counter for the fiftieth time. Today had been the slowest day ever and she was ready to tuck tail and go back to her room for a pint of Cookies 'n' Cream and a good Christmas movie.

She sighed as her eyes darted down the hall once more. Two days ago the most handsome man she had ever seen had checked in, and Ruth hadn't seen him since.

Not once.

It was almost as if she had dreamed the entire encounter. And maybe she had. With another long sigh, Ruth tucked her hair behind her ear. She patted the top, making sure the wig hadn't moved out of place.

Grandma Nan kept giving her grief about her hair, wanting Ruth to just go natural and let everyone know her survivor status, but Ruth just couldn't do it quite yet. And now knowing there was a handsome man walking around somewhere, there was no way Ruth was going to walk around looking like a fuzzy billiard ball.

Her hair had barely started to grow back and Ruth was eager for it to move faster. As soon as it actually covered her head, she was going to get rid of the itchy wigs and just rock something short and pixie-ish, but until then...she would do her best not to frighten the general public.

"Thank heavens for wigs," she murmured to herself as a reminder. Trying to be grateful had been one of the biggest boosts to keeping her spirits going when all seemed lost.

"I think we can do without them, thank you very much," Grandma Nan retorted as she came in the front door.

Ruth gave her a look. "Well, I'm glad we have them. So, don't rain on my parade."

The door opened and a younger woman followed Grandma inside. Her wide smile was warm and Ruth knew immediately she was going to like this newcomer.

"Hi, Welcome to Motel on Main. How can I help you?"

Grandma Nan waved away Ruth's greeting. "This here's Hadlee Mendez. Her husband is Felix...the boat captain?"

Ruth nodded. "Oh, yeah. I've met Felix." Ruth smiled. "Your husband was such a help in moving all my stuff down from Washington. Thanks for sharing him with me."

Hadlee's smile widened. "We're glad he could help." She walked over and held out her hand. "I was off work today and ran into your grandmother at the grocery store. She mentioned you would enjoy meeting a few of the younger people in town."

Ruth rolled her eyes and sent a look at her suspiciously busy grandma. "I'm not a little kid who needs you to find me friends," Ruth said.

Hadlee laughed, drawing Ruth's attention back. "Don't worry," Hadlee said. "She wasn't as pushy as all that. And I know the other ladies would love to get to know you." She held out a card. "We get together for a flower arranging class once a month. I know it's last minute, but it just happens to be tomorrow night. If you'd like to come, I'd be happy to introduce you to everyone."

Ruth took the card and felt her heart squeeze a little at the generous offer. "That's very nice of you, but I don't want to intrude."

"Oh, you're not," Hadlee assured her. "It's a public class and many women from the community come. But sometimes a few of us stay after and enjoy being with those in the less than sixty demographic."

Grandma Nan grunted. "That demographic is the sole reason you young'uns exist," she snapped.

Hadlee laughed again. "And we're grateful to you. But sometimes we also enjoy speaking to people who know what the letters LOL mean."

"Lots of love," Grandma Nan said, putting her hands on her hips. "What else could it mean?"

Ruth snickered. Grandma Nan knew exactly what it meant, and they both knew it, but still... "That's really nice of you. I'll do my best to make it."

"Great!" Hadlee said. She tucked her scarf a little deeper into her coat. "I'll keep an eye out for you." She moved back to the door and waved. "See you then!"

Ruth waved, then turned to her grandma. "What was that all about?"

Grandma Nan opened her eyes in innocence. "What are you talking about?"

"Grandma..."

Grandma Nan rolled her eyes. "She's right, okay? You need to spend your time with someone other than my quilting circle." She walked over to Ruth and cupped her cheek. "You're young. You need young friends. Go. Live a little!" She winked. "And if you find a handsome man, then enjoy that too!"

Ruth rolled her eyes. "Grandma, I'll get out eventually. When I'm ready." Grandma Nan was right. Ruth knew she should get out more, but there was a part of her that was still scared. What if they found out about her cancer and felt bad for her? She didn't want friends who only stuck around out of pity. Or what if they saw her without her wig on? Not everyone would be kind about it.

"Ruth Allen, you're the bravest person I've ever known," Grandma Nan said in a scolding tone. "You took on cancer like it was an annoying flea and you're standing here to tell the tale. But now you're acting like a coward."

Ruth jerked back, hurt at the truth of that statement.

"Those girls are some of the sweetest things to ever grace this tiny town,"Grandma Nan continued. "If you're lucky enough to be friends with them, then you'll have found something special."

Ruth smiled. "I already have something special. I have you and your friends."

"And we'll keep supplying you with pumpkin pie and homemade preserves until you start bursting the seams on those skinny jeans of yours," Grandma Nan assured her. "But you need to live a little. What good was saving your life if you're not going to do anything with it?"

Ruth dropped her eyes to the counter. "You're right," she agreed softly. "But I just don't know what I *should* be doing with it." She wanted everything Grandma Nan was talking about. The friends, the activities, the boyfriend...but somehow, Ruth's ever present hope was failing her in this instance.

She fingered her wig out of habit and Grandma Nan scowled. "You're beautiful," she snapped. "And anyone who doesn't think so ought to be shot."

Ruth shook her head, a small smile playing on her lips. "No shooting, Grandma. But if it makes you feel better, I'll go." She huffed a laugh. "Funny thing is, I've met a few of their husbands, so I suppose it's only right that I finally meet the wives."

"Good girl," Grandma Nan said, patting Ruth on the shoulder. "And if you insist on wearing that old thing, maybe we should go find you a hot pink one or something. That'll really get them talking."

Ruth shook her head. "You're incorrigible."

"I ought to be," Grandma Nan retorted. "I've had enough years of practice."

Ruth snorted through her laughter. "Grandma, don't ever change." She kissed the soft, wrinkly cheek.

Grandma Nan waved her off. "I'm also too old to fall for such flattery."

"I still have two pieces of pie left."

Grandma Nan stilled. "Two pieces?"

Ruth nodded.

"Well, we wouldn't want it to go to waste, now would we?" Grinning, she linked her arm with Ruth and the two of them headed to the back room for a little break.

JUDE WAS ABOUT READY to pull his hair out. He'd taken to running in the afternoons every day, just to get a break from all the holiday madness, but it wasn't enough. He needed some quiet time to recharge and that meant he needed to go back to his hotel room.

But *she* was there.

Or at least, he assumed she was. Truth was, Jude didn't know for sure. He hadn't been back since he'd checked in.

"Scaredy cat," he scolded himself under his breath. He sighed as another burst of laughter came from the kitchen. He should be in there, enjoying the talking and socializing. But instead he was moping like an idiot in the family room by himself.

He leaned his elbows on his knees and scrubbed his hands over his face. "What is wrong with me?" he muttered.

This was not his normal behavior. For the past month, Jude had been sulky, cynical, and anti-social. None of those were words that his friends would normally use to describe him.

But right now, everything was just so...overwhelming. His heart still ached from Elania's betrayal and Jude was having a harder time than he wanted to admit getting over it. The worst of it was, it was becoming less and less about Elania and more and more about feeling blindsided.

Jude still didn't understand how he could have read their situation so wrong. He had thought he loved her. Had thought she might eventually develop feelings for him as well, and then *bam!* She'd used him as a way to get to another man, leaving a trail of lies in her wake.

Jude had never felt so incompetent as he did every time he thought about the situation. He felt like he couldn't trust himself. If he had read Elania so wrong, what was stopping him from reading everyone wrong? Would Carson take off as well? What about Gray? Had Jude only imagined their friendship the same way he'd imagined the feelings between him and Elania?

"Would you get off your butt and get in here?" Carson called from the doorway.

Jude jerked his head toward the sound. "Get in where?"

Carson gave him an unimpressed look. "Where the people are."

Jude took a deep breath and stood up. "Yeah. Guess I should, huh?"

Carson narrowed his eyes. "What's up with you anyway? You keep avoiding the subject every time I ask."

Jude rubbed the back of his neck. "I know and I'm sorry, but..." He squished his lips to the side. "I don't want to talk about it." He moved to walk past Carson, but his friend stopped him.

"Jude...I thought we were friends."

"We are."

"Then what's going on?" Carson slowly shook his head. "You're not yourself."

Jude huffed. "Just give me time, okay? I'll get my head on straight soon enough." A flash of bright, blue eyes shot through his mind and Jude shoved it away. Thinking about another woman was *not* how he was going to get his head on straight, no matter how angelic she appeared. Hadn't he just been thinking about how he couldn't trust himself? Now was not the time to investigate something new when he was still such a mess.

Carson turned and slapped Jude on the back. "Well, there's no better way to do that than with a cup of Brook's eggnog in hand." He leaned in close. "Just drink slowly. It's a little thick."

Jude held back a gag. Eggnog wasn't exactly his drink of choice. "She made it herself?"

Carson widened his eyes and nodded, a slight look of horror on his face. "Yep." They walked into the kitchen. "And it's absolutely delicious!"

"What are you going on about now?" Gray asked, his arms folded over his chest as he leaned back in his seat.

"About how tempting your wife's eggnog is."

Brook beamed and Jude had to hold in a snicker. "It was my great grandma's recipe," she said, jumping to her feet. "Let me get you a glass," she offered Jude.

Jude started to hold up his hand, but Gray's glare made Jude snap his mouth shut. His lips twitched, however, when Caro hid what sounded like a giggle behind a cough.

"You do realize that we drink it all wrong?" Caro asked, spinning her own full glass at the table.

Jude raised an eyebrow.

"It's a Southern drink," Caro continued. "But..." She took a tiny sip. "It's missing a few ingredients."

"Ingredients that pregnant women can't have and none of us drink anyway," Brook said wryly as she handed Jude his cup. She leaned in. "I always thin mine with a bit of soda or nonfat milk," she whispered.

"What?" Carson cried. "You didn't tell me that!"

"Who says you get to know all my secrets?" Brook argued back.

"You mean to tell me I ate that entire glass, all because I love my sister-in-law, and I could have actually had it thin enough to drink like a normal beverage?"

Laughter erupted around the room and Jude couldn't help but chuckle. He eyed the glass and tilted it around a bit. It did seem more like a milkshake than a regular drink. "I think I'll take you up on that bit of genius," he said to Brook, who was now seated next to her husband again. Jude walked toward the counter where he had spotted an open bottle of lemon lime pop.

"Oh, no," Carson insisted. "You have to try it the same way I did."

"Apparently not," Jude shot over his shoulder. He grinned and winked. "Brook likes me better."

"I object!"

"A lawyer would," Caro said sarcastically.

Carson scrubbed a hand through his hair. "This isn't fair. Am I the only one who choked that stuff down in its original form?"

The whole room went silent as everyone looked around at each other, shrugging and answering the question without words.

"Unbelievable," Carson grumbled. He glared at Brook and pointed a finger her way. "You're going down."

"You'll have to get through me first," Grayson said easily, throwing one of his huge arms across the back of Brook's chair. "And judging from the results of our arm wrestling contest the other day, I'm not too concerned."

Carson strode forcefully to the table and sat down across from his brother, throwing his arm up. "Rematch."

Grayson raised an eyebrow. "You can't be serious. You want to be humiliated with an audience this time?"

Jude allowed himself to smile while he poured more than a little pop into his eggnog, thinning down the liquid significantly. He could still hear the good natured arguing going on behind him and for a moment...it felt as if nothing had changed. That he hadn't had his heart ripped out, that he hadn't lost his faith in humanity and his faith in himself. It was just like old times when he hung around the Cordova brothers and enjoyed the banter.

But when he turned around and caught Jack kissing his wife's temple and Brook leaning her head on Grayson's arm, it all came rushing back. Jude was surrounded by people, but all alone, and he didn't know how to fix it.

CHAPTER 5

The bell above the door jangled as Ruth warily pushed her way into the flower shop. She had visited her grandmother numerous times over the years, but not once had Ruth been inside this particular door.

The sweet smell of foliage and petals hit her nose immediately and Ruth closed her eyes to better concentrate on the wonder of it. Grandma Nan had sent flowers to Ruth on a regular basis and they were a personal favorite as far as ways to lift Ruth's spirits. The colors, the smells, the variations in texture and shape. Ruth had loved staring at them when she was feeling sick or had no energy to get up and move.

"You must be Ruth," a low, feminine voice said sweetly.

Ruth turned at the sound and her eyes widened. An absolutely stunning redhead was headed her way with a wide, welcoming smile on her face. "Yes," Ruth replied. "Ruth Allen."

"Grandma Nan's granddaughter, right?" The woman held out her hand and Ruth reciprocated.

"Right."

"You have the most wonderful grandma," the woman gushed. "I think she's basically adopted the entire town."

Ruth chuckled. "Sounds about right. And I'll bet she bosses all of you around like you're family as well."

The woman laughed. "But we love her for it. Oh! I'm Rose, by the way. My husband, Captain Ken Wamsley, helped you move down here."

"Oh my gosh! So nice to meet you, Rose. And thank you for sharing him."

Rose laughed. "Come on in and I'll introduce you around." Rose held out an arm and Ruth walked farther in.

"It's beautiful in here," Ruth said as they walked past a few of the displays.

"Thank you," Rose said sincerely. "Flowers are kinda my thing, if you couldn't tell from my name." She laughed. "My daughter's name is Lilly, so..."

Ruth's smile grew. "That's fantastic."

"I like it." Rose pushed open a door. "This is where we hold the arranging class."

Ruth walked in and felt a bit of her trepidation return. The room was filled with chatting and laughing women. They all seemed to know each other and Ruth felt very much like an outsider. She patted her hair, then immediately threw her hand down, not wanting to draw attention to her wig. She swallowed hard.

A tentative hand landed on her back. "Don't worry," Rose said softly. "Everyone here already loves Grandma Nan. They'll accept you just on that connection alone."

Ruth gave Rose a grateful smile. "Is it that obvious?"

Rose shook her head. "No. But I've been the new person. I know what it's like."

A small blur rushed across the room and grabbed Rose around the legs. "Mama!" the little girl said too loudly.

Ruth studied the darling. She was the spitting image of her mother and was well on her way to being just as stunning. But there was something different about the way she spoke.

"Inside voice," Rose said, her hands moving as she spoke.

Ruth's eyes widened and she studied the little girl's ears, noting a device attached. "Is she deaf?" Ruth asked before she could think better of it.

Rose looked up. "Mostly. But she can hear pretty well with her implants and she reads lips and sign language."

Ruth looked down at the little girl in awe. "That's amazing…"

Rose gave her a funny look. "Thanks."

"Sorry." Ruth shook her head. "I didn't mean for that to sound weird, it's just…she's so young and has already overcome something really big. I think it's wonderful."

As odd as it sounded, seeing little Lilly gave Ruth hope. As far as she knew, this group didn't know her story and Ruth wasn't going to tell them, but they'd obviously already adopted people who were imperfect and had struggles. Maybe, just maybe, they wouldn't mind taking in one more stray.

Rose rubbed her daughter's hair. "Thank you," she said with extra warmth. "We're very proud of her."

"Where's the best chocolate eater this side of the Mississippi?" a voice called out just behind Ruth.

"ME!" Lilly screamed, leaving her mother to dash to a very petite and very pregnant blonde woman.

Rose shook her head. "That's Caro." Rose smiled indulgently as Caro squatted down to hand Lilly a bag of goodies. "She and her husband own the chocolate and cookie store just a few blocks down from your grandmother's motel."

Ruth laughed softly. "And I'm guessing she also spoils your daughter rotten."

"You would be correct," Rose said, followed by a sigh. "But I can't complain too much. She's one of my best friends after all." Rose waved. "Caro! Come over here. I have someone for you to meet."

Caro straightened and waddled over with a grin. "Another victim, huh? Who'd we capture this time?"

"This is Ruth, Grandma Nan's granddaughter."

Caro's eyebrows shot up. "Really? That old coot has a granddaughter?"

Ruth snorted a laugh. "I'd love to see you say that to her face."

"Oh, she does, believe me," Rose drawled. "The two of them go at it like fighting roosters."

Ruth's smile was too wide, but she was enjoying herself. "I'd love to watch."

"You and every other person in Seaside," Caro argued good naturedly. She grinned. "I can't help it if we've both got sass for days. Too much in one room tends to be explosive."

Ruth had no answer for that, but the laughter continued.

"Why don't we get on with the arrangements?" Rose offered. "I'll introduce you to the rest of the women when it's over."

"I appreciate it," Ruth responded, following Rose to a spot at a table.

An hour later, the women were still chatting and laughing as they began filtering through the door to go home.

"Hang around," Caro told Ruth. "We'll introduce you to the gang."

The evening had been so pleasant that Ruth easily agreed and she did her best to remember all the names as they were thrown at her.

"You've already met Rose and me," Caro stated.

"And me!" Hadlee offered with a little wave.

"Hi, Hadlee," Ruth said with a smile.

"And this is Genni, Charli, Mel, Ally, and Brook." Caro winked. "There'll be a test later."

The groans were enough to have the room breaking into laughter.

"Ignore her," Brook said, stepping forward. She held out her hand. "Brook Cordova."

Ruth's eyes widened. "Oh my gosh. You're Grayson Cordova's wife! I saw you on TV when I was..." She bit off the rest of her comment. They didn't need to know it was during chemo treatments. "When I was laying around," Ruth finished lamely.

Caro snorted. "Don't remind us. Having Grayson around changes the whole town."

"Can you blame them?" the woman named Charli asked. Her hand rubbed her own large belly. It seemed several of the women were in the last stages of pregnancy together. "The man has the prettiest eyes I've ever seen."

"I'm telling Bronson," Caro teased.

"Go ahead," Charli argued back. "He already knows."

More laughter and tittering rang through the group. The warmth of it all calmed every nerve that Ruth had been holding onto. What she wouldn't give for a group of friends like this. They were wonderful!

"Ruth?"

She turned to Brook.

"What are you doing next Friday?"

"Uh...nothing, though sometimes I help out at the desk for Grandma."

Brook grinned. "Want to come join our Christmas party? You can meet a real live movie star."

Ruth's smile was wide enough to split her face. "Really?"

"Don't let it go to his head." Caro groaned.

Brook shushed her friend. "It'll send you the details. We'd love to have you."

JUDE STRETCHED HIS arms high above his head, barely reaching the spot where Brook wanted the garland. "Tell me why I'm doing this again?" he whispered to Carson.

Carson snorted. "You'd think Gray would just hire a bunch of people to decorate, but nooo...he had to marry a civilian."

Jude chuckled at Carson's choice of words.

"The kind of person who thinks hard work is good for the soul," Carson continued as his clumsy fingers tied a bow into place. "Isn't that why he got rich in the first place? So he could order people to do his bidding?"

Jude spotted movement out of the corner of his eye and froze. "Car," he said softly, but Carson didn't hear.

"All that money and we still have to work." Carson tsked his tongue and shook his head.

Jude widened his eyes on purpose. "Car!" he hissed.

"What good is money if you don't spend it, huh? Why make your family be slaves when you're perfectly capable of adding to the economic growth of an area by helping out some poor college student."

A throat cleared and Carson finally snapped his mouth shut.

Jude pinched his lips between his teeth.

"She's behind me, isn't she?"

Jude nodded, doing his best to swallow his laughter.

"Ahem," Brook said curtly.

Carson slowly turned around and spread his hands. "Brook! My favorite sister-in-law!"

"I'm your only sister-in-law," she said wryly. Her dark eyebrows shot up. "What's that you were saying about spending our money?"

Even Jude could see the blush on Carson's cheeks. Even his darker skin couldn't hide his embarrassment.

"I didn't say I wanted to spend it," Carson explained, putting a hand to his chest. "But there are starving children at UCLA. They need opportunities to feed themselves."

Jude's laughter couldn't be held back anymore and a loud belly laugh broke through. Even when Brook shot him the evil eye, he couldn't stop it. How someone who was as suave as Carson could constantly put his foot in his mouth was a complete mystery to the physical therapist.

Ask Carson to win over a jury and the job was done before a person could blink. Ask him to woo a woman and the guy was all thumbs, even with people he knew well.

It's not like you have any room to talk, a cynical voice said in the back of Jude's mind, which brought his laughter under control. It was true. He didn't. Jude wasn't exactly the aggressive type, alpha male who always seemed to catch women's attention. Most would probably describe him as the "nice guy", and lately he had really been understanding the saying that nice guys really did finish last.

"I'm just saying that if you've got money, you've also got the obligation to spend it!" Carson defended himself.

Brook pointed a finger at him. "Then spend your own money! The whole point of this was for us to enjoy time together as a family. Why pay someone else to do something we could all work on together?"

"Why not?" Carson shrugged. "Do you know anyone who tells stories about the good ole days when they got to hang mistletoe from every corner of the room?"

Brook threw her head back and groaned. "You're impossible!"

"What'd he do now?" Grayson asked as he sauntered into the room.

"He thinks you should spend a fortune hiring out the decorating, all so you can be in the poor house," Brook stated.

"What?" Carson cried. "Don't put words in my mouth, woman!"

"Don't speak to her that way," Grayson growled.

Jude put a fist to his mouth, holding back more laughter as he watched the scene unfold. Slowly he backed up, only slightly concerned it was going to come to blows. Many times he had seen the Cordova boys break down into playful, but physical violence.

"Don't make me smash you in another arm wrestling contest," Grayson warned. "I think we've seen enough how that turns out."

Carson rolled his eyes. "You and your muscles. Perhaps we should aim for a war of words instead," he offered. "Brains over brawn. What do you think?"

Brook frowned. "Uh...what?"

"Challenge accepted," Grayson said, grinning smugly. "This ought to be good." He looked over to Jude. "Sorry you're stuck with Car, but if you think I'm working with anyone but my wife, well..."

Jude grinned back. "I'll take my chances."

Carson rubbed his hands together. "Let's get on it!"

"What in the world is going on?" Brook demanded. "We have decorating to do."

Grayson stopped and turned. "She's right."

"Crud," Carson muttered. "Do we have to?"

Grayson glanced sideways at his wife, then nodded reluctantly. "Yeah."

"Fine." Carson went back to the garland. "First one done gets to roll first."

Jude hopped back into action. Going first was always a good idea.

"What is going on?" Brook cried as the men all sprang into action.

"Better get some snacks ready," Carson hollered. "Our games of Trivial Pursuit can be epic."

"And last for hours," Jude warned her.

Brook gaped at him. "You can't be serious."

Jude chuckled. "I've seen them go on for days. These two never know when to quit." He jumped up to hang the garland on the hook. This needed to be done quickly if they were going to go first. He and Carson were a pretty decent team, but Grayson always knew more than Jude expected him to.

He tuned out Brook's complaints and the brothers' banter, focusing solely on finishing their jobs. That same feeling from the night before was back. Before Grayson was married, before Carson and Jude banded together out of necessity, before Elania left him for another man...

There was something to be said for those years when things were smooth and carefree. But if Jude was being honest with himself, he wasn't quite sure he would change any of it.

Grayson had never been so happy. Carson was a pretty good friend, despite his flair for the dramatic. And if Elania didn't have the same feeling for Jude as he did for her, then maybe it was better to find out now rather than after he'd proposed and maybe after they'd been married for a year or two.

Slowly, Jude felt like he might be on his way to healing. Maybe. Sort of. Okay, he wasn't ready to tackle the world yet, but maybe he could start with something small. He was enjoying these moments where he felt happy again and wanted more of it. Like playing games with friends without being sulky or depressed. Or flirting with a girl at Brook's opening holiday party tomorrow night.

Those were all things the old Jude could handle with ease. Maybe it was time to start bringing him out again.

CHAPTER 6

Ruth adjusted her wig for the hundredth time and took in a deep breath. The house in front of her was more than a little intimidating! The seaside mansion was decked in lights and greenery and was unlike anything Ruth had ever seen outside of a television screen.

"Come on," Grandma Nan grumbled. "I'm freezing my skinny behind off out here and if we wait much longer, I won't be able to sit down for a month of Sundays."

Ruth shook her head and scrambled after her grandmother. "You're ridiculous, you know that?"

Grandma Nan snorted. "Nobody appreciates a body who tells it like it is," she snapped. "Just because I choose honesty doesn't make me ridiculous."

"What does it make you?" Ruth asked.

"Honest, of course," Grandma Nan retorted, then grinned. "You're beautiful tonight, honey. You know that, right?"

Ruth smiled back. "Only because you've already told me, like, a dozen times."

"Well, make it an even baker's dozen." Grandma Nan patted Ruth's cheek. "Some lucky guy is gonna grab your attention and never let it go."

Ruth chose not to answer. It just wasn't worth the argument and she didn't want to accidentally give words to her internal hopes. What woman wouldn't want a man to see past her obvious flaws and still love her? Life was precious. Ruth knew that more than anyone, and she would go through her cancer all over again if it meant finding the right person, but it just wasn't reasonable to expect a significant other to not care. Maybe after her hair had grown back or her body filled in with a few more curves, she could find a companion, but until then, Ruth would indulge her grandmother and go about her business.

"I'm so glad you made it!" Brook said from the doorway. She stepped forward to hug both Grandma Nan and Ruth. "Come in, come in." Brook took their coats and waved them farther into the house. "Everyone is inside. There's food, hot chocolate, and plenty of friends. Please. Have fun!"

"Thank you," Ruth said softly, smiling at her host. Brook was a total sweetheart and Ruth hoped they could continue to get to know each other. She stayed close to her grandmother as they walked inside and the noise of the party began to filter to her ears.

Ruth felt her jaw drop as she took in the decorating inside the mansion. It was like walking into a winter wonderland. Garland, lights, candles, mistletoe...everything a person could associate with Christmas was draped, hung, or standing in the space.

"A body can do a lot when they've got more money than Bill Gates," Grandma Nan grumbled.

"Oh, stop," Ruth scolded. "They don't have more than the Gates family."

Grandma Nan raised her eyebrows. "How do you know? Been looking at their bank account statements?"

Ruth just laughed and shook her head. "You love Brook, so don't pretend otherwise."

Grandma Nan waved her off. "Don't act like you know me."

"I see your quilting ladies," Ruth said in a cajoling tone. "Better hurry over so you can all gossip together."

Grandma Nan glared. "Watch it, sweet pea. Or you'll be out of a job come Monday."

"Promises, promises," Ruth teased.

Grandma Nan chuckled and started to walk away, then paused. "You'll be okay?"

It was moments like his that Ruth knew for all Grandma Nan's bluster and bravado, the woman really did love her. "I'll be fine. Go enjoy your friends."

Grandma Nan nodded and walked away, quickly joining her friends.

Ruth took a deep breath and patted her hair again.

"You're looking quite lovely tonight," Brook offered, coming up beside her.

Ruth smiled gratefully. "Thanks. You look amazing, as always, and your house is a wonderland."

Brook snickered. "Thanks. It, uh, wasn't without a bit of a fight, but we got it done."

"*You* did this?"

Brook shook her head. "I designed it, but I had help." She looked around the room. "There's my husband, Grayson."

Ruth nodded. "He's even more handsome in person." She grinned. "Lucky you."

Brook laughed. "Don't tell him that. We get enough groupies who won't leave him alone. If you'll notice, the entire group of people talking to him are all young women."

"I did notice," Ruth agreed. "That must be hard as his wife."

Brook shrugged and shook her head. "I know he loves me and he'd never stray." She looked around again. "There's his brother, Carson. He's a lawyer down in California, but up visiting for the holidays."

Ruth looked to where Brook was pointing and froze. It was him. Grayon's brother was very handsome, just like Brook said, but it was the man standing just behind Carson that caught Ruth's eye.

"Do you know everyone here tonight?" Ruth asked, her eyes never leaving the corner where the men were hunkered down, avoiding the crowds.

"Yeah, pretty much," Brook answered.

"Would you mind introducing me?" Ruth finally looked at Brook.

"To Carson?" Brook asked.

"Uh, yes, please."

Brook frowned. "He's been a little…" She chewed on her lip. "You know what? It's fine." She smiled. "Come on."

Ruth wasn't sure what Brook had been about to say, but she was grateful Brook was willing to go along with it. From the way the two men were chatting, Ruth was positive they knew each other, and if she could get an introduction to one, surely she could get an introduction to the other.

One way or another, Ruth was determined to know who this man was. He had captured her attention with just the slightest of looks the other day, and after his disappearance, she had been sure her vision was a hallucination.

But here he was. Tall, muscular, handsome, blond… Tthose blue eyes were roaming the room, looking sad, and it tugged at Ruth's heartstrings. She wanted to see him smile. Wanted to see him stand confident and sure of himself.

You don't even know him! she scolded herself. Why was he so intriguing? Ruth had met handsome men before. Carson Cordova was a handsome man. But there was nothing about him that drew Ruth in the same way his companion did.

Just find out his name, she told herself. *If I can just find out his name, then maybe I'll be able to calm down about it. It's just the mystery surrounding him. That's all.*

Maybe if she chanted that in her head a few thousand times, she'd actually come to believe it.

"DID YOU LAY THE LAW down with Brook?" Carson asked Jude as he casually sipped his punch,

Jude gave Carson a look. "No." He sighed. "I don't have the heart to."

Carson chuckled. "It's the only way you're gonna escape the noose."

Jude pushed a hand through his hair, messing up his normally well shaped style. "I like Brook. I don't want to hurt her."

Carson snorted. "I like her too, but that doesn't mean I'm all right letting her pick out a date for me."

"It's not like we're going to be here that long," Jude muttered, looking down into his glass of punch. His plan to step back out of himself was going miserably. Everywhere he looked, he found himself reminded of the fact that he was alone. Carson's disappearing acts kept leaving Jude to fend for himself and it was getting harder and harder. He needed to go take a break at the motel, but had been too worried he would run into that woman. She was *not* going to help him calm his stress levels.

Carson frowned. "Jude, man, I'm worried about you. Are you ever gonna tell me why you're so down?"

Jude shrugged and threw back the rest of the glass. "I guess I'm just getting old," Jude responded, stepping to the side in order to drop off his empty cup on a table corner.

"And what makes you say that?"

Jude folded his arms over his chest. "I'm just getting tired of it all," he admitted. "And at this point I'm not sure I trust my own judgment anymore."

"Hello, gentlemen." Brook's too perky voice drew Jude's attention and immediately let him know she was up to something.

Carson's look was anything but welcoming to his sister-in-law.

Brook gave him a helpless shrug.

Jude knew there would be another fight later.

The woman with Brook smiled shyly and tucked a piece of dark blonde hair behind her ear and Jude froze. It was her. The woman from the motel with the blue eyes. The very one he had been trying to avoid.

"You're Grayson's brother?" she asked.

"Yep," he said, popping the last letter a little too hard.

No way. After all this time, how did it come to this? The very woman who had caught Jude's attention, without even trying, was being introduced to Jude's best friend. Brook intended her for Carson.

Jude wanted to punch something. What was it about him that made him so easy to overlook? He dropped his gaze to the floor. Even looking at her was too much. He wanted those blue eyes to be stuck on him, not Carson. He wanted her shy smiles and the small talk that was currently going on.

You don't even know her!

Jude shook himself mentally. He had no claim to this woman. He didn't even know her name, let alone have any right to be jealous that Brook thought she was good enough for Carson.

"That's, uh, great. I'm Ruth. My grandma owns the Motel on Main." Her eyes went to Jude and he felt his heart go into overdrive. "Are you visiting as well?"

Jude nodded and put out his hand. "Jude Lisbon. Nice to meet you." His eyes went up to Carson's, then back to the lovely Ruth. "If you'll excuse me."

Walking away was one of the hardest things Jude had ever done. There was something about those eyes. They called to him. There was something haunting about them that made him want to stand up and be her protector.

But that's not what anyone else wants you to do.

How could Jude have been so stupid? Drawn to a woman that Brook wanted to introduce to Carson. Jude wanted to slap his forehead at his lack of foresight. It seemed to be just another example of his inability to trust himself.

"What's got you looking so glum?"

Jude jerked his head up and relaxed when he recognized Captain Ken. Jude shrugged. "Uh...nothing. Just not big into parties, you know?"

Ken narrowed his gaze. "No. That's never the impression I've gotten from you." He tilted his head. "It's something else."

Jude gave Ken a look. "It's nothing, all right?"

Ken put a hand in the air. "Fine. I won't pry, but between Brook's concerned looks and Carson's angry scowl, something fishy is going on."

"Sometimes you're a little too much of a policeman," Jude shot back, though he worked to say it in a teasing tone.

Ken grinned. "Guilty. I'm not ashamed about it." He nudged Jude's shoulder. "If you have woman troubles, trust me, no one else will understand like I will." He took a sip of his drink. "It took me five years to win my wife over."

Jude whistled low. "I've heard a little bit about it, but not the details. That's a crazy long time."

Ken nodded thoughtfully. "Yeah...she had some baggage she was hiding and *policeman* that I am," Ken joked, "I couldn't leave well enough alone."

"So, what? You bugged her until she let you in?"

"Something like that."

Jude chuckled. "I gotta give it to you. That's persistence."

"And now I have a beautiful wife and daughter." Ken raised his glass in salute. "Persistence means winning."

"I'm sure stalkers could say the same thing."

Ken laughed. "It's a fine line."

Jude chuckled again and reached for a passing tray for a drink, taking a sip of the sparkling cider.

"So?"

Jude frowned. "So...?"

"You never did say if it was a woman problem?"

Jude let his head fall back. "You've got to be kidding me."

"Because if it is, you might want to let the cute little thing working her way toward us know that you're taken."

Jude's head came jerking back. "What?"

Ken nodded subtly across the room.

Jude followed his gaze and once again found himself held captive. Those blue eyes were stuck on his and coming closer. He could feel his heart beat getting faster with each step she took. Why was she coming to him? Where was Carson? Weren't they getting to know each other?

"And my work here is done," Ken mumbled, disappearing from Jude's periphery.

Jude couldn't quite bring himself to say goodbye or even call back his friend. Instead, he was mesmerized by the woman who was arriving at his side.

"Hey," she said softly, tucking that hair behind her ear again. She patted the top of her hair as if looking for strays.

"Hey," Jude responded. *Wow. That was brilliant.*

"Um...I think maybe I saw you at my grandma's motel," Ruth continued. "Did you check in the other day?"

Jude opened his mouth, then paused. How could he tell her that he had booked a room in order to find a quiet space, but hadn't been back since she disturbed his peace? "Yeah," came the lame reply.

Ruth nodded. "Right." The silence grew awkward between them. "So..." Ruth ventured again. "How do you know Brook?"

"I'm Grayson Cordova's personal physical therapist," Jude responded automatically.

"Ah, so you met her through work?"

"I met her here," Jude explained. "It's kind of a long story. It was when Grayson got hurt. We came up here for him to recover and that's where he met Brook." Jude shrugged. "I was kind of a third wheel."

She smiled again. "I doubt that."

Jude felt his own mouth respond in kind. Considering that she was here with him instead of talking to Carson, Jude had a mind to test the waters just a bit. "Would you like to grab something to eat?" he asked. "I've been standing in the corner all evening and I'm starving."

"I'd love that," Ruth breathed.

Jude couldn't have wiped the smile from his face if he'd tried. "Then let's grab plates. I happen to know that Brook was really excited about the catering company she hired, so I'm guessing the food is good."

"Perfect."

Jude walked just behind her as they went to the food tables and decided that right at this moment, he couldn't have said it better himself.

CHAPTER 7

Ruth's stomach was doing flip flops. She couldn't believe that Jude had asked her to eat with him. His answers to her questions had been so stunted and short she had been sure he was trying to get rid of her. Her last flirtatious remark had been just that...her last. If he hadn't responded, she had already decided to walk away with her tail between her legs and hide in a closet until the party was over.

But instead, he had asked her to spend more time with him.

A feather would have taken Ruth to her knees, but instead, she held her head high and walked over to fill a plate. "Oh my goodness," she gushed. "It all looks delicious. I wish I had the stomach capacity for everything."

Jude smiled. "I probably have too much stomach capacity. Maybe between the two of us, we can make a decent dent."

Ruth laughed softly and tucked her hair behind her ear, then patted her wig to make sure it was in place. "I think I'll try one of these." She lifted a crostini with salmon and dill.

"Good choice, but I think I'm headed for something sweeter." Jude took a couple of pastries that were making Ruth's mouth water.

After several minutes, they both had full plates and were looking for a place to sit.

"Come on," Jude said, tilting his head. "I know a place where we can grab seats away from the crowds."

"Are you sure that's allowed?" Ruth asked, worried about doing something that would upset her new friends.

Jude chuckled. "Trust me. It's fine." He guided her down the hallway and ducked into a formal dining room. Using his elbow, he turned on the light and nodded his head toward the table. "Pick a seat. Any seat."

Ruth laughed. "Am I going to see magic?" She set her plate down on the table and shifted the chair so she could sit down.

Jude set his own food down and quickly reached over to help her adjust her chair.

"Thank you," Ruth said, surprised he would help her. Not many men did all the gentlemanly things anymore.

Jude nodded and took his own seat. He paused before eating and looked around. "It's kinda obnoxious how big this is with only two people in it."

"I like it," Ruth responded. "It's quiet."

Jude chuckled. "Well, that's true. I don't usually mind crowds, but sometimes they're overwhelming."

Ruth shrugged and poked at her food. "I can deal with them, but if given the choice, I like smaller settings." She leaned forward, taking a bite of one of the pastries she picked up. "Oh my goodness," she gushed through her full mouth. "This is amazing."

Jude eyed his plate, picked one up, and tried it as well. "Wow. That is good." He finished chewing and swallowed. "I wonder who made them. Seems odd to find a French pastry in such a small town."

Ruth wiped her mouth. "I'm guessing you find stuff like this all the time in Hollywood?"

Jude nodded, taking another bite before answering. "Yeah. We have pretty decent food down in California."

"So does Seattle," Ruth said before she thought better of it.

"You lived in Seattle?"

She froze. She hadn't meant to spill that because it could lead to questions...questions she didn't want to answer. Doing her best to act casual, she played it off. "For a bit, but now that I'm here in Seaside Bay, I don't know if I'll ever leave."

"It does kind of grow on you, doesn't it?" Jude asked, polishing off another treat. "I've lived in California my whole life and even I can't argue with the charm of this place."

"There's something cleaner about the air here," Ruth mused. She laughed at herself and shook her head. "Sorry. That sounded dumb."

"No, no, I know what you mean," Jude responded with a bright smile. "I think it has to do with the fact that life is just...slower here. People are friendly, for the most part, and it's a little like stepping back in time."

Ruth grinned. "There are downsides," she teased. "Like the fact that my grandmother's quilting circle knows everything about everybody."

Jude chuckled. "That's true. When everyone knows each other, there's not much of a chance of hiding secrets."

"And there's an older gentleman at the motel who would put your friendly theory to the test."

Jude gave her a look. "Really?"

Ruth nodded and swallowed her latest bite. "Yeah. Grandma Nan says he comes every year, and every year he does his best to suck the Christmas spirit out of everything."

"So you have a real life Grinch on your hands, huh?"

Ruth nodded. "That's a great way to put it." She leaned in a little closer, doing her best to ignore the cologne Jude was wearing. The musky scent of it was intoxicating. "He takes, like, five walks a day and every time he walks through the lobby I make sure to be as peppy as possible, you know, trying to bring a little sunshine into his life."

Jude raised his eyebrows. "And how does that go over?"

She straightened and shrugged. "About how you'd expect. He grumbles and complains, but never actually tells me to stop." Her smile widened. "I think, secretly, he likes it, but doesn't want to admit to such weakness."

Jude laughed, turning his face back to his plate. "You're something else," he said softly.

Ruth felt her face heat up and she patted her hair self consciously. "I just don't like to see people unhappy."

"Maybe he's happy in his grumpiness?"

"Who could be happy in that?" Ruth argued. "There's no way he would complain all the time if he felt happy inside."

"If you say so," Jude said, picking up his drink. "Remind me to give my compliments to Brook. Everything I've eaten has been delicious."

"Hear, hear," Ruth agreed. She held out her cup of punch. "To good food. May your holidays be filled with it."

"Now that's a toast I can get behind," Jude said with a laugh, clinking his plastic cup with hers. They both took a drink, then smiled at each other.

Ruth felt as if the very air of the room had grown thick and sticky. Their eyes were caught and just like the moment they first saw each other the other day at his check-in, something passed between them. Something intangible, but sweet. It put butterflies in Ruth's stomach and sent thoughts of fairy tales and Prince Charming's through her head.

Jude grunted and shook his head, effectively breaking their moment. "Sorry," he said curtly. "Not sure what came over me."

The same thing that came over me, Ruth wanted to say, but she held her tongue. She'd never quite experienced a feeling like this and didn't want to risk ruining it if he wasn't as intrigued as she was. "No biggie," she responded. "It's hard not to get caught up when talking about culinary masterpieces."

JUDE WAS AN IDIOT. He was a grown man and yet sat here staring at a pretty girl as if he was back in middle school.

He focused on the last bits of food on his plate, but for some reason, they weren't as enticing as they were before. What he really wanted was the woman beside him, but that was utterly ridiculous. He'd just met her!

"So, tell me about yourself," Jude said, clearing his throat. "What brought you down to Seaside Bay, after living in a place like Seattle?"

Ruth's face paled dramatically and Jude felt panic begin to stir automatically.

"Is something wrong?" he asked, looking her over. "Are you choking?"

"No!" Ruth shouted, then jerked back and shook her head. "Sorry. That came out much louder than I meant for it to." She tucked a piece of hair behind her ear and then patted her head, apparently making sure the hair was all in place. "Uh, I didn't love being in Seattle. It was kind of chaotic for me, so Grandma invited me to come live with her until I got my feet under me."

"Got your feet under you?" Jude tilted his head. "Sounds like things were a little rough."

She smiled softly and tucked the same piece of hair behind her ear again. "They could have been better." She shrugged. "But now I'm here and everything is going great."

Jude nodded. "Good. Do you plan to work for your grandmother forever?"

Ruth scrunched up her nose. "I don't think so," she said slowly. "Truth is, I'm not quite sure what I want to do." Her lips pursed as she thought about her answer. "I really enjoy meeting new people at the desk and hearing where they're from and why they came to Seaside Bay. But I don't think I'd be happy in the motel business forever."

"What do you want to do, then? Did you study something else in college?"

Ruth's face fell and she wouldn't look at him, and Jude once again felt as if he'd done something wrong.

"Hey, look, I'm sorry," he started. "I didn't mean to pry into things that are none of my business."

"No, it's fine," Ruth assured him, though Jude wasn't sure he agreed. "I just...don't have a good answer for you." She held up her hands in a helpless gesture. "I started college, but unforeseen circumstances kept me from finishing."

"I'm sorry," Jude said, not quite understanding, but definitely not going to dig any deeper.

"It's fine," Ruth said again. "I promise. I'm more embarrassed than anything."

Jude jerked back a little. "Why would you be embarrassed?"

She scrunched her nose again. "Because I'm twenty-five and have nothing to show for it." Her eyes darted to his before going back to the table. "I feel like I should have a degree or a good job or...*something* to prove that I've actually lived."

Jude shook his head and nudged her shoulder. Man, it was hard to keep his hands to himself. As he had leaned in to nudge her, he caught her perfume and thought the soft, floral smell was perfect. Shy but sweet and slightly romantic. Those are all words he would already use to describe Ruth, though most of his attraction had to do with her looks at this point. He was getting glimpses of her personality and it was starting to draw him in as well.

Their little chat had done little to push Jude away. He wasn't sure what exactly she was hiding as to why she didn't finish college or have a regular career, but he hadn't known her long enough to find out, and if she was embarrassed about it, then he saw no reason for red flags.

Truth was, he had been enjoying their time together and didn't want to go back to the crowded party. A part of Jude was afraid that Carson would spot them and steal away Ruth's attention, which Jude wanted for himself.

"I think the fact that you're here today showed us you lived," Jude said, trying for a little bit of humor. Her polite laugh did little to boost his ego.

"What was your favorite thing you ate tonight?" Ruth offered.

Jude snorted a laugh. "Nice change of subject."

She winked. "I thought so."

"Food is usually a safe bet." He took a deep breath. "Hmmm...I think those croissants take the top spot. The ones with the chocolate." He turned to Ruth. "And you?"

She nodded. "I have to agree with you, though the cheesecake bites were a close second."

"Yeah, those were great." Jude's eyes wandered to the wall clock. "Shoot," he said, pushing his chair back. "Brook is gonna wonder if I ditched the party."

"And my grandmother is going to think I'm hiding in a dark corner." Ruth also stood up and grabbed her plate.

"Let me get that," Jude said, taking it from her.

"That's very sweet, thank you."

Jude smiled. "Anytime." He used his elbow to indicate the door. "After you."

Ruth gave him another gracious smile, sending Jude's pulse into overdrive, and then led the way. She held the door open for him as he maneuvered through with full hands.

"I'm gonna drop these in the kitchen," Jude said, knowing he had no reason to ask her to wait for him.

"Oh, gotcha." Ruth looked flustered and it was adorable.

"Maybe I'll catch you around later?"

She patted her hair. It must be a nervous habit of hers. "Yeah. That'd be great." With a tiny wave, she walked away, heading back to the party.

Jude watched her go, unwilling to admit how much he wanted her to stay. Ruth was as sweet as sugar and obviously available. But

Jude was only here for a few short days. It didn't really matter that she had been the first woman to catch his attention in months...did it?

Besides, he wasn't himself. He was still struggling to find his old self and pull up the happy, friendly physical therapist who could have wooed Ruth in a matter of minutes.

What exactly could he offer the shy, soft spoken woman?

"Right now? Nothing," Jude muttered to himself as he stepped into the kitchen. He nodded at the caterers as he took the dishes to the sink. "It was delicious. Thank you for your hard work," he said.

"Thanks," a young man said cheerily. "Enjoy the party!"

Jude gave him a chin tilt and headed back out the door. The noise from the party was like rocks on his ears as he grew closer. Jude paused in the doorway. Everyone was mingling and chatting, filling the air with laughter and guffaws. The whole scene should have served to make him warm and content, but instead, he felt slightly sick.

He couldn't help but keep his eyes out for a dark blonde head, but from where he currently stood, Jude didn't see Ruth anywhere.

Good thing you know where she works.

The thought was more comforting than it should have been. He really shouldn't entertain ever seeing her again, but Ruth had been a bright spot in an otherwise hard vacation.

He couldn't seem to make himself move, and so, even knowing that Brook would be disappointed, Jude turned around and headed to his room. He just couldn't bring himself to hang out with the rest of the party, not when all he wanted to do was spend time with a blonde woman who was practically a stranger to him.

He was equal parts worried about the desire and eager for it. Only time would tell which emotion would end up being right.

CHAPTER 8

Ruth had her nose in a book, but her head was somewhere else. Which was probably why the appearance of Sir Grumpsalot caught her so off guard.

"This map is faulty," Mr. Portman growled, slamming the offensive material on the counter.

"Oh..." Ruth blinked a few times, trying to get her mind out of the clouds. "I'm sorry, Mr. Portman. Let me just take a look at that for you." She gingerly took the map and studied it, but could see nothing out of the ordinary. "I'm sorry. Could you tell me where the problem is?"

His eyes narrowed and Mr. Portman stepped closer to the counter, nearly crowding Ruth out of her space even though the entire desk separated them. "Right here," he stated in a growly tone.

Ruth glanced down. "What about it?"

The elderly man rolled his eyes. "It says it's an antique shop. That place is nothing more than a glorified flea market!"

"Um..." Ruth chewed on the inside of her lip. "Do they not sell antiques?"

He nodded once. "They do."

"Then I don't understand the problem." She could feel every muscle in her body tightened and on edge. Mr. Portman was not very tall, but the sheer size of his personality was enough to make Ruth intimidated. Funny how she felt fine about it when he wasn't directly confronting her, but now that Mr. Portman was fighting back, Ruth's courage was dwindling.

He rolled his eyes. "The owner restores the furniture! And she sells chocolates at the front desk!"

Ruth tried to hold back her frown, but it was difficult. "Maybe you could just start from the beginning?" she offered politely. "I'm afraid I'm really struggling to see what the problem is."

Mr. Portman grumbled as he snatched the paper back and worked to fold it properly. He was so upset, however, that he kept folding against the grain and ended up messing up the pamphlet, which only served to upset him more.

"Here," Ruth said gently, carefully prying the map away from his fingers. When it was done, she held it out and Mr. Portman jerked it from her fingers. "I'd be happy to help you settle your problem, Mr. Portman, but I don't understand what the issue is." Ruth tried to smile. "Perhaps you could explain it to me in different terms?"

"She's not selling antiques if she's repainting them, is she?" he grumbled. "Imagine, ruining perfectly good furniture by painting it."

Ruth's eyes darted to the older man's car in the parking lot. It looked to be a beautifully restored vehicle from the fifties era, though Ruth was a little unsure. Add to that his bowtie and fedora and suspenders and the man obviously had a deep love for the past. "Remind me again which shop you're talking about?"

Mr. Portman gave her a look before responding. "Antiques and Things."

Ruth smiled. "I think that's Charli's shop."

"A woman named Charli," Mr. Portman huffed. "What next?"

Ruth kept her laughter to herself. If Mr. Portman had been in the shop this morning, she guessed there had been major fireworks. Charli was part of the new group of friends that Hadlee had introduced Ruth to. She had married a man named Bronson and together they ran the antique/restoration shop as well as a charity. Ruth only remembered a few of the details from the Christmas party the other night. Charli was friendly, but loud spoken, and she definitely wouldn't have taken kindly to Mr. Portman's complaining, especially since Charli was in the last stages of her first pregnancy. "I know the owner," Ruth said. "Why don't I introduce you and we can talk about what's bothering you."

Mr. Portman huffed and grumbled, but didn't deny her.

Ruth just had this feeling that he needed to be heard. He needed someone to listen to his side and that maybe his bad attitude was a way to do that. She peeked into the backroom. "Grandma? I need to run an errand with Mr. Portman. Would you mind taking over the desk?"

Grandma choked on her cup of tea. "Excuse me?" she sputtered.

Ruth just smiled. "We'll be back soon." She came around from the desk. "I think it's within walking distance," she said to the older man. "Do you mind?"

"Walking is good for the soul," Mr. Portman said under his breath. "Young people don't understand."

Ruth ignored that cheap shot and grabbed her coat, tucking her scarf tightly around her neck and patting her hair into place. "I'm sure we can get this figured out in no time." She pressed open the glass door and held it, waiting for Mr. Portman to go through.

He growled softly and marched as if a gun were being held at his back.

Ruth shook her head and quickly caught up. "Do you enjoy antiquities?" she asked, trying to figure out if her suspicions were correct.

"They're hardly antiques when most of them came from my childhood," he snapped.

Ruth nodded thoughtfully. "I never thought of it that way. I suppose it would be difficult to have the things you knew and loved growing up be called old or disposable."

He grunted but didn't speak.

"I happen to know that Charli has a great love for turning pieces of furniture that aren't as well taken care of into something beautiful." Ruth chose her words carefully all while smiling at Mr. Portman's scowl. "I think you two probably have more in common than you realize."

The rest of the five-minute walk was done in silence, though Ruth wasn't uncomfortable in it. As they reached the sign that said *Antiques and Things*, Ruth once again moved to hold open the door.

Quicker than she would have guessed possible, Mr. Portman lunged in front of her and opened the door instead. "Don't even know the word gentleman," he grumbled.

Ruth bit back a laugh. "That's very sweet of you. Thank you, Mr. Portman." She did her best not to watch his face too much, but Ruth found herself sneaking glances all the same. There was just something about the grumpy old man that called to her. At least, it did when he wasn't trying to melt her into a puddle with his angry glare.

She hated to see him wasting so much of his life complaining rather than enjoying. Choosing to enjoy was one of the most important things that had gotten Ruth through her years of illness. She had learned a valuable lesson at a very young age.

Don't waste time complaining. It's the best commodity you have.

She could easily have lost everything at the young age of twenty-one, when she'd first been diagnosed, but somehow, through a miracle Ruth didn't understand, she was still here. And she didn't want to let it go to waste.

Mr. Portman had a life. He had a good one if his clothes and car and vacations were any indication. The fact that he didn't seem to enjoy it at all tugged on Ruth's heartstrings.

She wouldn't be in Mr. Portman's life for very long, but maybe, if she was lucky, Ruth could help teach him a thing or two. Perhaps even a lesson he would never forget.

JUDE STOOD WITH HIS hands on his hips, staring at the door to Antiques and Things. He was panting and sweat was coursing down his chest and soaking his shirt.

What is she doing?

Ruth had just walked into the store with an older man, who looked like he was ready to kill every person that crossed his path.

Jude hadn't seen Ruth since the party two nights ago, but he had never stopped thinking about her. Her sweet personality and way of looking on the bright side had stuck with him over the weekend, and Jude had fought with himself a thousand times over whether or not to go see her.

He'd been an idiot and hadn't bothered to get her phone number, which would have been a good way to start. It was less confrontational than just showing up at her place of work and she could easily have ignored him if she wasn't interested.

But now he was standing on the sidewalk, watching her and unable to look away. Staying away for so long had only made him want to see her more, rather than helping curb his longing.

Before he could think better of it, Jude was striding across the street, aiming directly toward the shop. He pulled open the door and stepped inside, only to hesitate for a second when he heard shouting.

"You're ruining them with your need for glamor!"

"Glamor? Are you kidding me? I'm giving those pieces new life!"

"Ruth!" Jude shouted, rushing farther into the warehouse-type space. He didn't like the sound of the arguing and didn't want Ruth to get stuck in the middle of something.

"Jude?" Ruth's head poked around a large armoire. Her smile lit up the dark space. "Hi! What are you doing here?"

Jude ran a hand through his sweaty hair. "I saw you," he said lamely.

"Jude?" Charli's face came next to Ruth's. She grinned smugly, looking back and forth between Ruth and himself. "Were you looking for someone?"

"I heard fighting," Jude said, hoping that was a better excuse than the one he'd used before.

Charli rolled her eyes. "Ruth was kind enough to bring this guy in here." Charli jabbed a thumb over her shoulder.

"Did you or did you not use chalk paint on that nineteen-twenties armoire?" a masculine voice shouted.

Charli huffed and turned around, disappearing.

Ruth made a face. "Sorry," she said softly as Jude approached. "I brought Mr. Portman because he was upset and I thought having the two of them talk would be good and help him be a little happier, but I might have been wrong."

Jude wiped his forehead on the sleeve of his shirt. "They certainly sound like a couple of alley cats going at it, don't they?"

Ruth nodded, wringing her hands together. "I probably ought to help."

"Maybe I'll come along." He grinned. "For moral support, you know?"

Ruth laughed. "I can use all the support I can get right now."

Jude followed Ruth a little deeper into the warehouse, to see Charli, her stomach large and bulging, facing off with the small, older man that Jude had seen come in the door with Ruth.

"Okay," Ruth said, loud enough to catch everyone's attention. "I didn't bring you back, Mr. Portman, so that you could berate poor Mrs. Ramsay about her choice of paint."

The man glared while Charli smiled triumphantly.

"But, Mrs. Ramsay, I did hope that you would be willing to listen to Mr. Portman's concerns and see if we could find some type of middle ground."

Jude covered his laugh with his fist as Charli's mouth gaped open and closed several times.

"I don't see how there's any middle ground to meet at," Charli finally declared. "This is my shop. If he doesn't like how I do my furniture, he's perfectly welcome to go somewhere else."

"There's nowhere else to go on this stretch of beach," Mr. Portman shot back.

Charli opened her mouth, but Ruth interrupted. "Mrs. Ramsay, do you always sell your furniture after fixing it up?"

Jude felt like he was in the middle of a ping pong match, his head whipping back and forth as he followed the seemingly random conversation. He had no idea what Ruth was aiming for.

"Sure," Charli said, her shoulders shrugging. "I sell both restored and non-restored."

Mr. Portman snorted, but Ruth ploughed on.

"Mr. Portman, did you have a particular piece of furniture that you were interested in?" she asked sweetly.

Mr. Portman hesitated and Jude found himself fascinated. The man had had no trouble speaking just moments before, but Ruth seemed to have hit on something.

Slowly, Mr. Portman moved. He glanced back at Charli, who was still glaring, and then Ruth, who nodded him on encouragingly.

Finally, throwing back his thin shoulders, the man walked to a display where there were several jewelry boxes. He picked up one that looked old and weathered and cradled it lovingly in his hand.

Jude's eyebrows went up when the man opened the lid and a soft, halting melody tried to play. It was obvious even without looking that the mechanism was struggling, but Mr. Portman didn't seem to care.

Snapping the lid shut, the reverence in his behavior gone, Mr. Portman marched back and shoved the box at Charli. "One of your paint jobs would ruin this," he snarled.

Ruth put up her hands before another fight could break out. "Mr. Portman," she said firmly. "I think it's wonderful you've found a treasure. And since this one has yet to be restored, I'm sure if we asked very nicely, we could negotiate a good price from Mrs. Ramsay, and then you can restore it the way you restored that beautiful car you drive."

Jude's eyebrows pulled together. What car was she talking about?

Mr. Portman put his chin in the air. "Well?"

"Well?" Charli challenged back.

"What are you asking for it?"

Charli looked ready to do battle, but when Ruth caught her attention, Jude saw Charli physically soften.

"I paid twenty-five for it," Charli admitted. "Fixed up, I would be asking about seventy-five, but as is, I'll give it to you for forty."

"Thirty."

Charli glared. "Thirty-eight."

"Thirty."

"That's not how a negotiation goes."

"Thirty."

Charli's lips were pinched. "Done."

"I know."

The two stood exchanging death looks until Ruth clapped her hands. "Wonderful. I'm so glad we could work that out." She sent a wide eyed look Jude's way before hurrying forward and linking her arm with Mr. Portman. "Let's just head up front and we'll get it paid for, hm? Then maybe we can grab some lunch on the way back to the motel?" She began walking to the front as if she hadn't a care in the world and Jude followed in their wake, helpless to do anything else.

He had no real reason to follow, but if Ruth thought Jude would leave now without seeing this whole thing through...she had another thing coming.

CHAPTER 9

To Ruth's delight, Jude followed her and Mr. Portman out of Charli's shop. "Thank you!" Ruth called to Charli as they slipped out the door.

Charli smiled widely and waved, rubbing her belly with her other hand. "Feel free to come back...without some of your present company," Charli concluded.

Ruth laughed softly. She looked at Jude, who was staring at her as if she had two heads. Automatically, Ruth's hand went to her hair. "What?" she asked.

Jude shook himself, then shrugged. "Nothing. I just..."

"A body can catch pneumonia with the pace you two walk," Mr. Portman grumbled.

Ruth pinched her lips between her teeth and hurried forward to catch Mr. Portman's arm. "Good thing you're here to help shelter me from the cold, then."

Ruth glanced behind them as Jude continued to follow. She couldn't believe how excited she was that he was here. Their time together at the party the other night had been wonderful, but Jude had given very little indication that she would be seeing him again. And with him here to purposefully visit friends, Ruth hadn't dared to hope.

Jude gave her a half smirk, to which Ruth grinned before turning her attention back to Mr. Portman. "What do you plan to do with it?" she asked, indicating the jewelry box.

Mr. Portman's lips thinned and Ruth decided maybe she had pushed him enough for one day.

"Well, whatever it is, I'm sure it'll be lovely." They walked in stilted silence for a few moments. "Are you interested in that lunch I mentioned earlier? I know a great cafe not far from here, and for dessert—"

"Is that all you ever think about? Food?" Mr. Portman snapped, though Ruth was positive there was a little less bite to the sound than normal.

"I have to say I'm quite fond of it," Ruth said cheerfully. She wasn't going to tell him *why* she was so excited to eat all the time, but the fact remained nonetheless that Ruth thoroughly enjoyed a good meal.

"I can attest to that," Jude said from behind them. "Ruth has a good appetite."

Ruth laughed, but Mr. Portman just scowled deeper and refused to turn around.

"Have you met Jude?" she asked, realizing she hadn't introduced the two. "He's a friend of mine." Ruth couldn't help but glance back to Jude's reaction to her words. It was a bit of a stretch calling them friends, since they barely knew each other, but she wasn't sure what else to call him. An acquaintance? Or a person she knew? No...friend should be fine, and Jude didn't seem off put at all by her description.

Mr. Portman grunted but didn't look back.

"Jude is a physical therapist," Ruth continued.

Mr. Portman gave her an unimpressed look.

"I've never worked with a physical therapist before," Ruth rambled. "Although one could have been useful after..." She bit her tongue so hard she was sure she would taste blood.

"Did you have an injury of some kind?" Jude asked, catching up to her side. "Do you still have trouble with something?"

Ruth shook her head. "Oh, no. Sorry. I was just rambling." Her smile was shaky, but there was nothing for it. Her free hand automatically went to her hair. "I, uh, was just making conversation."

Mr. Portman pulled his arm from hers. "I don't need a babysitter," he growled.

Ruth stopped walking and blinked when she realized they had arrived back at the motel.

Mr. Portman stormed inside as if he couldn't stand another minute in Ruth's presence.

"Thanks for the walk!" Ruth called after him. She really should have continued in as well, but she couldn't quite bring herself to leave Jude quite yet. She turned to her follower with a loud sigh. "Well. That was interesting."

Jude looked at her for a split second before bursting out laughing. He laughed so hard, he bent over, resting his hands on his knees.

Ruth laughed with him, though not as hard. Giggles broke free from her lips as she watched Jude, enjoying his amusement more than she was actually amused herself.

"That must be the guy you were talking about at the party," Jude said, gasping for air when he was finally done laughing.

"It was," Ruth said with the last of her laughter. She caught her breath and calmed down. "Though, today was the first time I pushed myself on him. Normally I'm content with saying 'hello' or 'have a good day.'"

Jude shook his head and pushed a hand through his sweaty hair. He grimaced at the touch as if just realizing he was still wet from whatever he had been doing before he came into Charli's shop. "Ugh. I'm gross," he muttered. "Hey, you wanna wait a few minutes and let me shower, and I'll take you out to that lunch you got turned down for?"

Ruth caught her breath, but tried to act as if she wasn't doing cartwheels inside. "Sure. Let me just clear it with Grandma, but I don't think it'll be a problem."

Jude nodded, his smile still wide. "Great. Just give me a few minutes." He pulled open the door and let Ruth proceed him inside.

Ruth headed straight to the front desk. "Hey, Grandma." Ruth kissed Grandma Nan's cheek as she came around the counter. "Have you met Jude Lisbon? He's friends with Grayson and Carson Cordova."

"We've met," Jude said softly. His amused smile had fallen since they came inside and Ruth was unsure what had caused it.

Hadn't they just been having fun a few minutes ago? What happened between then and now that caused Jude to lose his smile?

"That's right, we have," Grandma Nan said with a wink. She wrinkled her nose. "Looks like you've been exercising."

"Grandma!" Ruth scolded.

Jude rubbed the back of his neck. "I have and I'm just about to go clean up." His eyes met Ruth's. "I'll, uh, be out soon."

"Okay," Ruth said, forcing a perky note into her voice. "I'll be ready when you are."

Something was definitely wrong.

"Right." Jude ducked his head and headed down the hall. It was the first time Ruth had actually seen him go to his room since checking in several days ago. In fact, now that she thought about it...why was Jude staying at the motel? There was more than enough room at Grayson's house. Wouldn't he be staying there?

"He seems nice," Grandma Nan said innocently after Jude was gone.

Ruth gave her grandmother a look. "He is nice. But don't be getting any funny ideas." *I have enough of them myself.*

Grandma Nan's eyes went impossibly wide. "Why not?"

Ruth huffed and folded her arms over her chest. "Because he's just visiting, Grandma. He's really nice and I'm excited to go to lunch with him, but in a few days he'll go back to California and I'll never see him again."

Grandma Nan shrugged. "We'll see."

"Whatever." Ruth shook her head and went to the back room in order to make sure her wig was in place and looked all right. She had no idea if there was any chance of something happening between her and Jude, but for once, Ruth had to admit that she hoped her Grandmother was right.

WHAT WAS HE DOING? Jude scrubbed his face for the tenth time, knowing he should get out of the shower, but not quite ready to leave the sanctuary he'd created. Ruth was a beautiful, kind woman, but Brook had planned her for Carson. Was it wrong of Jude to take her out instead?

Ruth didn't seem to have any qualms with it and as far as Jude knew, Carson and Ruth hadn't gone out at all. He groaned and turned off the water. Life shouldn't be this complicated.

He was a grown man who should be able to handle himself and his feelings. So why was he filled with an emotional tornado inside? Bitterness, interest, attraction, curiosity, hope, and even shame seemed to make his stomach nearly curdle with anxiety.

He felt like most women he loved had, at one point, lied and left him. He was attracted and even interested in Ruth. He saw a spark of hope that maybe there was something good left for him. But he was ashamed at the fact that the woman he finally found interesting was the very one that his friend was being set up with.

How was one person supposed to handle all that at once without going stark raving mad?

"She's waiting," Jude reminded himself as he threw on a set of clothes. They weren't exactly the type he normally would wear on a date, which try as he might, there was no getting around that that's exactly what this was. But he hadn't had dates in mind when he'd stored a few things at the hotel room. His athletic pants and sweatshirt would have to do.

After a fortifying breath, he headed out into the hallway and toward the front desk. When he spotted Ruth, her face lit up with that stunning smile and Jude felt almost every inhibition melt away. There was just something so carefree and joyous in her smile.

He wanted to sit in her radiance and let it warm all the parts of him that had become cold ever since Elania's betrayal. He wanted to somehow capture that sunshine and bottle it for a rainy day.

Jude shook his head. He was becoming a poet and as much as he wanted a little more happiness in his life, he wasn't looking to become a sap.

"Hey," he said lamely as he got to the desk.

"Feel better?" Ruth asked brightly.

Grandma Nan narrowed her eyes and studied him as if he were a bug under a microscope. "Ya look better."

"Grandma!" Ruth scolded.

Jude laughed and pushed a hand through his half dry hair. "I should hope so. I don't usually get done with runs looking like a million bucks."

"Oh, I wouldn't say that," Ruth began, then snapped her mouth shut and turned red.

Jude grinned. Knowing she found him attractive was exactly what he needed at the moment. "But I do finish them absolutely starving. Ready for that lunch?"

Ruth nodded, her cheeks still bright. "That sounds great."

"You'll take care of her?" Grandma Nan questioned.

Jude paused. "Uh, yeah. I promise I'll be a perfect gentleman."

Grandma Nan nodded. "And make sure she—"

"I think we're ready to go, Grandma," Ruth interrupted, kissing Grandma Nan on the cheek. "Let's go," she said to Jude with a tight smile and a quick pace.

Jude frowned, but hurried after her. "Here. Let me," he said, pushing open the door.

Ruth's shoulders and smile relaxed. "Thank you," she said softly, tucking her hair behind her ear, then patting the top of her head.

Jude recalled he'd seen her do that several times before. Her hair must have a tendency to be fuzzy or something, the way she was always patting it. It was an interesting little quirk. *I wonder if she even knows she does it,* he mused as he followed her out into the chilly air.

"Geez," Ruth said, wrapping her coat tighter around her. "If there's sunshine, you'd think there'd be heat. I feel like we're being lied to."

Jude chuckled. "Since it's usually gray around here, I'm not sure most people see it that way."

"True." Ruth tilted her head as they walked. "It's surprising that this area becomes so, so...colorless during the winter," Ruth said softly. "Now that I'm thinking on it, I guess snow is white, which is completely colorless, so I suppose winter in general lacks color."

"And does that make you like it more or less?" Jude asked. His hands were stuffed in his pockets, trying to keep warm, but he found himself completely intrigued by the conversation. It sounded like a simple topic, but he could tell there was a deeper meaning to her observations... Hhe just wasn't sure what yet.

"I think less," Ruth admitted with a shrug. She finally turned to look at him. "I like color. Bright, achingly vibrant color." She grinned. "There's just something about it that screams life."

"And let me guess...you like life."

Ruth's grin turned into a smile. "You got it!"

Jude smiled back, but that ache picked back up inside. He used to enjoy life, but not lately. All that had been sucked out of him, as if Elania's choice had been the last straw to break the camel's back. Seeing Ruth's optimistic outlook made Jude jealous. He wanted to be the same way, but how? How do you find a spark that has been smothered to the point of ceasing to exist?

"We're here," Ruth announced cheerily.

Jude looked up from his mental wanderings. "Yep." He reached forward to grab the door. "Have you eaten here before?"

Ruth nodded. "Yep. Grandma Nan has taken me out several times since I got here." Ruth smiled at the hostess. "Hello, Rachel."

"Ruth! So good to see you." Rachel looked at Jude and her smile widened. "This isn't your grandma," Rachel teased. "Who'd you bring in today?"

Ruth sighed and shook her head. "Rachel," she scolded.

Jude smirked and waited.

"This is Jude, a friend of mine," Ruth said, her cheeks showing off her embarrassment. "He's visiting for the holidays."

Rachel's smile never left her face. "As much as I love your grandma and the ladies from the quilting circle, it's nice to see you eating with someone your own age."

Ruth groaned and let her head drop back.

Jude laughed softly and put his hand on the low part of her back. "Come on," he urged. "Let's go sit down." He was liking this girl more and more. With each tidbit he learned, he found that he wanted to learn more. She was sweeter than anyone he'd ever known before, she was beautiful, and now he discovered she obviously had a deep respect and love for her grandmother, her grandmother's friends, and grumpy old men.

How many other people in their twenties could say they had that kind of appreciation for their elders? Especially the ones that were downright cantankerous.

Jude shook his head. Who was this girl? And how deep should he let himself get involved before it was too much?

CHAPTER 10

"Thank you," Ruth said to the waitress, handing off her menu. After she and Jude were alone again, Ruth found herself struggling to come up with a topic of conversation. She had made a complete fool of herself while walking over here and to top it off, the hostess's teasing had been enough to send Ruth into the grave!

"So," Jude said, leaning onto the table with his elbows. "Tell me about your family."

Ruth pinched her lips between her teeth. "My family?" she squeaked.

"Yeah." Jude grinned. "You know...the people who raised you? The siblings who tormented you?"

Ruth had trouble looking him in the eye as she spoke. "There's, uh, actually very little to tell. My parents are gone and my only sibling lives out of the country."

"Wow." Jude made a face. "I guess I've gotten really good at sticking my foot in my mouth."

"And I've gotten really good at making my life sound like something on a Lifetime drama," Ruth said, shaking her head. "Sorry. I didn't mean to bring down the mood."

"No, no," he assured her. "It's fine. I just...didn't realize you had it so rough."

"I didn't have it rough," Ruth said quickly. "I've got Grandma Nan and a few cousins I see once in a while." She grinned. "And the quilting circle, of course."

"Of course," Jude agreed with a laugh.

"And yours?"

"My quilting circle?" he teased.

Ruth laughed as intended. "If you know how to quilt, I'll eat this tablecloth."

His eyebrows rose up. "I know you enjoy your food, but that's a bit extreme, isn't it?"

The humor fell from her face. "You can't be serious. You really know how to quilt?"

Jude chuckled and folded his arms over his chest. Even in his bulky sweatshirt, it was a beautiful sight. "Nah. I'm just giving you a hard time."

"Whew!" Ruth wiped at her forehead dramatically. "You had me going for a minute."

"I don't think Grayson and I would ever have become friends if I was into quilting," Jude joked.

Ruth smiled. "So being a personal physical therapist sounds like a pretty sweet gig. How'd you get into that?"

Jude scratched his chin. "Not quite sure, actually. I'm part of an outpatient clinic and we have a section of our therapists who do home visits. Which is very enticing to people with more money than time."

"Like celebrities," Ruth added.

"Exactly," Jude said. "I didn't usually do that kind of thing, but a call came in for an ongoing contract and somehow I was the only one available. I didn't plan on it being more than just a few visits and then I'd hand them off to another person, but once Gray and I got to know each other..." He shrugged.

"Bromance at first sight?" Ruth teased as she picked up her water for a sip.

Jude laughed. "Not quite, but we found we got along really well and I just never asked to be removed from the situation."

"You mentioned that you were with him when he got really hurt a couple years ago," Ruth said quietly. She leaned onto the table. "Is it okay to ask what that was like?"

Jude was quiet for a minute and Ruth worried she had asked something she shouldn't have.

"I'm sorry," she said hurriedly, straightening up. "I'm sure there's confidentiality problems with that question."

Jude waved her off. "It's no biggie. Gray has told me it's all right to talk about it and plus, like you said, it was a couple years ago." He sighed. "It was kind of a hard time though, you know? Watching my best friend go through something so difficult." Jude's eyes dropped to his water glass and he began to twist it from side to side. "He...Gray...was different. He'd lost himself in the pain and became very...I guess bitter is the right word."

Ruth wanted to cry. She hadn't thought about how much a story like this would affect Jude. Didn't guys usually just joke about injuries like they were a scratch, even if they'd broken a bone? But to see things from the outside perspective, when someone you knew and loved had been hurting, must have been devastating.

I need to be more grateful to Grandma, Ruth mentally told herself. It had to have been just as hard on Grandma Nan as it had been on Ruth to go through the cancer ordeal.

"I had to give him some tough love," Jude said with a soft laugh. "But it turned out I wasn't what he needed at all." Jude shook his head. "Look at me getting all sappy on you. I'm sorry."

Ruth reached across the table and put her fingers on his hand before she could stop herself. "Don't be sorry. I think it's wonderful that Grayson had such good friends with him."

Jude smiled and Ruth started to pull her hand away, but he stopped her. Twisting his palm he gripped her fingers and slowly ran his thumb over her knuckles. "Thanks," he said softly. "I'm not sure I've ever actually told anyone my side of the story. It felt good to share it."

Ruth knew then and there that she would have to continue to hide her past. Jude had already been through a life altering situation with Grayson and it had been difficult. He didn't need to experience something similar with her.

I mean...if we ever got to be close friends, that is, she corrected herself. But as his thumb continued to caress her gently and their eyes continued to hold each other, Ruth knew that for her personally, she was definitely in danger of growing that close.

"The pasta primavera?"

The two of them jerked away from each other as if they'd been caught with their hands in the cookie jar and Ruth felt her cheeks automatically heat up. "Uh, here," she said, then cleared her throat when her voice was raspy.

"That means the BLT is yours," the young woman said with a smile, placing the plate in front of Jude. "Anything else I can get you two?" she asked, looking back and forth.

Ruth didn't trust her voice and simply shook her head.

"I think we're good, thanks," Jude said.

The young woman nodded and left, leaving an awkward silence in her wake.

Ruth wasn't sure what to say now. She was pretty sure they'd just experienced a moment, but the interruption made her unsure how to handle it.

"Smells good," Jude said, closing his eyes and taking a whiff. "I think maybe I should have ordered yours."

"Ah, but you have bacon," Ruth pointed out. "That's worth something."

"True." Jude picked up his sandwich and took a bite. "And it's good bacon. Nice and crispy."

"Oh man," Ruth teased. "You've now been cleared to be my friend. I don't do the whole chewy bacon thing."

JUDE SNORTED HIS LAUGHTER and had to throw a napkin over his mouth.

Ruth was smiling as she twirled pasta on her fork.

"Warn me next time, huh?"

"What? When I'm going to be hilarious?" Ruth asked.

"Pretty much," Jude tossed back. He couldn't seem to wipe the smile from his face. Any reservations he had had during his shower were not even registering in his mind. Ruth was proving to be amazing...and apparently, quite funny. If Carson had a problem with it, they were two grown men. They could talk it out.

Ruth leaned in. "Then I guess I should warn you, it's a constant thing."

Jude chuckled through another bite. "Good to know," he replied. He wiped some mayonnaise from the side of his mouth. "If you could be anything in the world, what would it be?"

"Whoa." Ruth set down her fork. "Decided to go straight for the jugular, I see."

Jude laughed. "If that's what you want to call it." He took another bite and waited. Yeah, it was a big question, but Ruth had him honestly curious. She was such a happy person, yet she didn't seem to have an actual direction. He wanted to figure out what her dreams and aspirations were. He wanted to know why she'd quit college. He wanted to know what she was going to do if she ever stopped working for her grandmother.

"Anything, huh?" Ruth mused.

Jude nodded, still chewing.

"Well, I've always thought being a wizard would be fun." She twisted some pasta onto her fork. "Ooh! Or maybe I could help out with a zombie apocalypse team. I think I'd be pretty good at that."

Jude's laughter started out small, but it grew with each new outrageous idea she came up with.

"Or maybe I could be an ice cream taster. I hear they have to insure their taste buds and I think that sounds awesome."

"Okay, now you've finally landed on one I would enjoy," Jude interrupted.

"That does sound like a sweet gig, doesn't it?" Ruth took a bite of her meal.

"Eating ice cream all day? Yeah." Jude paused. "But what about when you're trying the stuff that doesn't make the cut?"

"Do you really think there's anything that terrible?" Ruth asked. "I'm not saying all of them are *good*, but are any of them actually disgusting?"

"I would hope not, but I've seen some make it into stores that I thought sounded gross, so I guess you never know."

Ruth frowned. "Like what?"

Jude scratched his chin. "Okay, I know a million people love this, but I hate bananas. So any ice cream with bananas in it is enough to make me want to gag."

Ruth put a hand to her heart. "And after bonding over crispy bacon," she said breathlessly. "How did we go so wrong?"

"I take it that's a deal breaker?" Jude pressed.

"You can say that." Ruth tsked her tongue and shook her head. "Haven't you ever had a fluffernutter?"

"Of course, but what does that have to do with bananas?" Jude asked.

Ruth looked shocked. "There are bananas on fluffernutters."

"No, there aren't."

"Yes, there are."

Jude scowled playfully. "I think I would know if there's been a banana on a sandwich made of nothing but carbs and sugar."

"Sugar and chocolate," Ruth pointed out. "And banana."

Jude continued to shake his head and Ruth whipped out her phone.

"Let's just settle this once and for all, huh?"

"Go for it," Jude challenged. "I always enjoy being proven right."

"Oh, ho," Ruth laughed, her eyes on the screen. "So confident."

Jude was still grinning as he took another bite of food and waited for her to look it up. She was too cute. He popped the last bite of sandwich in his mouth, suddenly sad that their time was going to come to an end. He wasn't ready to let go of this light-hearted argument they were having.

"Huh," Ruth said, setting her phone down and pursuing her lips.

"It's all right, you can just say it," Jude taunted.

"Well, what do you do when two people are right?"

"Wait...what?" Jude reached for her phone, but Ruth kept it away from him. He narrowed his eyes. "How can I know you're telling the truth if you won't let me see?"

"Use your own phone," she teased, though the words were slightly shaky. "I don't know you well enough to let you use mine. What if I have weird pictures on it or something that I don't want you to see?"

Jude rolled his eyes and pulled his own phone from his pocket. "I wasn't going to look at the pictures," he teased back, though some of the enjoyment was gone momentarily. He wasn't quite sure what was off about her response, but something had been lost. He read the definition of a fluffernutter. "Huh."

"Exactly what I said," Ruth cried, waving a hand in the air. "What are we supposed to do with that?"

"It said the original is without any additives," Jude said. "So clearly, I should win."

"It said adding bananas is typical," Ruth pointed out. "Typical means most people do it. So clearly, I should win."

"But the original means it came first."

"Typical means they learned how to make it better," Ruth argued.

"I don't think that's what it means," Jude said slowly.

"It does in my book." Ruth folded her arms over her chest.

"And your word is law?"

"It is today."

Jude laughed. "I guess there's only one way to settle this," he stated, laying his hands down on either side of his plate.

"Why am I suddenly afraid to ask?" Ruth gave him a wary gaze.

"We'll just have to set up a time to make fluffernutters and compare." Jude stilled after the words were out. It wasn't that he didn't mean them, he did. He just hadn't thought them out very well before tossing the idea into the mix. "I mean...only if you want to," he hurried to add. "I wasn't trying to presume—"

Ruth shook her head and put up a hand to stop his rambling. "I'd like that," she said when he finally shut up.

Jude relaxed into his seat. "Great. I mean, that's great. It'll be great. The whole thing will be..."

"Great?" Ruth offered, still grinning.

Jude nodded. "Yeah." Could he get any more stupid? How many times did he need to say something was great? And his word vomit made him appear like a kindergartner for heaven's sake!

"I think so too."

And just like that, all the negative words rushing through Jude's head were done. This was Ruth. He might not have known her long, but this was the woman who smiled at grumpy old men. Who spent time with gossip groups who pretended to be quilting circles. Who worked at a cheap motel and greeted guests as if it were a five star resort. Of course she would be kind about his semi-nervous chattering.

"Tomorrow?" he asked, praying he wasn't reading this whole thing completely wrong.

"Tomorrow."

"Great," he said with a wink, reveling in her laugh. "It's a date."

CHAPTER 11

Want to eat sandwiches for dinner tonight?

Ruth laughed at the text, then glanced around to make sure no one knew what she was doing. The front desk had been extremely slow today and her little texting thread with Jude was a life saver.

Her thumbs hovered over the keys as she debated her answer. She *definitely* wanted to have their fluffernutter competition tonight, but she also wanted to not appear like a drooling fangirl, nevermind the fact that she was one.

Jude had been hard to get to know at first, but he was starting to open up and Ruth was really enjoying everything she saw. He was totally handsome, which she had known from the start, but he was also a gentleman. He was kind. He was funny, smiled and laughed a lot, and he didn't seem put off by her need to help the people around her.

Some of the guys Ruth knew thought her desire to help others feel better was dumb. If they'd seen her with Mr. Portman, they would have said she was wasting her time, but not Jude. He'd simply followed along and smiled the whole time.

Ruth's stomach erupted in butterflies at the thought. She had been so surprised when he'd followed her back to the motel from Charli's shop, only to take her to lunch as if they'd had a date planned the whole time.

Only if you're ready to realize I'm right.

You can dream, but those don't always come true.

She grinned. **Bananas make everything better.**

Bananas are the Brussels sprout of the fruit world.

Her laughter couldn't be held in this time, and Ruth snorted in her humor.

"I didn't realize an empty room was so entertaining," Grandma Nan said wryly as she came in from the back room.

Ruth shoved her phone in her pocket and shook her head. "It's not."

Grandma's eyes narrowed. "Please tell me you weren't watching cat videos."

Ruth's eyebrows shot up. "Nope."

"The World's Dumbest Criminals?"

"What in the world are you talking about?" Ruth asked, throwing up her hands.

Grandma Nan pointed a finger at her granddaughter. "I want to know what put that twinkle in your eye."

Ruth looked away. "Nothing," she said more softly.

Grandma Nan stepped over and took Ruth's chin, pulling her gently back. "It's Jude, isn't it?"

Ruth rolled her eyes. "How did we get from dumb criminals to Jude?"

Grandma Nan smiled. "I *knew* it. Just wait until I tell that old crone she was wrong."

"Wait...what?" Ruth's dreamy feelings immediately turned to panic. "What are you talking about?"

This time it was Grandma Nan trying to look innocent. "Just a little thing from the circle." She turned away. "Nothing for you to worry about."

"Grandma..." Ruth warned. "What have you old biddies been talking about?"

"Biddies!" Grandma Nan spun and put her hand on her chest. "I take that personally!"

"You should," Ruth shot right back. "If you can call your friends crones, I can call you biddies." She folded her arms over her chest. "Especially if I'm your topic of conversation."

Grandma Nan blew a raspberry and waved a hand through the air. "We're grandmas. We can talk about whatever we want."

"Not if it's about me."

Grandma Nan was unimpressed. "I hate to break it to you, sweetie, but we've been chatting about you for years."

Ruth's arms fell. "I know." She dropped her eyes to the ground. She put her hand over her eyes. "I'm sorry," she whispered, hoping Grandma couldn't hear the held back laughter. "I didn't mean to be such a burden."

Tapping fingers caught Ruth's attention and she carefully peeked through her fingers, before dropping her hand and sighing.

Grandma Nan was slowly shaking her head. "I've lived too long to fall for that."

Ruth put her hands on her hips. "It was worth a try."

"And yet ultimately, a waste of my time."

Ruth laughed and tucked a piece of hair behind her ear before patting her head. "Apparently so."

"It wasn't a waste of time to go to lunch with Jude, however."

"Nice segway," Ruth said dryly.

"I've had years of practice."

"I'll just bet you have."

"And I still want to know who you were talking to."

Ruth smirked. "I thought you knew."

"Did he invite you out again?" Grandma Nan's eyes were wide and hopeful and Ruth found she couldn't quite bring herself to keep arguing.

She bit her lip and nodded. "Yes."

Grandma Nan squeezed her eyes shut and clenched a fist in victory. "I knew it!" Her eyes popped open. "When are you getting together? Do you need time off?"

"Whoa…" Ruth put her hands in the air. "Not so fast."

"Well?" Grandma Nan pressed.

Ruth laughed and shook her head. "We're having dinner tonight. It's no big deal."

"It *is* a big deal," Grandma Nan urged. "What did he say about the cancer?"

Ruth froze.

Grandma Nan's smile fell. "Ruth."

This time Ruth's shame was real as her eyes hit the ground. "We barely know each other," she mumbled.

"That boy deserves to know you," Grandma Nan snapped.

"We're getting to know each other," Ruth argued. "But there's no way I'm pulling the victim card until, or better yet if, we ever get deeper into a relationship."

"Victim?" Grandma Nan scoffed. "You're a survivor! Not a victim! Any man worth his salt will know that."

"Well, I don't know if Jude is worth his salt or not," Ruth said in exasperation. "Because we're just getting to know each other."

Grandma Nan was somber as she shook her head. "You're doing him a disservice."

Ruth felt her stubborn side rising to the surface. She didn't get this way very often, but this…this was too close to home. There was no way she could tell Jude about the cancer. At least not at this point in time. And especially not the hair. Ruth's scars were still too tender for her to want to share that side.

If…and it was a big if…she and Jude ever got serious, then she would tell him. Maybe…probably…yes. Yes, she'd definitely tell him. But not before then, and absolutely not right now.

"He's only here for a few more days," Ruth said firmly. "Odds are I'll never see him again. I'm not spilling every skeleton in my closet when we'll only ever be friends."

Grandma pushed past Ruth and paused at the door. "We both know you're hoping for more than that. I'm hoping for more than that." Grandma's eyes were misty when she met Ruth's gaze. "You deserve something wonderful, but heaven knows so does he. I know who his friends are...and that means Jude is a good kid. Give him a chance to show you."

JUDE COULD HEAR CARSON in the bathroom up ahead and he stuffed his phone in his pocket. He wasn't ready to admit to Carson that he was seeing the girl Brook had set him up with. The bathroom door was wide open and steam filtered through the air. "Got a hot date?" Jude asked with a grin.

"Heading to the grocery store," Carson said without looking at Jude.

"You just went a couple days ago." Jude crossed his arms over his chest. "Why would you need to go again?" Something was up. Carson had been disappearing right and left lately, and it left Jude suspicious.

"Maybe Brook's sending me." Carson turned and mimicked his friend's pose.

"Eh." Jude made the sound of a buzzer. "Try again." Now he really needed to know. Was Carson spending time with someone? Was it Ruth? Panic hit Jude in the gut, but he forced himself to slow down. Ruth didn't seem like the type to play with two men.

Carson rolled his eyes. "Maybe I don't want to tell you."

Jude narrowed his gaze. "It must be a woman." There. That should do it. Carson never could resist a good argument.

Carson's eyebrows slowly rose. "What makes you say that?"

"Because you're one of the most talkative people I know," Jude said wryly. "You only clam up when it comes to women, and even that you don't do very much of, because most of the time you complain about how all they want is Gray."

"I've seen you with female company yourself, lately," Carson shot back.

Jude rubbed the back of his neck. "Yeah. So?" *Crap.* Just what had Carson seen? Did he know Jude was seeing Ruth? Or had he seen him talking to someone else?

"So, nothing," Carson said easily. "You do your thing. I'll do mine."

Jude sighed, frustrated he hadn't gotten the answers he wanted. But if Carson thought he had his own ammunition, Jude wasn't going to fight. "I suppose." He stopped Carson as he tried to walk through the door. "It isn't..." He swallowed. No...he couldn't let it go. He needed to know. "It's not the lady from the opening party, is it?"

Carson frowned. "She was there. She was refilling the dishes."

Now it was Jude's turn to frown. "Refilling? Like, she was working? With the caterers?" Wait...could they be talking about two different women? Hope flared to life in his chest.

Carson nodded. "Who else would it be?"

"No one," Jude said quickly, stepping back and leaving room for Carson to leave. "It's no big deal." Jude didn't say another word as Carson bid him farewell and darted down the hall to escape. *It isn't Ruth.* A slow grin spread across Jude's face. *He isn't after Ruth.*

Jude had no idea who the woman was that Carson was hurrying to see, but all in all, he didn't care. If Carson wasn't interested in Ruth, then Jude wasn't going to feel guilty about it anymore.

He liked her. He wanted to spend more time with her and now, nothing was in his way.

He pulled his phone back out. **What time are you available tonight?** "Shoot." Jude crinkled his nose. He would need to hit the grocery store as well if he was going to have the necessary ingredients for his sandwich tonight.

Six?

Perfect.

That gave Jude plenty of time to freshen up, grab the ingredients, and head out. He turned to walk downstairs and paused. "But where?" Jude was here as a guest. He didn't technically have a kitchen for them to have their date in. They could probably have it at Ruth's, but she lived with her grandmother. Would that be weird? And would it even be polite to ask if they could have it there?

Jude scrubbed a hand down his face. Ruth had seemed really uncomfortable when her grandmother wouldn't stop teasing them. She probably wouldn't want to hang out at home.

He glanced down the stairs and sucked in a deep breath. "Nothing for it," he whispered to himself. Marching down to the family room, he searched for Brook. This went against everything Jude would normally have planned, but what else could he do?

"Hey, Jude!" Brook snickered and Jude rolled his eyes.

"If I had a dollar..." He groaned.

Brook laughed. "I know, I know." She held her hands up. "But we haven't seen much of you and I thought it'd be funny." She wiped her hands on her jeans and surveyed the tree she had been setting up. "What do you think, Gray? Was it funny?"

Jude hadn't known Grayson was in the room, but when his grunt came from the other side of the tree, there was no mistaking it. "Absolutely hilarious." Grayson groaned as he straightened and rubbed his back. "Just like it was the first million times."

"Thank you!" Jude exclaimed, throwing a hand toward his friend. "Your back okay?'

Grayson chuckled. "Always worried about injuries, I see."

Jude stuffed his hands in his pockets and shrugged. "Second nature, I suppose."

Grayson nodded. "I figured, but I'm fine." He playfully glared at his wife. "If *someone* would stop asking me to put up a thousand trees, then I'd be even better."

Brook snorted. "We're having a tree decorating competition. What else are we supposed to do?"

"Hire a couple of teenagers?" Grayson offered.

"It's only, like, ten trees," Brook argued. "Why do I need to hire out for that?"

"Because your husband is getting old," Jude offered with a grin.

Grayson's eyebrows shot up. "Old? Really? You're only two years behind me, buddy."

"Ah..." Jude rocked nonchalantly on his heels. "Two years of youth shall yet be mine."

Brook laughed while Grayson grumbled under his breath. "Don't make me show off the guns this early in the day," Grayson threatened.

"Need your beauty rest?" Grayson lunged toward Jude, who danced out of the way, laughing. He hadn't had this much fun with any of his friends in what felt like a long time. At this moment, the joking and taunting made him realize just how far he had sunk into the abyss. He felt like he was coming up for a breath of fresh air after being shut in a prison cell for too long. "Can I use the kitchen tonight?" The words were out before Jude could stop them. His easygoing feelings vanished and he bit his tongue so hard, he was sure he was about to taste blood.

Brook tilted her head. "Sure, but why?"

Jude cleared his throat and scratched his jaw. "Uh..."

"You've got to be kidding me." Gray snorted. "Both of you?"

Jude felt his neck heat up as Brook looked back and forth between the two of them. "What? What do you mean, both of you?"

Jude made a wordless yet imploring plea toward his best friend.

Gray laughed some more and shook his head. "When do you need it?"

"Maybe between six and eight?"

"Would somebody please let me in on the conversation?" Brook demanded, putting her hands on her hips.

Grayson's eyebrows shot up as he smirked. "Want us to set up some mistletoe? I hear it worked wonders for Carson."

The heat intensified. "Nah, that's okay," Jude said, backing up. He should have spoken with Gray alone. Or Brook alone. Either way, it would have been better than just blurting out something he wasn't quite ready to explain.

"Oh my gosh," Brook gushed. "Are you bringing over a woman?"

Grayson's laughter followed Jude as he turned and practically sprinted out of the room. Now was the perfect time for that run he'd been neglecting this morning. Perhaps if he was fast enough, he could outrun his embarrassment and have just enough time to get ready for Ruth before their dinner date.

And avoid Brook.

Sweet as she was, Jude was going to leave the heavy lifting to Grayson's guns. He was married to Brook. Surely he could handle her just fine.

CHAPTER 12

Ruth's heart was beating so hard, she wondered if she hadn't been running a marathon. It seemed the last time she had been so worked up was before a treatment or waiting for the results of a test.

She wrung her hands together and paced the lobby of the motel, internally scolding herself for being such a ninny.

"You'll wear a hole in that carpet," Grandma Nan said dryly.

Ruth forced herself to sit down and relax, though her nervous system still didn't get the message. "Sorry."

"Not a big deal, hm?" Grandma Nan's knowing smirk was a little obnoxious this evening.

Ruth chose to ignore, rather than get defensive, and picked up a magazine. She hadn't been on a date in years. Not a real one anyway. Sure, she and Jude had gone out to lunch the other day, but that had been a hastily thrown out suggestion that he'd been nice enough to help fulfill. This had been a real, boy-ask-girl, spend time together because we like each other, date.

Headlights flashed through the glass front doors and Ruth jumped to her feet. She began walking to the door, but Grandma stopped her.

"Don't you dare not give that boy a chance to come inside and be a gentleman," she scolded.

Ruth blew out a breath. "It isn't the nineteen-fifties, Grandma. And he's not a boy."

"Maybe not, but any *man* unwilling to step inside for a minute to collect a beautiful woman isn't worth your time."

Ruth plopped back down in the seat. "Fine." The door opened and Ruth was back up in a flash. Her eyes widened and she had to consciously keep her jaw from dropping. She had seen Jude in sweats, shorts, T-shirts, and even a dress shirt at the party. All of them had been marvelous, but tonight he looked...amazing.

His hair was slicked back and his peacoat showed off his strong shoulders, allowing his long, athletic legs to stand out in well-fitting jeans. It was a look in between the casual and formal and it was perfect.

She must have squeaked or something because Jude jerked his head in her direction, then stopped and stared.

Ruth's hand went up to pat her hair, making sure it was in place as he studied her from head to toe.

"You look beautiful," Jude said softly, breaking the silence between them.

"So do you," Ruth responded with a small laugh when Jude scratched his chin. "Handsome? Is that better?"

He made a face. "I think most men prefer it, yeah."

"Pretty men," Grandma Nan grumbled from the front desk. "They've been around since the dawn of time; just ask Eve."

Ruth frowned. "What? How do you know what Adam looked like?"

Grandma Nan put her hands on her hips. "Why else do you think she wanted him to leave the garden with her? A smart woman would have gotten herself kicked out just to get a little space, but no...Eve had to take Adam with her." Grandma pointed a finger at Ruth, then Jude. "Only explanation? He was pretty to look at."

"Oh my goodness," Ruth said under her breath. "And that, I think, is our cue to leave." She dramatically opened her eyes at Jude as he chuckled.

"Thank you," Jude said to Grandma. "I think."

Grandma Nan threw her hands in the air. "Can't even give a compliment anymore." She groaned.

Ruth was still shaking her head as they headed outside. "Night, Grandma! Thank you!"

"Tell him!" Grandma shouted behind her.

Ruth stiffened but forced herself to keep going. Grandma was going to go too far one of these days.

"Should I even ask what that's all about?" Jude asked, still laughing as he opened the passenger door for her.

"Nope," Ruth said in a chipper voice. "Believe me, you don't want to know."

"I'll take your word for it," Jude said just before closing her door.

Ruth deflated for a second, blowing out a long breath as he walked around. She set her bag of ingredients on the floor at her feet and tried to calm down her ire. This was not the night to spend being upset at her grandma. It was her first date in years with a guy Ruth liked much more than she should, and she didn't want to ruin it. Cancer and grandmas were off limits tonight.

Jude plopped into his seat and locked his seatbelt. "Ready?"

"Yep." Ruth waited a moment as they pulled out into the street. "So, where are we going? Obviously, we're not doing this in your hotel room..." She raised an eyebrow at him, though he probably couldn't see it in the dark.

"Brook and Gray said we could use the kitchen."

Ruth gulped. "The Cordovas?"

Jude nodded and glanced her way before going back to the street. "Is that a problem?"

"Are they joining us?" Ruth tried, but failed at keeping the worry from her voice. Brook had been so sweet the other night, but Ruth wasn't sure she could handle the movie star husband. Plus...she just didn't want to share Jude with anyone. She and Jude would only have a few days together before he went home and she couldn't help but feel possessive of that time. *He came to Oregon to see THEM*, she reminded herself. It wasn't fair of her to be jealous of something that wasn't hers in the first place.

"Not tonight." Jude waited a beat, then continued. "I mean, I'm sure they could if you want them to. They're really nice people, but I...hadn't planned on it."

Ruth's shoulders relaxed. "No, that's fine," she said too quickly. "I mean...I'm fine with it being just us."

There was no way Jude didn't catch onto her relief and when a smirk grew on his face, Ruth knew she was busted. "I'm fine with that too," he assured her.

Ruth's heart took off once again. She glanced at his lips, then quickly looked away. It wouldn't do to dream too hard, but man...Ruth was having a hard time reining in her imagination. Apparently, it had been left alone for too long to be rational in any way, shape, or form.

"Here we are," Jude said, parking in the large driveway. "Let me come get your door."

Ruth waited patiently, then stood as he waited for her. "Thanks."

"Anytime. Got your stuff?"

Ruth held up the bag. "Am I ready to win? Isn't that what you meant to ask?"

Jude laughed. "Close enough." He took a step back and held out his hand, waiting for her.

Ruth glanced at his face, where he looked hopeful, but patient. Slowly, she slid her fingers into his, enjoying the sweet sensations that began to jump up and down her arm.

Jude's smile was brighter than the driveway lights as he gripped her fingers gently and took her inside. They slipped through the front door and navigated the quiet hallways with ease until they reached the large chef's kitchen.

Ruth's eyes couldn't take it all in as she looked around in awe. The white granite, the gray backsplash, the spots of colorful dishes bringing life to the room. It was magnificent. "Whoa…"

Jude grinned, still holding her free hand. "It's something, huh? I guess it pays to be a movie star."

Ruth squeezed his fingers, drawing his attention. *Tonight is a time to be bold,* she reminded herself. *Life is too short and precious to waste any of it.* "The room is nice," she said, forcing herself to keep meeting his eyes. "But it's the company that makes it great."

JUDE COULD BARELY FIND the self discipline to look away from those penetrating blue eyes. How could a woman be so soft spoken and yet so clear about where she stood? He had sort of expected someone as kind as Ruth to be a little more shy about her feelings, but in the end, he wasn't complaining.

One of the worst things about dating was trying to figure out how the other person felt. Jude should know. He'd held out hope for months with Elania. But here was someone who was offering her thoughts without playing coy or trying to dance around the question. She liked him. It was that simple.

And he liked her too.

Her fingers felt perfect in his grip and he was already mourning the fact that he would need to let her go in order to get their evening started, but he promised himself there would be more hand-holding later.

It felt as if his knuckles were creaking in protest when he let go of her hand and walked farther into the room. "I'll grab plates. Would you like anything to drink?"

"I think something like this calls for milk, don't you?" Ruth asked.

Jude grinned. "Sounds perfect." He grabbed what they needed and set it all out on the counter, Ruth doing the same with her supplies. "Okay...now what?"

"Now, I show you how it's really done," she teased. Her eyes went around the counter. "Knife?"

Jude went over and grabbed one out of a drawer. "Should I be concerned that you're asking for weapons?" He handed her the small piece of silverware.

Ruth gave him a wink. "Guess you'll find out."

"And here I thought you were so sweet."

"Just goes to show that you never know," she said breezily.

The familiar feelings of panic and anxiety began to build in Jude and he stilled for a moment.

"Jude?" Ruth dropped what she was doing and came to stand in front of him. "Are you okay? You look pale all of a sudden." She put a hand to her forehead. "I'm such an idiot. I'm sorry. I was just teasing. I promise."

Jude shook himself out of his depressive reverie and focused on the concerned face before him. "No, no, no," he hurried to say. "It's fine. I promise." Ruth still looked upset and Jude's hands came up to frame her face, catching her attention. "Ruth," he said, his voice dropping as the intimacy of the touch sank into his consciousness. "It's fine."

Her eyes were wide and concerned as they looked up at Jude. There was something in them that Jude couldn't read. Hope? Fear? He wasn't quite sure, but the warmth from her skin felt too good for him to pull back just yet. Instead he just stood, holding her and waiting to see what she said next.

"If you say so," she whispered. Her voice had a slight rasp to it, and Jude felt his attraction surge to the surface.

When she didn't pull away, he allowed his thumb to slowly move, tracing along her cheekbone. Her skin was so soft...softer than any person he'd ever met. What was this woman doing to him? The more he got to know her, the more Jude wanted from her. He wanted time, he wanted to keep touching her, he wanted to know everything about her, and he wanted to share everything about himself.

Somehow this woman he barely knew had started to dig into places in his heart that Jude had only ever shared with one person, the person who had sent him running from California like a dog with its tail between its legs.

Ruth had found him and was slowly coaxing out the man that Jude used to be, and the feeling was exciting.

"Ruth," he breathed, coming in a little closer.

"Yes?"

"Can I kiss you?"

The edges of her lovely pink lips tilted up. "At this point, I'd be disappointed if you didn't."

A soft laugh escaped Jude before he closed the rest of the distance. At the first touch of her mouth, he felt something jolt to life inside of him. Something that had been dormant for too long and was now being revived.

Again, he kissed her, his hand sliding down her neck, while the other trailed to her back so he could pull her closer. When her arms came up around his neck, and she rose up on tiptoe for better reach, Jude took the chance in deepening the kiss and bringing her fully into his arms.

Over and over he kissed her, quickly realizing that he would never be able to satiate himself. Their moments went from soft and gentle, to hungry and hurried, but stopping just didn't seem to be an option. When she sighed and melted against his chest, Jude thought he would lose control for sure. His hand crept up her back in order to move into her hair, ready to feel the silky strands between his fingers, but just before he was able to do so, Ruth pulled back, gasping for air.

"I'm sorry," she said, one hand on her head and the other over her bright red lips. "I'm sorry."

Jude was a little confused, wondering why she had stopped and why she was apologizing. "Uh...I..."

Ruth's cheeks were bright red and her fingers were shaking. "You must think I'm...that I..." Groaning, she put her face in her hands. "Where is an earthquake when you need it?" she grumbled.

Realizing she was worried he was going to take things too far, Jude laughed and pulled her hands away from her face, then ducking until she was willing to look him in the eye. "Hey...I'm sorry," he said. "I shouldn't have attacked you like that on our first kiss." He gave her a half smile. "Although, I'd be lying if I said I regretted it."

Ruth hung her head, but she was smiling. "I don't regret it either, and I can't decide if that makes me a floozy or just desperate."

Still chuckling, Jude pulled her into his chest and hugged her, laying his cheek against her head. "Well, you're definitely not a floozy, and I was just as into it as you, so I guess that makes us desperate together, huh?"

Ruth pulled back, though she looked reluctant about it, and patted her hair again.

She's really worried about that hair, Jude mused. He shrugged it off, figuring it was just something he would have to get used to. After all, no one was perfect, right? If Ruth was worried about her hair, he would just have to show her that he could respect that. "Ready to try my masterpiece?" he asked, trying to break the tension in the room.

Ruth's smile was relieved as well as stunning. "You're on," she said, turning back to the counter.

Jude couldn't help himself. He stepped up behind her, crowding her just a little, and whispered in her ear. "I think the winner should earn a kiss. What do you think?"

Ruth looked over her shoulder, her blue eyes sparkling. "Doesn't that just mean both of us get kisses no matter what?"

Jude shrugged a little. "I guess that just makes us both winners, right? Don't they encourage that nowadays? Participation trophies for everyone?"

Ruth laughed. "Sounds like a plan."

Leaving a quick kiss on her temple, he stepped to the side and rubbed his hands. "Then let's get this going. I have a kiss to win." He winked. "Or give."

CHAPTER 13

"You're humming again."

Ruth stopped the Christmas carol she had no idea she'd been singing softly and did her best not to blush. She failed.

Grandma Nan tsked her tongue. "I can't believe you won't tell me what happened last night."

Ruth shrugged. "I'm a grown woman, Grandma. I don't see why I should have to spill everything to you."

Grandma Nan huffed, but didn't argue more.

Ruth laughed softly and finished filling the bowl full of mints on the front counter. She couldn't seem to stop smiling today. Last night had been, in a word, amazing.

Ruth wouldn't deny the fact that getting a kiss from Jude had crossed her mind more than once, but she hadn't really believed it would happen, at least not last night. After all, it was their first date. But it had happened, and it had been glorious.

If angels still came to earth to announce wonderful tidings, this was surely one of them. At the first touch of his lips, Ruth felt as if her whole being had suddenly lit up. Her heart had fluttered, her breathing had become nonexistent, and her brain had floated into the cloud covered sky.

Unfortunately, the touch of his hand coming into her hair had been enough to pull her right back down to earth. There was no way he wouldn't have figured out her hair was fake if he had been playing with it.

"You need to tell him."

Ruth threw up her hands. "Do you have telepathy for something? I'm the one who went through radiation! Why didn't I get the superpowers?"

Grandma Nan grinned, despite the seriousness of the situation. "Honey, it's just like a Band-id. It's better if you just do it all at once, rather than wait or move too slowly." Her smile fell. "The longer you wait, the more it's going to hurt. He's going to feel lied to."

"I'm not lying to him," Ruth defended. "I'm just not telling him everything."

Grandma turned away, shaking her head.

Ruth knew in her gut that Grandma was right, but how could she do it? She *really, really* liked Jude. And his kisses last night were the stuff dreams were made of. But how could she look him in the eye and tell him that she ate so much because she had been unable to eat for years? That her figure was due to medications rather than genetics or being a big exerciser? That she had no direction in life because she had been unsure she would even have a life?

That she was bald and looked like an alien instead of a woman without her wig on?

Grandma Nan's fingers gripped her chin. "Give him a chance," she said softly. "He likes you. Anybody can see that. Give him a chance to show just what kind of man he is."

Ruth pulled back. "Not yet," she said hoarsely. "When the time is right, I'll do it, but not until then."

Grandma Nan opened her mouth, but never got to speak again as they were interrupted when Mr. Portman came storming into the room. "Can't get a decent fish sandwich around here anywhere," he snapped. "Been coming here for fifty years, and now they decide they can't make one?" He shook his head and headed toward the hallway.

Grandma Nan rolled her eyes, but Ruth smiled. Why were grumpy old men so funny? "Something wrong, Mr. Portman?" she asked, giving him her best smile.

The elderly man stopped and turned to glare at her. "Fifty years I've been coming here," he said. "Fifty years I've been buying the same fish sandwich at that stand by the marina. But it's not the same, I tell you! Not the same!"

Ruth frowned sympathetically. "I'm sorry. Did they go out of business?"

He shook his head and waved her off. "Don't understand. You young people know nothing of tradition and making things last."

Ruth deflated a little when he left.

"I can't figure out why he comes," Grandma Nan grumbled, poking around at the computer.

"I feel sorry for him," Ruth said, her eyes still on the hallway.

"What? Why would you do a foolish thing like that?"

Ruth turned to her grandmother. "Because it must be miserable to go through life like that. Plus, I don't think most of us are born that way. Something happened to make him grumpy and I feel bad that he had to go through something hard and bad that affected him for so long."

Grandma Nan waved her off and headed to the backroom. "I'm taking a break."

Ruth watched her go, then went back to the hallway. There was just something about Mr. Portman that called to her. She didn't like seeing him so upset. Surely there was something she could do. But what?"

The bell on the door rang again and Ruth turned her attention toward the noise.

"Hello, beautiful." Jude stood in the doorway with his hands in his jeans pockets.

Ruth melted just a little bit inside. "Hey." She watched him saunter closer. "I thought you said you were busy tonight."

Jude nodded, his face looking down as his eyes glanced up. "I was."

"But?"

"But I decided I'd rather be here with you."

If she wasn't a puddle before, she certainly was becoming one now. "Wow."

Jude's face came up and he raised his eyebrows. "Wow?"

"Yeah. Wow."

He chuckled. "Is that good?"

"Very good." Ruth fanned herself. "What woman wouldn't want to hear that?"

He laughed again and leaned on the counter, cocking his hip out behind him. "So...whatcha up to?"

Ruth shook her head, her smile uncontrollable. "Just guarding the counter while Grandma takes a break."

"Guarding? What exactly are you protecting?"

"The mints." Ruth nodded toward the bowl. "People try to take two sometimes."

Jude frowned and slowly shook his head. "For shame."

"Seriously!" Ruth said, holding back her laughter. "I'm not sure the average public realizes just how terrible that is." She got down on her elbows, putting her face close to Jude's. "Now, you're one of the privileged few."

"I feel special," he said, his voice low.

Ruth's heart leapt when his eyes darted to her lips and back up.

"Think your grandma might let you spend some time with me when she's done with her break? Or do fluffernutter losers also lose privileges for dates?"

"I think my grandma would be elated to end her break if she knew you were asking," Ruth admitted with a grimace. "Especially since you're a fluffernutter loser." She leaned forward and put a hand to the side of her mouth as she fake whispered, "Grandma doesn't like bananas either."

Jude chuckled and reached out to tuck her hair back.

Ruth tried not to flinch, but quickly followed his hand with her own, making sure her hair stayed in place. She could just imagine his look of disgust when her entire head moved and he realized she was bald. It wouldn't take a genius for him to figure out everything.

Jude cleared his throat and stood back, stuffing his hands in his pockets. "Um...I have to admit I didn't really have much of a plan when I showed up. What would you like to do?"

Ruth opened her mouth, then paused and turned her head to look back at the hallway again. She grinned. "I have an idea."

JUDE SHIFTED THE HOT paper bag from one hand to the other so he could open the motel door. "You're sure about this?" he asked Ruth for the thousandth time. "I'm pretty sure Mr. Portman hates me."

"He hates everyone," she said breezily, waving off his concerns.

They stepped into the heat of the front lobby and Jude shook a little, as if ridding himself of the chilly temperatures they'd just left behind. They waved at Grandma Nan, who rolled her eyes good naturedly.

"If you had just seen him," Ruth continued as she led him down the hall to Mr. Portman's room. "He was acting all mad, but really, I think he's just sad."

"How can you tell?" Jude asked, not quite sure he believed her. He'd seen Mr. Portman in action at Charli's store and the man looked anything but sad. He'd looked downright dangerous. If Mr. Portman had a cane, Jude was positive someone would have left the warehouse with a concussion.

Ruth shrugged as she bounced to a stop in front of a door. "I just can." She tucked her hair behind her ear, patted her head, then knocked.

Jude studied her hair. He was trying hard not to be offended by her odd fetish with it, but when she basically drove off his touch earlier, it was hard not to feel a little weird about it. He wasn't sure if he should address it or not and so had chosen to just stay quiet. So she had a personal bubble she didn't want breached. That was fine, right?

Before Jude could think on it anymore, the door opened and they were faced with a very *not* sad, but definitely angry, Mr. Portman.

"What do you mean by interrupting me?" he demanded. His slight stature made him hard to take seriously, but the narrowed eyes and nearly nonexistent lips were a pretty strong indicator of his emotions.

Ruth smiled, the one that seemed to light up a room in Jude's eyes, but Mr. Portman was unmoved. "We brought you a fish sandwich!" she declared, showing off the bag that Jude was holding.

Jude tried for a smile, but it felt more like a grimace as he held the bag up higher.

Mr. Portman blustered. "What do you think you're doing?" he snarled. "Why would you do that?"

Ruth tilted her head to the side. "Because you said you wanted one." She leaned in with a conspiratorial grin. "I discovered that the sandwich shack you were referring to wasn't closed down, just moved. They're farther down the boardwalk in a more populated zone now."

Jude couldn't help but smile at the way she was trying so hard to entice the older man.

Mr. Portman's eyes went back and forth between the two of them. "Fine," he snapped. He reached for the bag, but Ruth shook her head.

"Nope," she said cheerily. "We brought enough for everyone! We're going to have a picnic together."

When Mr. Portman shook his head adamantly, Jude bit his tongue to refrain from saying it hadn't been his idea. He'd ditched Brook's tree decorating party early in order to spend time with Ruth, and adding a grumpy old man to the mix was definitely putting a damper on his plans.

"I'm not having a picnic with you two," Mr. Portman stated bluntly before starting to close the door.

Ruth folded her hands in front of her. "I brought extra tartar sauce."

Mr. Portman paused and looked over his shoulder. "How did you know I like extra tartar sauce?"

Ruth just smiled.

Rubbing his face as if he'd been backed into a corner, Mr. Portman groaned. "Fine. But only this once." He shuffled into his room, coming back with a coat and hat.

"Wonderful," Ruth said. She stepped back, closer to Jude as Mr. Portman closed and locked his door. "Let's eat on the patio," she suggested. "It's not raining, but there is a bit of wind, and that patio is pretty well protected." She stepped up and took Mr. Portman's arm, walking at his pace as they made their way down the hall.

Jude followed in shocked silence. He couldn't believe that Mr. Portman had agreed. Jude had been sure the old man was going to chew them up, spit them out, and then walk away without a care in the world. But not with Ruth, apparently. He'd never seen someone so set on helping others and it made Jude feel bad for not only doubting her, but letting her eccentricities bother him.

Why did it matter if she was really particular about her hair? Her hair wasn't why Jude was falling for her. But her sweet spirit that she shared with everyone around her? Yeah. That was enough to pull him along all day long.

"Ooh," Ruth said, tucking herself into her coat collar. "It's colder than I thought."

Jude paused where he held the door, wondering if they were really going to sit out in the freezing winter weather.

"We can't stay out here," Ruth said firmly.

Mr. Portman grunted, but Jude could see the old man starting to shake a little.

"Looks like our picnic is inside today," Ruth decided. She smiled at Jude as he continued to hold open the door. "Grandma won't mind if we use the break area. We'll just have to pretend we've got blue sky above us."

Jude glanced up. "I think we would have been pretending anyway." The sea of gray was anything but inviting.

Ruth laughed and stretched up on tiptoe to kiss his cheek. "Thank you," she said softly, before turning back to Mr. Portman. "Ready to go in?"

"Make up your mind, girl," he grumbled, but even Jude could hear there was less bite than before in the tone.

"I have," Ruth said without sounding defensive. "And we're eating inside."

Jude shook his head and chuckled, but followed the pair back inside and into the break room.

"Have a seat and I'll grab plates," Ruth directed.

Jude gave Mr. Portman an awkward smile as they both sat down.

"She always this bossy?" Mr. Portman asked loudly enough for Ruth to hear.

Jude smiled. "Yep."

Ruth gasped. "Just for that, you two can get your own silverware." She sat down, passing out the plates and forks, contradicting the punishment she had just handed out.

A harsh sounding noise broke free from Mr. Portman and at first Jude was worried the old man was choking, but after a moment, he realized Mr. Portman was laughing.

Laughing!

"You remind me of Judy," Mr. Portman said, wiping his eyes.

"What a nice thing to say," Ruth replied, handing out the wrapped sandwiches. "Who's Judy?"

Mr. Portman's smile plummeted. "My wife."

The good humor in the room was immediately gone. It didn't take a genius to figure out that if Mr. Portman was here by himself, there was a reason for it.

Ruth put her hand on Mr. Portman's hand. "I'm sorry," she said softly. "I've lost people I love too."

I'm in deep. The words were a surprise, but not unwelcome. There was no possible way for Jude to continue to spend time around this woman and not be affected by her. His attraction seemed to be growing stronger by the minute and it had nothing to do with her beautiful looks. At the rate they were going, Jude was going to be a goner long before he ever headed back to California.

CHAPTER 14

Ruth knew she was in trouble. What man in his right mind would follow along with her hairbrained scheme to buy lunch for an old, cranky gentleman who was sad and lonely?

Only an extraordinary one.

Jude was slowly stealing pieces of Ruth's heart and she wasn't trying hard to pull them back. She couldn't seem to stop herself from watching as his eyes crinkled when he laughed, or the way one side of his mouth pulled up just a little higher than the other when he was smiling extra wide.

A wave of self consciousness ran over her and Ruth noticed her hand was already on top of her head. She quickly pulled it down, hoping the men didn't notice her weird tendency to check her wig. She was going to give herself away if she didn't stop.

"Well?" Ruth asked as Mr. Portman wiped his mouth with a napkin. "Was it just like you remembered?"

The older man grunted and folded his arms over his chest. "I suppose," he grudgingly admitted.

Ruth smiled. "I knew it!" She leaned onto the table and put her chin in her hand. "When did you and Judy first start eating them?"

A person could have heard a pin drop with how quiet the room went and Ruth felt herself freeze as she waited for Mr. Portman's response. Had she finally pushed too far? She knew from experience that people like Mr. Portman were simply lonely and in need of love. She'd seen enough harsh, defensive behavior in the cancer ward to last her a lifetime, but that didn't mean she had the right to dig into his backstory.

"Back in ancient days," Mr. Portman finally said gruffly.

Ruth's eyebrows went up and she looked meaningfully at Jude. "Ancient, huh? You look pretty good for being ancient."

One side of Mr. Portman's mouth quirked as he replied, "I was born in the nineteen hundreds. Practically another era."

Ruth immediately laughed and smiled wider when Jude's humor joined her own. "Believe it or not, I was also born waaaay back in the nineteen hundreds," Ruth said.

Mr. Portman huffed. "Barely."

"Okay, I'll give you that."

Mr. Portman began to stand up and Ruth immediately jumped to her feet.

"Are you leaving? Don't you want to stay and chat?"

One white eyebrow went up and Mr. Portman looked from her to Jude and back. "I think I've already overstayed my welcome."

"That's not true," Ruth argued. "We love having you around, don't we, Jude?"

"Of course," Jude replied without missing a beat.

Ruth wanted to give him another kiss of gratitude, but held herself back.

"I'm too old for that kind of nonsense," Mr. Portman said in his gravelly tone. He shuffled to the door, and just as Ruth was sure that he was about to leave without saying anything more, he paused.

Ruth held her breath, her fingers somehow finding Jude's shoulder and squeezing tight.

"Thank you," the older gentleman said before slipping quietly out.

Ruth sunk into her seat, all the energy suddenly gone from her body. Two simple words. That's all it had taken to let her know the cheer and company she had brought to Mr. Portman's life was all worth it.

Jude reached out and took her hand, bringing the palm to his lips. "You're a miracle worker," he said quietly.

Ruth smiled, suddenly tired, and shook her head. "*You're* amazing," she corrected. "I don't know many people who would go along with my crazy plans."

"Anyone who has a heart would," Jude assured her. "You're like some Christmas angel, bestowing your kindness on those who need it most."

Ruth laughed and leaned forward. "Are you saying you've been praying for a Christmas miracle?"

Jude shook his head. "No. I was one of the weirdos who didn't know they needed a miracle."

Ruth closed her eyes and shook her head while leaning back. "Considering how much you've helped me since arriving in town, I think you've been my miracle." She tilted her head to the side and pursed her lips. "Or perhaps, just a gift. Having you around is a gift for someone like me."

"Someone like you?" Jude made a face. "You make it sound like something's wrong with you."

If only he knew... Although, there wasn't anything wrong with her that time wouldn't eventually fix, Ruth reassured herself. "While I'm sure there's lots wrong with me," Ruth said with a tight smile, trying to make it a tease, "I mean it when I say you've been such a blessing."

Jude stood and stretched. "Well, why don't you come be a blessing to me and help me walk off that fried fish?" He held out his hand. "I had already eaten lunch and wasn't really hungry when we pulled off this mid afternoon meal."

"Why didn't you say something?" Ruth asked in exasperation. "You didn't have to eat it."

"Yes, I did." Jude led her out of the backroom.

"No, you didn't," Ruth argued. "You could have said you weren't hungry."

"No, he couldn't have," Grandma Nan interrupted.

"Grandma," Ruth said wryly. "You don't even know what we were talking about."

"Doesn't matter," Grandma said, her eyes on the computer screen. "If he said he had to, then he had to."

"Thank you," Jude said emphatically. "It's nice to be proven right once in a while."

Grandma looked over her reading glasses and winked. "Just don't get used to it."

Jude laughed and tugged Ruth toward the door. "Mind if I steal her for a bit?"

Grandma waved them both off. "Just don't stay out long enough to turn her into a pumpkin."

"Never," Jude vowed. He helped Ruth put on her coat and then put a hand on her lower back, guiding her outside.

"Bye!" Ruth said to Grandma, not even hearing a reply. "I think I should be concerned with how easily she gave me away," Ruth teased, tugging on her gloves.

Jude caught her hands and took one of her gloves off before stuffing it in his pocket. He then intertwined their fingers. "I'll keep this one warm," he said with a wink.

"Are you real?" Ruth asked, her heart beating double time in her chest. When she'd said he was a Christmas miracle, she meant it. How did she get so lucky that after years of heartache, pain, disappointment, and loneliness, the first man she was getting to know was some kind of saint who knew just what to say and when to say it?

Jude patted his chest, looking down. "As near as I can tell."

Ruth laughed softly, tucking her hair back, then patting it into place.

"Why do you do that?"

She froze. "Uh...what?"

Jude pressed his lips together and shook his head. "You know what? Nevermind." His smile was just a little smaller than before. "Ready to walk?"

I should tell him.

The thought lasted a whole three seconds before Ruth pushed it away. This was too perfect. And that meant she was feeling too self-ish at the moment to lose it all. She wanted Jude around and wasn't ready to lose him. Spilling her story would definitely do that.

"Yep," she said, squeezing his hand. "As ready as I'll ever be."

RUTH'S HAND FELT SO fragile in his own, yet so right. Jude had to fight to keep from beaming at every person they walked past as they strolled Main Street. It wasn't the best of days to be out and about. The wind was still whipping, the air felt moist and icy, and the light was quickly disappearing as the sun set, but not even the less than ideal conditions could keep Jude from enjoying the moment.

"Did you always want to be a physical therapist?"

He looked down at her. "What? You mean, like, as a kid?"

Ruth nodded, her hand hovering around her hair as if to try and keep the wind from messing it up.

He looked forward, ignoring the odd behavior. He couldn't be-lieve he had called her out on it earlier. While it always struck Jude as a little off, it wasn't like it was a deal breaker. So she was worried about her hair? So what? She was also worried about the people around her who were hurting or lonely and that was much more im-portant.

"Actually, I think I wanted to be a fireman," Jude mused, his eyes narrowing as he tried to remember. "My dad was a school athletic di-rector and that was fun, but I didn't really find myself heading in that direction until college." He grinned. "A fireman sounded awesome though. I needed to be in shape, which was fine since we were a big sports family, and I still got to do dangerous things. A boy's perfect dream."

Ruth laughed and ducked into his arm a little, obviously escaping the cold. "It does sound like the perfect career, doesn't it? Saving the damsels in distress never gets old."

"I don't think I considered that side of it," Jude admitted, letting go of Ruth's hand to wrap his arm around her. He ran his hand up and down her coat sleeve. "You're shaking. How about we head back and get something to warm you up?"

She gave him a sheepish grin. "Sorry. I get cold easily and have a hard time warming up once I'm shivering."

"No biggie." Jude glanced around and spotted a coffee shop. "Want to grab something there? Then it can help warm you up as we walk back."

"That sounds lovely. Thanks." She held up a finger. "But can I get hot chocolate? I'm not a caffeine person."

"Works for me." Jude led her across the street and into the small shop. He grinned when she sighed at the warmth of the shop. "Want me to hang up your coat?" he offered.

Ruth shook her head. "No, thanks. I really would rather take it to go, if that's all right with you."

"Ready to get rid of me?" he teased.

"No!"

The panic in Ruth's eyes warmed Jude as well as made him laugh. "Sorry. I was just teasing." He tugged her in a little closer and kissed her temple. "I promise not to ditch you quite so early."

Ruth melted into his side. "Sorry. I'm sure that made me sound desperate, but..." She scrunched her nose and looked up at him. "I really like spending time with you."

He moved to leave a peck on the tip of her nose. "I like spending time with you too."

"Next!"

Jude looked up and realized they were falling behind. "Sorry," he said, smiling at the barista. "Two hot chocolates, please." He glanced at Ruth. "Anything extra in it?"

"Can I get some mint syrup?"

"Of course," the barista said, punching some keys on the register. "Anything else?"

Jude reached for his wallet.

"Is it all right if I get a pastry?" Ruth whispered, her blue eyes wide and concerned.

Jude chuckled. "Your ability to eat is amazing."

Ruth's cheeks colored and she shrugged. "I've learned to appreciate food, I guess."

"Get whatever you want," he hurried to say. While he was impressed with her appetite, he hadn't meant to embarrass her. What idiot questioned a woman about what she ate? Or how much? "I think it's great." *Hello, foot. Come into my mouth.* Just how dumb could he get at the moment?

When the barista snickered, Jude felt his neck heat up. Even a teenager knew how badly he'd messed up.

Ruth stretched up and gave him another one of those sweet kisses on his cheek. "Thank you," she whispered.

Jude scratched his chin and nodded. "Anytime." He backed up and let her finish ordering. Right now was probably the time to just be quiet before he choked himself on another stupid move.

When they had their order, they once again braved the elements and began walking toward the motel.

"Should we bury ourselves in the break room again?" Ruth asked.

"Would you, um..." Jude debated whether or not to ask, but in the end, figured it wouldn't hurt. "Would you like to come into my room and watch a movie?" He winced a little. "I promise to be a gentleman, but I'd really just like to spend some time with you where no one can interrupt us."

Ruth laughed softly. "I think that sounds great. And I completely trust you."

The power of those words were more powerful than Jude would have ever imagined. Who knew that a woman putting him on a pedestal would feel so good while also being frightening. Nothing could keep a man from straying too far like a woman who said those three little words.

"Then let's hurry," Jude urged. "Because if we're both Popsicles when we get there, I don't know who's going to warm up whom." He walked faster, pulling lightly on Ruth, enjoying her laughter as they made their way back.

Once inside, they snuck in the back door and slipped into his room. The place was pristine, since he hadn't been inside for the last couple of days.

"You know, I never did figure out why you rented a room here when you have friends in town," Ruth mused, taking off her coat. "I figured you would stay at Grayson's. It's not like he doesn't have enough room." As soon as the words were out of her mouth, she closed her eyes and hung her head. "Oh my gosh. I'm so sorry."

"For what?" Jude asked, dumping his own coat on a chair.

"For being rude!" Ruth exclaimed. "It's no business of mine where you stay or if your friends have people stay with them or not."

Jude chuckled and walked across the room to give her a quick kiss in order to stop her rambling. "It's fine," he assured her, enjoying the pink of her cheeks. "I am staying with Grayson and Brook, but I like my privacy sometimes, so I rented a room in order to get time away when I needed it." *And to avoid all the married couples, but she doesn't need to know that.*

"Ah...gotcha." Ruth grinned. "What movie should we watch?"

Jude grabbed the remote. "Any requests?"

Ruth shrugged. "Nope. Anything is fine. I like it all."

"Even action flicks?"

She nodded and Jude put a hand to his heart.

"Woman. Where have you been all my life?" He frowned when her blush drained away and Ruth looked down at her hot cocoa. "Did I say something wrong?"

She shook her head and took a sip of her drink. "Nope. I think I'm just a little cold."

He knew it was more than that, but the desire to hold her and have her to himself was stronger than his curiosity at the moment. "Then come on over and we'll figure it out together."

They cuddled up on the couch, found their movie, and settled in. Jude rubbed her arm, bringing heat back to her skin, and almost groaned when she sighed and relaxed into his chest. This was perfect. There was no better way for him to spend his holidays than holding a beautiful woman.

Maybe it was time to start rethinking how long he was going to be in Oregon.

CHAPTER 15

"Here's your key," Ruth said, handing the couple the card. "And this is a map of Seaside Bay's Main Street shops. There's some really fun, little stores, but the best is Sassy Sweets and Cookies Up! You *have* to give them a try while you're in town."

"Thank you," the woman said with a smile, taking the offering.

"You're welcome." Ruth set her hands on the counter. "Be sure and let me know if there's anything else you need." She pointed to the left. "Your room is down that way."

The man nodded and put his hand on his wife's back, leading her away.

Whatcha up to?

The buzz in Ruth's pocket made her jump and she smiled when she read the text.

Not much. Just selling rooms as fast as I can.

Is there anything you can't do?

Ruth laughed and her thumbs flew.

I can't fly. I hate asparagus. And I can't get off work today.

"That's a pretty specific list."

Ruth jumped again and gasped, whirling to find Jude grinning from the side entrance. "Oh my gosh," she said breathlessly. "How did you get there?"

Jude's eyebrows rose and he looked at the door before coming back to her.

Ruth rolled her eyes. "How did you get in without me hearing you?"

"You were too busy offering advice to that couple," Jude stated with a grin. He sauntered over. "I'm sure they'll appreciate it. So will Caro."

Ruth smiled and shook her head. "Well, with treats like hers, they deserve to be talked up a bit."

Jude glanced at his phone screen. "So you really can't get off today?"

Ruth sighed and slumped onto the stool they kept at the desk. "No. Grandma isn't here."

"Does she normally run this place all by herself?" Jude asked, leaning his hip against the counter. "How did she manage before you got here?"

"She had a couple of teenagers who helped her out," Ruth explained. "But both of them decided they'd rather take some time off when I showed up." She laughed. "I think they were bored to death. I mean, I enjoy meeting people, but most teens aren't that into socializing with strangers."

Jude nodded and glanced around before his eyes landed on her stool. "Is there another one of those in the kitchen?"

Ruth looked then and frowned. "I think so. Why?"

Jude walked purposefully past the desk, straight to the break room. "Just a moment." He came back out a few seconds later, carefully maneuvering the stool so as not to hit the walls.

"Jude," Ruth exclaimed. "You don't really want to hang around the desk with me."

"Why not?" he asked, setting the seat down and joining her.

"Because it's boring," she said plainly. "I just explained that."

"Are you here?"

Ruth paused. "Yes."

"Then it's not boring."

Ruth couldn't help herself. She reached out and cupped his face, pulling him in for a soft kiss. "Careful, Mr. Lisbon," she whispered against his lips. "You'll sweep me off my feet."

"Then my work here will be done," he said before taking her mouth in a much more heated exchange than Ruth had initiated.

Not that she was complaining. Jude's kisses were worth every bit of pain she went through to get down to Seaside Bay.

The bell above the door made Ruth jump for a third time and she couldn't seem to stop the giggle that broke through. "Sorry," she said in an aside to Jude, who was smirking like he'd won the lottery. She shook her head and turned to see who had come in, only to immediately blush when Mr. Portman stood giving her an evil glare. "Hello," she said lamely.

The elderly gentleman rolled his eyes, grunted, and shuffled down the hall.

As soon as he was gone, Ruth broke into more laughter, with Jude joining her.

"I don't think he appreciated the free show," Jude said between his gasping breaths.

"Nah," Ruth responded, her smile wide. "A guy like that could probably use a bit of romance in his life."

Jude's laughter softened into a low chuckle. "Romance, huh? Is that what they call it nowadays?"

"You have a better word for it?" Ruth finished up the reservation from a few minutes before, her fingers dancing along the keyboard.

"Making out?"

She snorted. "I suppose that would be more technically correct, but less..."

"Politically correct?" Jude offered.

"Romantic," Ruth said instead.

Jude shook his head. "So romance is romantic? That sounds like a double negative or something."

Ruth put her hands on her hips. "And what's wrong with that?"

"Not a thing." Jude reached out and pulled her back to him, settling his hands on her waist. "Your grandma said I shouldn't get used to being right. Guess *she* was right."

Ruth slapped his shoulder playfully. "Don't listen to Grandma. She's a troublemaker." Reaching out, she began to run her fingers through his hair. Working at the desk had never been so fun, although Ruth was a little worried about what their customers would think. A small smile played on her lips as she pushed his soft locks back off his forehead. Jude had really nice hair. A dark blond with short sides. The top was just long enough for her to feel the texture and enjoy playing with it a little.

I wonder if my hair will be the same when it comes back...

Ruth paused her perusal when she realized Jude was giving her an odd look. Yanking back her hand, she tucked them behind her back. "Sorry. Guess I should have asked permission."

Jude shook his head, though his thoughtful expression remained. "No. You're welcome to run your fingers through my hair anytime," he stated. "I was just curious."

"About?" Ruth asked, though she was afraid she knew the answer.

"Does it bother you to have my hair messed up?"

Ruth almost barked out a relieved laugh. He thought she had a thing about her hair being messed up.

Although, I guess that's sort of correct in an odd sort of way.

Her humor fled when that thought entered her mind. "I, uh...no." She tried to smile. "I kinda like it, actually. Makes you look boyish."

His eyebrows rose. "And that's a good thing? Are you saying I'm too old?"

Ruth laughed. "Definitely not. Although...do you think I'm too young? Does it bother you that I'm several years younger than you?"

Jude shook his head. "Nope. Not unless it bothers you. I mean…" He scrunched up one side of his face. "If you were eighteen or something, that'd be weird, but at this point, I don't find it to be a big deal."

"Good." Ruth clasped her hands behind his neck, grateful for the change in topic. "Neither do I."

"So you don't mind if this old man hangs around a bit?"

"Maybe I'm going to keep this old man captive," Ruth teased. "I won't let him not hang around."

"I think that's the opposite of the word hanging around," Jude mused.

"Eh, who cares," Ruth said. "I'm just glad you're here." She leaned down and Jude met her halfway. Yeah…this was definitely the most fun she'd ever had while running the motel.

JUDE SAT BACK AND WATCHED with a small smile as Ruth helped another couple who were checking in. These two were quite a bit older than the ones from earlier and were sort of fun to watch. Apparently, they liked to keep their marriage lively, if their banter was anything to go by.

"He won't remember a thing," the woman said, waving a hand at her husband. "Better give me the directions."

"Don't tell me what I won't remember," the man snapped. He reached for the map Ruth was holding out and held it over his wife's head. "How's that for forgetting?"

The woman put her hands on her hips and glared up at him. "What's the map for?" she taunted him. "Do you remember where we're supposed to go?"

"It doesn't matter," the man huffed, stuffing it in his back pocket. "The only important places around her are the marina and the fishing boats."

"Oh?" his wife said. "You don't want to eat dinner at any point? Or maybe breakfast?"

Jude chuckled as the man scowled.

"Tell you what," Ruth said with her usual kindness. "I've just happen to have two maps." She held another out to the wife with a smile. "How about you each keep one, and then both of you can get where you want to go."

"You're such a dear," the older woman said, accepting the gift. She immediately turned to her husband and frowned. "Unlike other people I know."

"Well, you've dealt with me for fifty-seven years," the man said with a snort. "I'm sure you can handle a few more."

The woman shook her head, gave Jude a discreet wink, and then headed away from the counter. "And every white hair on my head has come from those years," she bantered back.

"It's not my fault you chose to have kids," the man grumbled, dragging their luggage behind him. "Where's this room again?" he asked Ruth.

"I told you you wouldn't remember," the wife called from the hallway.

"Maybe I just wanted to speak to a pretty woman!" he shouted back, grinning and pumping his eyebrows at Ruth.

Ruth laughed and pointed the same direction his wife had gone. "She's right," Ruth said to the man.

"Shoot," the man grumbled. "She usually is." He leaned in. "But don't tell her I said that."

"I heard that!"

"Fifty-seven years didn't affect your hearing any," he mumbled. Giving Ruth a shrug, he took the luggage and followed his wife. "Where's the fire?" he called after her.

Ruth's laughter drowned out any more arguing between the two guests and Jude couldn't help but join her.

"Oh my gosh, they're too precious," Ruth said as she gasped for air.

Jude scratched his chin. "That was pretty funny," he admitted. "But you gotta wonder why they stick together if they argue so much."

"They argue because they enjoy it," Ruth explained.

"Enjoy?" Jude pursed his lips. "I guess some people do enjoy that, but I don't understand it personally."

"You've never started an argument just to enjoy bantering with someone?" Ruth asked as she finished putting the reservation in the system. "Not even for a little bit of flirting? Just because you wanted to hear the person speak?"

"Now that you put it that way, I guess I have," Jude admitted. He paused. "That explains a lot, actually," he mumbled.

"Hmm?"

"My friend, Carson." Jude paused a second. "Do you remember him?"

"The movie star's brother?" Ruth said, turning his way. "Sure. Why?"

Jude let out a breath he hadn't known he was holding. For a moment, he'd worried yet again that her interest was in Carson since that's who Brook had tried to set her up with.

When he didn't respond right away, Ruth turned around to look at him. "Did I get it wrong? Was Carson someone else?"

Jude frowned, momentarily distracted from his original point. "You don't remember for sure? But..." He stopped. This probably wasn't a road they should go down.

"But what?" Ruth pressed, folding her arms over her chest and resting her hip against the counter.

"Nevermind."

She shook her head. "No. Not nevermind. You have something on your mind. Ask me. Ask me anything."

"I'm just surprised you don't remember who he is for sure. I mean, you're right. He's Grayson Cordova's brother, but I would have thought you'd remember him in exact detail."

"And why is that?"

"Because he's the one Brook tried to set you up with." Jude felt his neck heat even as he spoke about it. It all felt so ridiculous now. Ruth had been open to Jude's attention, even seemed to want it, and Carson had an interest in someone else. Why should it bother Jude that Brook had tried to get them together? It wasn't like this was some kind of high school romance or something. They were all mature adults. It should be no big deal.

"Brook tried to..." Ruth's face contorted and then she began laughing.

Jude jerked back. "I don't understand."

"Actually..." Ruth's humor calmed down quickly. "I suppose I should be embarrassed about that situation, but now it's just kind of funny how pathetic it was."

He rubbed his forehead. "I'm so lost."

Ruth grinned. "Brook introduced me to Carson because I asked her to."

"So, you're interested in him?" Jude began to stand, but Ruth rushed forward.

"No, no. Let me finish." She sighed and her cheeks turned pink. "I was never interested in Carson," she admitted, making a face. "I had seen you when you first checked in here."

Jude nodded. "Yeah. I remember getting a quick glimpse of you from the entrance to the break room."

"Well, I wanted to get to know you." Ruth shrugged and turned away. "So I asked Brook to introduce me to Carson."

Jude frowned. "Okay. Spell it out in man terms, huh? I'm still lost."

Ruth spun and threw her hands in the air. "I thought you were handsome, okay? You were so handsome and looked so sad that I wanted to get to know you. But I didn't want Brook to know that, so I asked for an introduction to Carson because you were standing right next to him and I knew I would get introduced to you as well."

Jude gaped, then began to belly laugh. He leaned forward and put his hands on his knees, trying to get himself under control, but the irony of the situation just wouldn't be contained.

Ruth sat on her stool, her hands on her cheeks as if that could stop the blush from overtaking her face, but it was a useless endeavor. Jude could see the flaming pink spread clear down her neck and under the collar of her shirt.

"Ruth," he said as he worked to catch his breath. He took her face in his hands, careful not to mess with her hair, and gave her a fierce kiss. "You're a gem."

"Because I acted like a star-struck teenager?" she asked breathlessly.

"Exactly," he responded, sealing that with another kiss. "And just so you know, you can walk over to Carson anytime...as long as you're really coming for me."

"I'll remember that," she said softly, her blue eyes searching his. "You promise you don't think I'm pathetic?"

Jude decided that with the lobby empty and her confession hanging in the air between them, actions were much better than words right now. It shouldn't be too hard to convince her of his sincerity...and if it did? He didn't mind at all.

CHAPTER 16

Despite the fact that Jude wasn't standing behind her and taking her attention away from her work, Ruth could barely concentrate on her job. When she was with Jude, she wanted to pay attention to him. When she wasn't with him, she could only think of how much she wanted to be with him.

"It's a good thing I didn't fall in love during college," Ruth mumbled before freezing. *Love him...?* She hadn't even thought about the words as they'd left her mouth, but now they were all she could think about.

Do I love him?

Can someone fall in love this fast?

What about the fact that he lives in California?

Could he feel the same? Or is he just having fun during his vacation?

He's supposed to go home next Sunday...then what?

Ruth pressed the bottom of her palms into her eyes. There were way too many questions swarming her head, and not one of them had an answer. "One thing at a time," she whispered to herself. "Live for the moment. Enjoy what's here."

The words, however, ones that had gotten her through many dark times in the not-so-distant past, fell flat.

She didn't want to just enjoy the moment with Jude. She wanted to enjoy more than a moment. As her heart slipped further and further away from her own grasp, Ruth had to acknowledge that she wanted something much more long term. Possibly even lifelong.

Ruth had learned not to wait when she saw something she wanted. Life was fleeting and all too easily snuffed out. Having Jude down in California would surely slow down any possible progress they could make as a couple. Provided, that is, that he was even willing to do the long distance thing.

Should she consider moving to California? What could she do down there? Right now she had a job and a home, and none of that was guaranteed if she took off with no marketable skills into one of the most expensive states in the country.

"What's bothering ya, girl?"

Mr. Portman's rough voice caught Ruth off guard and she blinked several times, trying to get out of her own head. "Oh. Hello, Mr. Portman," she said with a forced smile. Her soaring heart had had a wake-up call and now Ruth's happiness was nonexistent, having been replaced with worry. "How's your day going?"

"You're ignoring the question," the older gentleman snapped. He pointed a gnarled finger at her. "Something's picking at ya. I can see it. It was the same way with my Judy."

Ruth's smile became more natural. "Would you tell me about her? I'd love to hear about such a remarkable woman."

Mr. Portman paused, then shook his head. "I'm not so easily distracted."

Ruth laughed lightly. "Darn," she said, snapping her fingers for emphasis. "I was hoping."

"Is it the cancer?" Mr. Portman asked bluntly. "Did your man say he couldn't do it?"

Ruth's jaw dropped. "The...what?"

"The cancer." Mr. Portman pointed to her head. "Your wig is good, but I've seen it all before."

"Judy," Ruth said breathlessly. "Judy had cancer."

Mr. Portman nodded. "She did. And I watched her adjust her wig a thousand times before the end."

Ruth's hand shot up to her head before she realized her reaction and brought it back down. "I just..."

He scowled. "You haven't told him, and fool that he is, he hasn't noticed, has he?"

"He's not a fool," Ruth argued. "I've worked hard to hide it from him."

"Eh, a boy in love doesn't notice much anyway," Mr. Portman grunted.

"He's not…" Ruth bit her lip and turned away. Jude wasn't in love with her, though Ruth had high hopes it would go that way. But the crux of the matter was that Mr. Portman knew her secret. "I'm sorry about Judy," Ruth said softly, not wanting to continue the line of their conversation.

Mr. Portman grunted again but nodded. "It's life."

"Would you like to have a cup of tea and talk about it?"

"You need to tell him."

Her stubborn side began to overcome her compassion. "I will," she defended. "When the time is right."

"If he's half the man I think he is, he'll not care either way," Mr. Portman said.

"I'm not telling him until I'm sure," Ruth said, the strength of her argument waning.

"Sure about what?" Mr. Portman gave her his best scowl. He stepped forward. "A man in love won't care, but if you wait past a certain point, it becomes betrayal."

The words were like a knife to the heart. Ruth didn't want to betray anyone. She just wanted to be seen for who she was, not for the disease her body had housed at one point in time. Was that so bad? She didn't want to be a cancer victim or even a survivor. She just wanted to be Ruth. "I'm scared."

Those weren't the words she had meant to say. She had wanted to argue, to defend her actions, to make Mr. Portman understand why she was hiding something so big. But somehow, those bushy, furrowed brows had pulled something else out of her. The truth. The bald, naked, ugly truth. The one she didn't want to admit to any-one...even herself.

Ruth had gotten through years of treatment and doctors by putting on a brave smile. She'd been praised for her attitude and looked to as an example of how everyone should handle the struggles in their lives.

And she was scared.

Scared of being alone again. Scared of losing the man she was falling in love with. Scared that if someone saw the curled up little girl inside, she would lose all the ground she had gained. That the lie would be all she was known for, rather than her determination and choice to live.

"Fear is an odd enemy," Mr. Portman said, his gruff voice softer than usual. "It somehow has the ability to separate us from every-thing good in our lives. Makes us think we're alone, desperate, and that there's only one way to survive."

He deflated a little. His already rounded shoulders sunk farther and for the first time since he'd arrived, Ruth thought he looked vul-nerable. His gruff manner was gone, and left in its place was an old man. A tired old man. "But in separating you...it feeds." Mr. Port-man's dark eyes were deadly serious. "And as it grows, it makes the ex-act things you feared in the first place come true." He shook his head. "Don't be a victim, Ms. Allen. Stand on your own two feet."

A tear went down Ruth's cheek as she watched the gentleman leave. This was not how she'd expected her afternoon to go, especially after realizing that she was falling in love.

Jude...

As much as she hated to admit it, Mr. Portman was right. She needed to come clean and she needed to do it now. The deeper they got in the relationship, the harder it would be to hear.

Ruth took in a long breath through her nose. Tonight. She would tell him tonight. No more excuses, no more waiting. If he couldn't handle who she truly was, well...

Ruth swallowed hard. She didn't want to think about that. But still, she would share it all. Both her grandmother and Mr. Portman were right. Jude deserved to know.

JUDE POKED AT THE BEAUTIFUL dinner sitting on his plate. It had been designed to catch the eye and had looked stunning when it had been placed in front of him, but he had no appetite. No matter how delicious it probably was.

"What's up?" Carson elbowed Jude's rib cage. "Not hungry?"

Jude shrugged. "I don't know."

Carson stuffed a bite in his mouth, looked around at all the happy, smiling couples, and then dipped his head back down. "Jude, you've been like this since we got here. For a few days I thought you were coming out of it, but now it's back. Do you need to see a doctor?"

Jude's fork froze, midair. "What?"

"Look, it's not a big deal," Carson said soothingly. "It's okay to need help once in a while. I deal with people all the time who get help for their emotional struggles."

"I don't need a doctor," Jude whispered harshly under his breath. "Can a guy not just sit around contemplating life without being asked if he needs medication?"

Carson gave him an unimpressed look. "He can, but being dramatic isn't like you." Dark eyebrows rose high. "What's. Going. On?"

Jude sighed. He also looked around at their surroundings. The house was huge, beautiful, and perfectly arranged. The couples were smiling, celebrating, and having a wonderful time. Jude really liked all of Brook's friends. They were good people, but he didn't want to be here.

He had finally found a woman to shake him from his doldrums and Jude was stuck spending time with everyone but her. For the last two days, he'd had a hard time getting away from Brook's parties and now he was set to leave in less than forty-eight hours. It was eating at him. He didn't want to go, but he wasn't sure if he should stay. He wanted to spend every waking hour with Ruth, but he had an obligation to his friends.

How would he handle it all? It wasn't like he could never see Ruth again. They could certainly talk on the phone and visit each other, but it just wasn't the same. Long distance relationships were a mess. Everybody knew that.

He couldn't kiss her long distance, or hold her, or watch her fuss over cranky old men.

"You've got to be kidding." Carson's loud pronouncement brought a hush to the table.

Jude blinked out of his wandering thoughts and turned to his friend. "What? Who's kidding?"

Carson had the good grace to look abashed before he put his hands in the air. "Nothing to see here, folks. Sorry."

It took a couple of minutes before the table buzzed with activity again, but several suspicious glances kept coming back to Jude and Carson.

"What are you doing?" Jude asked under his breath.

"You're in love with her."

Jude jerked, not caring that he was catching more attention. "What are you talking about?"

"Your brooding," Carson explained with a wide grin. "It's because you're in love."

Jude rolled his eyes. "That's ridiculous." The words were sharp on Jude's tongue. Truth was, he wasn't quite sure how deep his feelings ran. He liked Ruth. A lot. More than he should after such a short amount of time, but he was definitely not ready to jump into saying he was in love. "Don't you have your own female situation to worry about?" Maybe throwing the bus in the other direction would get Jude out of the limelight.

Carson scrunched his nose. "Yeah...but things are a little rough right now."

Jude frowned. "How so? Did you two break up?"

Now it was Carson's turn to poke at his dinner. "No, but she's..." He shook his head. "Nevermind. I'm sure we'll work it out." He straightened in his seat. "Are you having troubles?"

Jude shook his head. "Not with Ruth."

"Ah...the secret has a name."

Jude rolled his eyes.

"Then what?"

Jude debated for a moment more, but in the end, he found he wanted some advice. "I'm supposed to go home."

"Ah...and the lady is staying here." Carson nodded and took a long swallow of his drink. "And you're not ready to go."

Jude shook his head. "Nope. But I have a job I need to get back to." He glared at Carson. "I can't just help people from here like you can."

"I don't know..." Carson drawled. "Just send them a list of exercises. No biggie."

Jude chuckled. "Yeah...I'm sure my boss would like that a lot."

"Look," Carson said, his voice going low. "If you love her, which I think you do, then it'll all work out."

"What are you? The positive vibes fairy?"

The insult rolled right off Carson, who was busy staring into space. He finally tilted his head, his gray eyes nearly smacking Jude with their intensity. "Wait a second. You were upset when we came and that was before you met Ruth. Being upset now because you're going home is fine, but what about before? Why were you so upset then?"

Jude cleared his throat, gulping his glass of water as if it were his last lifeline.

"Jude..."

He sighed and leaned back in his seat. "Look, it's over. Something happened several months ago with another woman."

Carson's eyebrows went up.

"Remember Elania?"

"Your friend who eloped?"

Jude nodded.

Carson's eyes narrowed, then shot wide. "You loved her."

Jude shrugged. "I thought I did."

"But she...oh."

"Yeah...oh." Jude could feel the heat climbing his throat.

"And your feelings about Ruth?"

Jude looked sideways. "Are stronger than they should be." That was all he would admit to at this point in time.

"Good."

Brook's interruption into their conversation had both men nearly jumping out of their seats.

Brook was smirking like the cat that caught the canary. "You can bring her to dinner."

Jude choked on air. Grabbing his napkin, he tried to cover his mouth and catch his breath. "What?"

"Tomorrow night," Brook stated proudly. "Gray and I will treat you and Ruth to dinner at the Crab Pot." She winked. "I'm excited to meet her again, now that I know who she really has her eye on."

Jude's mouth flapped open and shut a few times and the table broke into loud noise. Everyone wanted to know what was going on and who Brook was taking to dinner and why Jude had kept it all a secret.

Jude's jaw set and he glared at Carson, who was grinning as widely as Brook.

"Don't blame me that you don't know how to whisper," Carson said with a laugh.

"If you think I won't—"

"I brought Belle to the tree decoration party, remember?" Carson winked. "I took evasive action to avoid this exact scenario." He slapped Jude on the back. "Good luck."

Jude groaned and rubbed his forehead. With the entire friend group in the mix, Jude knew he was going to need it.

CHAPTER 17

"I'll have the salmon, please," Ruth said with a soft smile to the waitress. She handed back the menu. "Thank you."

"Thank you," the young woman replied. She smiled at the table. "I'll get these put in." Her eyes went to Grayson Cordova. "And I'm sure you'll have your food very quickly."

"Thanks," Brook replied, looking completely at ease even though the waitress couldn't stop looking at her husband.

Ruth waited until the worker was gone, then leaned forward. "How in the world do you stand it?" she asked with a soft giggle.

Brook shrugged and took a sip of water. "I've gotten used to it."

Grayson's hand came up and rested on the back of her neck.

"Besides, it's not like I'm worried about him straying or something."

Jude shook his head. "I don't know if I'll ever get used to being in public with you, man."

Grayson made a face. "It's not like I encourage it." He waved. "I bought us a private spot on purpose, but we still have to see some of the workers."

"Speaking of," Ruth replied, "thank you. It was really sweet of you to invite me...us...to dinner." Her stomach had been in knots all day after getting the invitation. She had been trying to figure out how she was going to tell Jude the truth, and then this had fallen into her lap. It would be perfect if they could spend a little time together after the dinner. Then Ruth could spill the beans. At least that way she had one last date with him before he ran away.

He's not going to run away, she assured herself. *He likes you. It'll all work out.* Her litany of positive chants weren't being as helpful as usual. They had gotten her through a lot of dark times, but right now, Ruth wasn't just worried, she was terrified.

"You're welcome," Brook said cheerily. She leaned in. "So...tell us about yourself, Ruth. I know you're Grandma Nan's granddaughter, and truthfully, I've probably met you once or twice over the years since I grew up here, but I'm afraid I can't remember it."

Ruth shrugged. "I didn't do a lot of socializing when we visited. And now my parents are gone, so visiting is a little different than it used to be."

"I'm sorry." Brook's dark brows were furrowed. "That must be hard. Where were you before you came to stay with Grandma Nan?"

"Seattle." Ruth took a sip of her water. She'd have to be careful.

"Seattle?" Brook paused and tilted her head. "Are you the granddaughter that—"

Ruth panicked. "I'm afraid I wasn't a very good student," she interrupted with a forced laugh. "I've been jumping around trying to figure out my life, but you know...things just haven't really settled into place."

"Of course." Brook's tone was curious, as if she were trying to put pieces of a puzzle together.

She knows, Ruth realized. *Of course she knows. She's lived here for years. There's no way Grandma didn't mention at some point or another that her granddaughter was sick.*

Ruth kept eye contact with Brook, silently begging her to play along. "I came down here to help out Grandma and so I could take some time to figure out what I want to do."

Brook's eyes weren't quite as warm as before, but she gave a subtle nod, as if agreeing to the plea.

"And have you?"

Ruth jerked her head toward Grayson. "Have I what?"

Grayson paused, confusion furrowing his brow as he held his glass in the air. "Have you figured out what you want to do?" he asked slowly, as if unsure of the question himself.

"Oh..." Ruth nearly collapsed against the back of her seat in relief. "I'm...still working on it."

"I'm sure you've got plenty of time," Brook inserted, still looking quite serious. She more than likely didn't appreciate Ruth not telling the truth to one of her friends, but Ruth would assure her hostess later that it was being taken care of.

After all, it's happening tonight. Tonight I'm confessing.

"It won't take too much longer," Ruth stated, still keeping eye contact, hoping Brook would get her message.

Brook's smile was clear. Things were all right again.

"When did you know you wanted to be an actor?" Ruth asked, turning the conversation around. She sent a coy look at Jude when he reached over to take her hand. She loved it when he touched her.

Grayson chuckled. "I kind of got roped into it when I was a teenager and it spiraled out of control."

"Well, teenage girls everywhere thank you for your sacrifice," Ruth teased, earning laughter from the whole table.

"Such a sacrifice," Jude muttered into his water glass.

Brook tsked her tongue. "Don't make me call an arm wrestling match, Jude."

Jude's face went slack. "Low blow, Brook."

Ruth's head jumped back and forth between them. "Wait...what? Brook can beat you in arm wrestling?"

Jude looked so offended that Ruth couldn't help but laugh when Grayson and Brook both broke into their own amusement.

"That would be amazing," Brook said, wiping tears from the corner of her eyes. "But no, I'm afraid not."

"She can't beat me," Jude said, sending a scathing look to Grayson, who was still chuckling. "But she's not above using her husband's stupidly massive muscles to win what she wants."

"Hey, now," Brook argued. "He's not stupid." She smiled and leaned over to kiss Grayson's chin. "And I like his muscles."

"You would," Jude muttered.

Ruth pulled his hand farther into her lap and stroked it with her other hand. "Yours aren't so bad, you know," she whispered.

Jude relaxed a little. "Thanks," he muttered. "But I'm self aware enough to know that I'll never be as big as Sasquatch over here."

"Hey!"

"After all, I'm one of the people who helps him keep those balloons puffed up."

Ruth laughed as the banter continued. Grayson threatened violence, Brook rolled her eyes, Jude continued with the teasing. It was wonderful. What would it be like to have a group of friends like this? Ruth had never had the time to form that kind of bond in college before she'd had to quit.

Sure, a couple of her roommates had checked in on her at first, but that hadn't lasted long. They had their own lives, their own schedules, their own midterms to get to, and spending hours with a bedridden acquaintance wasn't part of the plan.

Ruth wasn't bitter about it, but that didn't keep her from longing for that kind of connection. It made her all the more nervous to share her secret tonight. If Brook had cancer, Ruth knew Grayson would move heaven and earth to be with her. It was spoken in every movement of his body. But Ruth and Jude weren't married, and she wasn't even sure if he loved her.

No. No more excuses. It has to be done.

Firming her resolve, Ruth put on a smile and forced herself to relax. She would enjoy tonight and allow tomorrow to take care of itself. It might be all she had.

JUDE WAS EQUAL PARTS embarrassed and entertained as he sat through the dinner with his best friend and the woman he was dating. Grayson had a way with people, it's part of what made him such a good star. The unfortunate part was, the stories Grayson was sharing were all ones that were embarrassing to Jude.

Ruth's amusement though, was almost worth the severe blush that had become a permanent addition to Jude's neck.

"Did you really use lard?" Ruth asked through her laughter. "You just rubbed fat on his shoulder?"

Jude chuckled at the memory. "Yeah…I mean, what was I supposed to do? We were in the middle of nowhere and getting real massage oil would have taken forever." He shrugged. "Can I help it if there was a pig farm nearby? It worked great."

"But then I smelled like pork for a week," Grayson pointed out, bringing the table into even more laughter.

"I don't think it hurt your reputation with the ladies at all."

Grayson turned to his wife. "Would you still love me if I smelled like pig?"

"Pig or bacon?" Brook teased.

"Which one means I don't have to sleep on the sofa?"

Jude laughed.

"The bacon, definitely," Brook said seriously. "That smells good. Muddy animal does not."

"Truth," Ruth said, pointing her finger at Brook. Afterward, her hand automatically went to her hair and Jude held back a sigh.

One of these days he was going to have a chat with her about her hair. It was such a constant source of worry for her and he had to wonder why. She didn't seem to be self conscious about anything except her hair and there had to be a story there.

"Jude?"

He blinked and looked around the table. "Yeah?"

Grayson hid his grin behind a fist. "We were asking if you and Ruth had plans for the rest of the evening?" With a very fake yawn, he wrapped his arm around his wife. "I'm beat and we're going to head home."

Jude wanted to roll his eyes at the display. For being a world renowned actor, that was a poor display of his skills. "I thought Ruth and I might take a walk down to the marina?" He phrased it like a question, raising his eyebrows at Ruth, since he hadn't passed the idea by her at all yet.

"That sounds great," she said, swallowing hard.

Jude frowned. If he didn't know any better, he'd say Ruth was nervous. But about what? They were just taking a walk. A walk where Jude had decided to tell Ruth about his past and see what her thoughts were for the future, but still...she didn't know that. "Is that going to be okay?" he asked softly, while Grayson settled the check.

"Yeah," Ruth said, nodding too quickly. "I, uh, I think us having some alone time to talk would be a good thing."

He nodded. "I thought the same thing. There's some stuff I'd like to tell you."

Ruth's face blanched. "You...want to tell me something?"

Jude nodded. "I think with my trip home coming up, we need to get some things settled." He tilted his head. "Don't you think?"

Again, her nod was faster than normal. "I suppose we do."

"Okay, you lovebirds," Grayson said, rising to his feet and pulling out Brook's chair. "We'll see you around."

"Thank you so much for everything," Ruth gushed. "The meal and company were wonderful." She flashed Jude a smile that was tight, but still beautiful. "I'm so glad Jude has such good friends. It's a wonderful gift."

Jude took her hand and squeezed it reassuringly. If all went well, he hoped that his friends would eventually become her friends. He might not be ready to say he was in love, but he was in very, very strong like, and Jude knew it was time to share more of himself with her. Hopefully a strong connection between them would help when they weren't in each other's physical presence any longer.

It was time to open himself to everything that a relationship could be. She had proven she was sweet, kind, thoughtful, service oriented, had a good sense of humor, and even through an evening with a movie star, her looks had been for Jude and Jude alone.

What more could he ask for?

"Ready?" he asked, taking Ruth's hand and bringing them both to their feet.

"Yep."

Her smile still said she was nervous, but Jude put it out of his mind. Once he got her alone, he would help ease whatever was worrying her. She was probably just upset that he was leaving in one more day. He was upset about it too. Hopefully that would give them a starting point to talking about them and where they were going.

The evening was cold, but the wind wasn't as bad as normal, much to Jude's relief.

"We'll see ya later," Grayson said with a wave.

"Don't be a stranger, Ruth!" Brook called out. After a moment's hesitation, she let go of Gray and came over to give Ruth a hug.

Jude stepped back and let the women embrace. He was so grateful for Brook's kindness in helping Ruth feel at home. Other than himself and Mr. Portman, Jude hadn't noticed Ruth spending a lot of time with other people. She hadn't introduced him to any friends of her own. But with her grandmother taking up so much of her time, and the town being as small as it was, it made sense that it would be difficult to find other younger people to hang out with.

Ruth was pale again as Brook stepped back. Brook nodded and Ruth nodded jerkily in return before grabbing Jude's hand like it was her lifeline.

Jude waited until his friends were gone before looking down at Ruth. "Are you all right? What did Brook say that upset you so much?" His mind whirled. He had thought that Brook and Ruth had gotten along, but that was the second time that evening that something had passed between the two women.

"She just wanted to make sure I'm taking care of you," Ruth said with a shaky grin. "I assured her I was doing my best."

Jude scratched his chin. "That's odd. Brook isn't usually the threatening type."

Ruth shook her head, then tugged on Jude's hand. "It was fine. I meant it when I said I'm glad you have such good friends. We'll get it all worked out in time."

Knowing he had a big confession coming up, Jude agreed and pushed the thoughts out of his head. After all, the women had only met twice. It might take a little time, but he was sure that Ruth would fit in beautifully with those he considered friends and family.

"Come on," he said, picking up his pace. "Let's walk."

CHAPTER 18

Twenty-four hours...

The words wouldn't leave Ruth's head. Jude was going home. But where did that leave them? Was he going to say it'd been fun, but now he was back to real life? Were her feelings deeper than his? Did she dare try to tell him she loved him? What would she do if he didn't feel the same? Would his feelings change when he found out about the cancer? Would he be repulsed by her bald head?

So many questions and so few answers.

"I can't believe how dark it gets here," Jude murmured as they meandered to a stop. The light breeze teased his hair and Ruth had the urge to reach up and push it off his forehead.

She loved seeing his eyes, but he was right. It was dark. Too dark to get a good look at the beautiful blue color he sported. "I guess that's what happens when you move away from the big city," she said, meaning to tease, but the words were too soft to be taken that way.

"What's wrong?" Jude asked, gathering her into his arms. "Something has been off most of the evening." He tilted his head down in order to look her in the face. "When I mentioned taking a walk, you got all nervous. What's the matter?"

Ruth shook her head. "I'm just...being stupid." She cleared her throat. "Didn't you say there was something you wanted to talk to me about?"

Jude studied her for a minute, then finally sighed and nodded. "Yeah. I...I wanted to talk about...us."

Ruth swallowed hard. Her throat had been dry ever since he'd announced they were going for a walk. It was like she had swallowed a piece of cotton. Nothing she did seemed to alleviate the distress.

She just wasn't ready to tell him, but she knew she had to. Since he wanted to talk about his leaving, maybe it was best to find out his feelings first. If he didn't want to have a long distance relationship, then she had no need to spill the beans about her secret.

"I'm leaving," Jude said carefully. "My flight is first thing Sunday morning."

Ruth nodded again. She couldn't speak.

"I'm hoping that you're willing to talk about a long distance relationship," he said slowly.

Ruth blinked. "You want to keep seeing each other after you go back home?" Relief warred with a burst of anxiety.

Jude frowned and nodded. "Yeah. Don't you?"

"Yes!" Ruth shouted, then covered her mouth and laughed. "Oh my gosh, I'm sorry. I didn't mean to shout."

Jude chuckled and gave her a weird look. "Are you sure?" he asked. "I know long distance isn't easy, but..."

Ruth put her hands on his shoulders. "I wasn't sure how you would feel about it," she admitted. "I wasn't ready to end this thing between us, but thought maybe you wouldn't be interested in continuing."

Jude dropped his chin to his chest and shook his head before coming back up to meet her eyes. "I think I should be offended that you thought I would just use you like that, but I'm too happy to worry about it."

He gathered her close and Ruth wrapped her arms around his torso, hugging tight. When she felt him kiss the top of her head, she pulled back, her hand going to make sure her hair was in place. At Jude's knowing look, Ruth forced her fist down to her side. "I promise I didn't think you were fickle or anything like that, but there's plenty of people who refuse to do long distance." She made a face. "It just wasn't something we had ever talked about before."

Jude nodded. "I know."

This was it. Ruth knew joy one moment and sorrow the next. He wanted to keep seeing her. Wanted to stay in touch even though they lived in different states. And she had promised that if he said that, she would tell him about her hair.

Her heart started to pound and even in the cool night air, she felt sweat begin to bead on the back of her neck. She wasn't ready! She didn't want to lose the happiness of knowing he liked her enough to keep dating. But how could she keep something so big from him?

Just as she opened her mouth, Jude continued. "But before we commit to anything, I feel that there's something I should tell you."

Ruth's mouth stayed open before she caught onto what he said. "Oh?" she asked hesitantly. What could he possibly want to discuss? Her mind spun, but she couldn't think of anything.

"I, uh, wanted to tell you a little bit about my past."

Her heart was pounding for a different reason now. Did Jude have a secret just like her?

"I've been in love with the same girl for over five years."

That pounding heart went from speeding to a standstill in a matter of moments. "You're...in love?" Ruth managed to gasp. "With someone else?"

Jude dropped his head back and groaned. "Hold on, that came out weird." He shook his head hard. "I'm over her, but what I was trying to tell you was that I *used* to be in love with someone else." He pushed a hand through his hair. "I met a girl in the physical therapy program at college and we became good friends. Over the years I grew to have feelings for her, but after a couple of dates, Elania admitted she didn't feel the same."

Ruth's knees were shaking. This was definitely not anything like how she had expected this to go.

"Geez, you're freezing," Jude said, rubbing her arms. "I can feel you shivering." He linked her hand through his arm. "Come on. We can walk back while we talk and I'll get you a hot chocolate."

Ruth was completely numb. She followed him only because her arm was attached to her body, but her legs were stiff and she couldn't seem to get into a good rhythm.

Jude tucked her in close to his side. "I'm so sorry. I didn't mean to freeze you to death."

"I'm f-f-fine," she stammered.

"Anyway..." Jude cleared his throat. "This is kind of a hard story for me, so I'm sorry if my words are kind of jumbled." He took a deep breath. "Even though Elania made her feelings plain, I decided it was still worth sticking around." He chuckled without humor. "Looking back, I was so stupid, but..." He shrugged.

"It's not stupid," Ruth finally managed to get out. "We love who we love."

"But I should have known enough to back off," Jude growled. He sighed. "Sorry. I'm getting off topic. Elania and I stayed good friends, with me just hiding my feelings." He squished his lips to the side. "Although, I must not have hidden them very well because one day she up and disappeared."

Ruth gasped. "What?"

Jude glanced down at her and nodded. "She eloped with a guy I'd never even met." Jude looked off into the distance. "I think, now that I'm looking back, that she knew I would have had a hard time, so rather than talk to me about it, she just...left."

"I'm so sorry," Ruth said softly. Inside, her heart was breaking. Who would do something like that to their best friend? It didn't matter if Jude had unrequited feelings, he still deserved enough respect to be treated like an adult.

"It probably wouldn't have hurt as much as it did, except that when I was a kid, my mother did the same thing."

Ruth stumbled. "Your mother left you?" she asked weakly.

Jude nodded. "Don't get me wrong. I've got a great stepmother and I had all the love I needed, but when I was eight, my mom packed up and left." He shook his head and rolled his eyes. "I guess when Elania did it, it felt the same as when I was growing up, knowing my mom hadn't cared enough to stick around."

A tear tracked down Ruth's cheek. "Jude," she whispered hoarsely. "How horrible."

He nodded. "Yeah. It was rough." His smile wasn't as wide as usual when he looked down at her, but it was still genuine. "But I'm mostly over it. I'm still sad Elania didn't talk to me about it, but I'm not still in love with her. She lied to me and that's one thing I just can't seem to forgive."

She lied...

I lied...

Ruth's confession was stuck in her throat. She opened her mouth several times, but no words came out. Sweat beaded on her forehead and her stomach churned with nausea, but she couldn't do it. Jude had been abandoned twice, by women he loved, but the thing that bothered him the most? The fact that Elania lied.

Ruth knew that if she told Jude about the cancer, he'd call her a liar and leave. She couldn't do it. She couldn't lose him that way. She had been scared from the beginning, but now she was downright terrified.

It can't end like this, she told herself. *I won't let it. I won't let him down the same way the others did.*

But she already had...and Ruth knew it. What she didn't know was how to fix it.

SOMETHING WAS STILL wrong with Ruth, but Jude wasn't quite sure what it was. Was she upset that he was leaving? Was she upset about the story with Elania? Maybe he shouldn't be telling another woman about someone he'd been in love with in his past. But his point had been to explain why he'd been so reticent when they'd first met.

Ruth had been a lifesaver. She had pulled him out of his dark disposition and slowly, he was starting to see the sun again. But how did he explain that without going too far? He wasn't ready to say he loved her yet, though he thought there was a good chance that would eventually come. Maybe. Hopefully.

Gah! Why is it all so complicated?

He was falling for her. That was a fact. But he wanted to see how the distance factored into the situation. After all, distance had played a huge role in the other women in his life. What if being apart made her feelings change? Or his, for that matter?

"So I guess my point in telling you all this was to explain why I was kinda..." He rubbed the back of his neck. "Kind of rude when we first met."

Ruth looked up at him. The sadness that lurked in her gaze just about tore his heart apart, but the tear was the clencher.

He pulled her in close and whispered in her ear. "I'm sorry. I'm not trying to upset you. I just wanted you to understand." Leaning back, he was careful not to mess with her hair, though he desperately wanted to tuck it behind her ear or run his fingers through the strands.

"No, it's fine," Ruth said, though the tone of her voice said it was anything but.

Jude closed his eyes and sighed. "No...it's not fine. I hurt you and that wasn't my intention." He opened his eyes and tried to show her everything in his heart. He couldn't quite say the words yet, but hopefully she could understand. "I wanted you to see how much you've helped me," he whispered. "I was depressed and hurt, and you changed all that."

Slowly, Ruth's face slid into a slight frown. "I did?"

"Don't you see?" Jude laughed softly. "Somewhere in between losing my best friend and the women I thought I loved, I also lost myself." Leaning in, he gave her a sweet kiss on her forehead. "But you gave it back to me. Your kindness, your patience, your determination to do what's right and enjoy life to the fullest." Jude slowly shook his head. "You helped me get my head above water again. I can't let you go just yet, Ruth. I know long distance will be hard. I know there'll be times when I'm missing you something fierce, and truthfully..." His shoulders slumped. "It's probably kinder to let you go so you don't wait for someone who lives hours away, but I'm too selfish. I don't want to give you up." He wiped another stray tear. "I don't know what the future will bring between us, but I feel like there's something here worth developing. Something worth holding onto and fighting for."

Ruth's eyes were wide and she seemed to be holding her breath, though her body had stopped shaking, which Jude hoped was a good sign.

"So I'm asking you to not only keep in touch, but I want you to be my official girlfriend. Exclusively." Anticipation and fear battled for the winning spot in Jude's chest. "How would you feel about that?" he asked hoarsely, his voice having given into his emotions.

Ruth's cold, trembling hand came up to cup his cheek. "I think I would be the luckiest girl in the world if I had you to wait for."

Jude laughed. "It sounds like we're in some kind of fairy tale."

Ruth's laughter was softer but still music to his ears. "I suppose it does." She shrugged and began to walk again. "Is there something wrong with a charming prince coming to rescue a damsel in distress?'

"No. But you're not a damsel in distress." Ruth was quiet for a moment and Jude looked down. "Are you?"

"Not that I know of," she said with a smile.

Jude relaxed a little more. He'd been worried for a moment. "Did my story freak you out?" He pressed his key fob since they were coming up on the parking lot of the restaurant.

Ruth shook her head. "No, but I'm sorry you went through all that."

Jude waited to respond until they were both in the car. "It's fine," he said, taking her hand and kissing her palm. "It's what brought me to you, right?"

Ruth still didn't seem quite herself, but she laid her head against the headrest and smiled. "Right."

"Best place to get hot chocolate?" he asked as he started the car.

"Probably my grandma's," Ruth said.

Jude could hear the smile in her voice and it made him feel better. It had probably just been the cold and his too personal story. Now that they were warming up, she would relax and be herself again. "Grandma Nan makes a mean cup, huh?"

Ruth nodded, her head barely visible in the dark car. "Yep. She's had years to perfect it." She put her finger to her lips. "But don't tell her I said that."

"What? That she makes great hot chocolate or that she's older?"

"Both."

Jude chuckled. "Why? I don't get the feeling that she'd be upset about it."

"Because we have an ongoing feud about who makes the best cocoa and I don't want to admit that it's not me."

"And the age thing?"

Ruth shrugged. "It's just not nice."

Jude shook his head as he smiled and drove them back to the house. Parking in the driveway, he paused. "Are you sure it's okay for me to come in?"

Ruth opened her door. "Grandma's with her quilting circle. This is the best time to come in."

He hurried out of the car and rushed around to finish helping her out. "Are you saying we'll have the house to ourselves?"

Ruth glanced at her cell phone clock. "For about another forty-five minutes."

Jude whistled low. "They go that late? Those ladies must really live it up."

Ruth rolled her eyes and stepped back to take his hand before leading him to the front door. "Sure. They live it up by talking about other people's lives."

"Are you saying they gossip more than they sew?"

Ruth glanced over her shoulder as she unlocked the door. "Is there any other way?"

Jude found himself laughing as they walked inside the dark house. Before Ruth could turn on the light, he grabbed her around the waist and pulled her into his chest. "You know...I think maybe I could warm you up without having to go through the hassle of making Grandma's hot chocolate."

"You do?" Ruth asked in an innocent voice. "And just what would that entail?"

Jude spun her around, enjoying her arms wrapping themselves around his neck. "Kisses," he said in a husky tone. "Lots and lots of kisses."

"I'm not sure I can give into that, Mr. Lisbon," Ruth said sweetly. "It sounds scandalous."

"It's a form of heat therapy," Jude threw out. "I learned about it in PT school."

"Wow. I've never heard of it before."

Jude began to leave feather light kisses against her cheekbone, slowly working his way down to her mouth. The shift in her breathing cast out every worry he'd had from her odd response to his chat tonight. "Trust me," he whispered against her skin. "I'm a doctor."

Ruth laughed breathlessly. "Show me," she said softly.

"I thought you'd never ask," Jude responded just before bringing their mouths together. He wasn't sure how he was going to leave in a few hours, but he knew...he *knew*...that having her waiting for him was the best thing he could have ever asked for.

CHAPTER 19

Guilt was eating at Ruth's stomach, worse than any food poisoning she had ever known. On top of that, she couldn't seem to stop the flood of tears as she was cuddled into Jude's chest, standing in the middle of the airport.

His hand rubbed her back, but never touched her hair, making Ruth want to break down even more that he'd figured out she didn't like having it touched.

"We'll see each other again soon, okay?" he whispered. "Maybe one of these days I'll convince you to come down to California." Jude leaned back, giving her a smile that didn't even come close to meeting his eyes. "I think you'd like the warm weather down there."

Ruth nodded and wiped at her wet cheeks. She needed to tell him. It didn't matter that he had problems with women leaving and lying to him. She needed to tell him.

Jude pulled her back into his chest. "I can't tell you how much it means to me to know that you're here waiting for me. The only thing better would be if we lived in the same place."

Ruth's guilt just about came spewing through her mouth. Why did he have to go saying things like that? She couldn't do it. She just couldn't hurt him that way. "I'm going to miss you," she croaked. And she would. She wasn't lying in the least. She knew, with the way her heart wrenched with each plane being boarded, that she was completely and utterly in love with Jude.

What she didn't know was if his feelings were as deep as hers. If they continued their relationship, the hair thing would come up. There was no way around it. But maybe if he was in love with her, the blow would be less harsh. He would understand that she wasn't planning to leave him and that her lie of omission had been necessary. By then, he would trust her.

A tiny bit of relief pecked away at the edges of the guilt. That had to be enough. She would tell him when he said he loved her. That way he would be too invested to freak out about it...maybe...hopefully...

It was the best Ruth had and for now, she was sticking to it.

Jude kissed her cheek. "I gotta go."

"I know," she whispered, gripping the edges of his coat. "Doesn't mean I have to like it."

Jude laughed softly. "I'll call you, all right? I'll let you know when I land."

"Okay." Ruth wiped her face and forced herself to step back. She put a shaky smile on her face. She was really good at smiling when she wanted to cry. Today would be no different. "Be safe."

Jude's smile was sad. "You too."

"And enjoy the sunshine while I waste away in the gray, gloomy weather here."

His laughter was more genuine this time. Reaching out, he trailed a finger down her cheek. "You're amazing."

Yeah. Amazing at lying.

Ruth swallowed hard. "Likewise."

"I'll call."

She nodded, her eyes refilling as he backed up.

"And text."

A laugh broke through her tears. "Okay."

"And email."

"I wouldn't have it any other way," Ruth said, her smile wide even as her heart broke in two.

Jude gave her a little salute, then turned and was immediately swallowed by the security line.

Ruth waited, hoping to catch one more glimpse of him, and was rewarded with a final wave just as he went through the metal detector. With heavy legs and a heavier heart, she finally turned and made her way back to the parking lot.

It was a long drive back to Seaside Bay and Ruth wasn't excited about all the time she'd have to dwell on her cowardice and her broken heart. Alone time right now seemed like a horrible idea, but there was nothing for it.

Biting her cheek until the tears cleared, she got in her car and headed home. Just as suspected, the ride was slow and long. By the time she pulled into the motel parking lot, Ruth felt as if she was going to throw up.

Her appetite, which had been immensely healthy since arriving in Oregon, was gone and Ruth had little hope of it coming back soon. *Should I call him?* Maybe she could get the confession out over the phone.

"He deserves more than that," she whispered to herself. Ruth acknowledged the truth with a long sigh. Jude had been the ultimate gentleman and boyfriend. He deserved more than an awkward phone conversation about her past disease.

"How'd it go?" Grandma Nan asked softly from the front desk.

Ruth took in a shaky breath. "About how you'd expect."

"I meant the cancer, silly girl," Grandma scolded. "How did he respond to you telling him about the cancer?"

Ruth was silent. She couldn't even tell Grandma the truth.

Grandma Nan slapped her hand on the counter. "You've really stepped in it now."

"Grandma!" Ruth said in shock. Hurt mixed with the guilt. Ruth knew she was in the wrong. But she had hoped for a little compassion, not being called out for being stupid.

Grandma threw her hands in the air. "What do you want me to say? That it'll all be all right? That the boy's heart won't be broken? That every fairy tale has a happy ending?"

"Yes," Ruth argued back, her chaotic emotions finally turning to anger. "I've spent most of my adult life seeing everything *except* a happy ending, Grandma. I've seen death, both from friends and almost myself. I've been through hell and back and I did it all with a smile on my face." Ruth's chest was heaving. Now that the words she'd thought for so long were starting to spill, her mouth just wouldn't stop. "For years, I've said I was fine. I've smiled, I've laughed, I've done my best to see the bright side of life, but you know what?" Ruth pounded at her chest. "I'm not all right!"

Grandma's face fell.

"I'm scared. No...that's not enough. I'm absolutely, positively TERRIFIED! I'm terrified about big things like my cancer coming back. Or whether or not I'll be able to have children someday. I'm terrified about small things like whether or not my new hair will be the same color or if I'll even like it." Her vision blurred. "But most of all, I'm terrified that once Jude knows about it, he'll say he can't handle the thought of another woman leaving him and instead, he'll choose to leave first. Or worse yet, he'll call me the liar that I am and never forgive me." Her shoulder drooped and the words stopped. She hadn't meant to blow up at Grandma Nan, but the emotions raging through Ruth's system were simply more than she could handle, and unfortunately, Grandma's scolding had broken her self restraint.

Grandma wiped at her face and Ruth's guilt came soaring back to the forefront. "I'm sorry," Ruth began, but Grandma held up her hand.

"No...I'm sorry." Grandma shook her head. "I've spent so much time worrying about whether or not you'd get a chance to have a life that when it was finally here, I pushed too hard." Her teary gaze met Ruth's. "Sometimes, we old ladies get too caught up in seeing something happen that we don't remember real people are going through everything we gossip about in the first place."

Ruth snorted through her tears.

Grandma Nan held out her arms. "Can you ever forgive an old woman?"

"Always," Ruth promised, rushing over for a hug that she knew from experience would cure every ill. She held her grandmother carefully, not wanting to hurt her. "I know I need to tell him," she whispered. "But I don't know how."

Grandma Nan patted her back. "It'll come to you," she said softly. "And when it does, I'll be right here to help. No matter what his response."

HAVING A WINDOW SEAT had always been Jude's favorite way to travel, but as he spent a few hours in a plane, leaving Oregon, all he could think about was how much land was passing underneath him. Land that was putting distance between him and Ruth.

Her tears had tugged at his heart and Jude knew one of these days he was going to have to admit just how deep his feelings for her went. He thumped his fist against his knee. *I probably should have just told her.*

He shook his head. No. It was too early. It had taken him a couple of years to fall in love with Elania. There was no way it could happen in a matter of days with Ruth.

Closing his eyes, Jude prayed the trip would go quickly and soon enough he was ducking under the door of the plane threshold in order to walk into the airport. He gathered his luggage and walked out to grab a ride home.

It took another hour for him to be settled at the kitchen counter, twisting a glass of water in his hand. He didn't want to be here.

The sun was warm, the city bustling, the smell of restaurants enticing, his mail overflowing with cards and letters, and yet Jude wanted to be back in a small town in Oregon.

"Idiot," he grumbled to himself. He picked up the glass and drained it. "You're an adult. No pining like this. Ruth has agreed to keep dating you, but you're man enough to handle the separation."

Grabbing his phone, he sent her a quick text.

Made it home safe and sound. As he moved around to start doing laundry and be ready to begin work the next day, Jude refused to admit that he was waiting for her response. Luckily for his nerves, he didn't have to wait long.

Yay! Did you have any troubles?

Nope. Smooth as silk. Just doing laundry.

I'm so glad.

Jude hesitated before responding again. What did he say? I miss you already? Please move to California? Are there any physical therapy jobs in Oregon?

No.

It was all so ridiculous. He couldn't be in love after this amount of time. He liked Ruth. He liked her a lot. But a little separation wasn't going to kill them. He'd seen her just that morning. There was no way he was craving her touch already. No way that the sunshine outside didn't feel as warm as normal. No way that right now he'd prefer gray, overcast skies to palm trees and heat.

He stuffed the phone in his back pocket. He'd call Ruth later. They'd agreed to keep dating and that's exactly what a good boyfriend would do, but he wasn't going to allow himself to groan and mope around like a lovesick fool.

He dragged his suitcase down the hall to the washer-dryer unit in the closet. He needed to get his clothes clean, and then he needed to go to the grocery store. His fridge and cupboards were embarrassingly bare.

The day wore on and by dinnertime, Jude was even more miser-able. The more he tried to push Ruth out of his thoughts, the more she stayed put. If this was how his week was headed, Jude wanted no part of it.

He trusted Ruth. She wasn't going to leave him like Elania or his mother, but that didn't mean he wanted to be so dependent on her.

Jerking open the fridge door, Jude grabbed the package of lunch meat he had picked up that afternoon and plopped himself on the couch. He picked up the remote, found a basketball game, and set-tled in. He opened the meat package and tore off a chunk before stuffing it in his mouth.

The saltiness was nearly as potent on his tongue as usual and yet the flavor of the meat fell flat. Ignoring the issue, Jude continued to eat it, keeping his eyes on the screen. After ten minutes, however, he realized he didn't even know who was playing.

Cursing under his breath, he dug out his phone and dialed Ruth. They needed to set some things straight. She needed to know that he wasn't ready for something serious. That he had issues he was still working on and that if he didn't speak to her every day, it wasn't a re-flection on her.

"Jude!"

For the first time all day, Jude felt his shoulders relax and he slumped into the couch, the package of deli meat sliding to the side. He sighed and let his chin fall to his chest. "Hey, Ruth."

"How was your day? Did you get your grocery shopping done?"

How could such a mundane question sound so wonderful? "Yeah, yeah. Shopping is done. Things are...good. Quiet." He chuck-led. "Much quieter than Mr. Portman's grumbling, but good."

"I'm so glad," Ruth gushed. "You should have seen Mr. Portman today. He accused me of not knowing how to decorate the Christmas tree we have in the lobby."

Jude sat up. "The one we did together? What was his problem with it?"

"Said we had too many ornaments up high. How was a body supposed to see them all if they were way up in the stratosphere."

Jude couldn't help but laugh. That old man could find dirt on a rainbow. "I suppose coming from his height, the complaint is valid."

"Probably," Ruth agreed with a laugh.

The line grew quiet and Jude found himself just listening for her breathing. He couldn't figure out the score on the television, but he could listen to Ruth's inhales all day.

I'm in so much trouble.

"Tell me about your day," Jude said softly. He hadn't meant to sound quite so vulnerable, but it seemed he couldn't keep hiding from himself.

He was in love with Ruth Allen. The thought was equal parts terrifying and exciting. The question was...now that they were apart, what in the world was he supposed to do about it?

CHAPTER 20

"If you just walk straight toward Main Street, the store will be on your left," Ruth said with a bright smile. She'd gotten lax in her ability to be happy even when she was sad. Jude being gone, however, had given her the incentive she needed to figure out how to put on that happy face again.

Grandma, however, wasn't as thrilled with the skill. She said Ruth needed to work her way through her feelings, but Ruth knew better. Just like a week ago when she had snapped at Grandma, Ruth knew that if she gave into the heartache inside or the guilt that ate at her, she would drown and might never find her way to the surface again.

"Thank you," the woman said, only her smile was genuine. "I'm excited to relax for the weekend."

"This is the perfect place for that," Ruth assured the woman and her husband. "Our town is quiet, but it has everything you need to unwind."

"Great." The woman laughed. "Leaving my five kids is hard, but sometimes..." She shrugged. "It just has to happen, you know?"

Ruth's eyes widened. "Wow! Five? You're a supermom!"

The husband wrapped his arm around his wife and kissed her temple. "That she is. But even supermoms sometimes need a break."

"Well, I'm sure you'll get everything you need while you're here." Ruth passed them another couple of pamphlets. "Be sure and take the time to walk down Main Street in the evenings. Everyone has Christmas lights up and it's beautiful right now."

"Oooh, that's perfect," the woman gushed. "Thank you again."

"Any time." Ruth watched them leave, then sighed and finished the details on the computer. She missed when Jude would put his arm around her and tuck her into his side. She missed sipping hot cocoa with him and laughing at something Mr. Portman had done.

Speaking of...

Mr. Portman hadn't been seen the past couple of days and Ruth was beginning to worry about him. Grandma said he always stayed through the new year, so it seemed odd that he would stop taking his afternoon walks.

Glancing around to make sure no one was coming in the front door any time soon, Ruth walked around the counter and headed down the hall. She nodded at a couple of guests. "Hello."

"Hi!" the little boy shouted and waved enthusiastically.

"That cafe you mentioned was wonderful," the mother called over her shoulder. "Even Logan enjoyed it." She gave Ruth a meaningful look.

"That's fantastic," Ruth responded, clasping her hands at her waist. "I'm so glad I could help."

"Bye!" Logan shouted again as they left the hallway and disappeared toward the front door.

Ruth smiled as she waved. She allowed the happiness of the moment to linger. It felt so good to smile and mean it. Moments like this had been few and far between with Jude gone, but there was still just something so wonderful about helping other people. It always served to lift Ruth's spirits, no matter how heavy they were.

Ruth found the right number and knocked. She waited, listening for sounds inside the room, but nothing was forthcoming. She knocked again. "Mr. Portman? Are you in there?"

Finally, some grunting could be heard from the other side and the door was thrown open. "What?" he asked, his voice lower and more hoarse than usual.

Ruth froze. Dark circles hung under the elderly man's eyes and his skin seemed saggier than usual. "I..." She blinked, pulling herself out of her stupor. "I'm sorry to disturb you, Mr. Portman, but I've noticed you haven't been taking your afternoon walks this week. I wanted to make sure you were doing all right."

Mr. Portman snorted and shifted his weight. "Just can't leave a body alone, can ya? When I come on vacation I want to rest, not be kept up all hours with nosy busybodies." Without another word, he slammed the door in Ruth's face.

Ruth blinked rapidly, trying to process what had just happened. She tried hard not to take it personally. She knew that his rudeness was his armor, but geez, it was hard not to. Especially when her emotions were already struggling.

"I'm just down the hall if you need anything," Ruth called out, sighing when she heard more grumbling. Her shoulders were slumped as she walked back to the desk. Mr. Portman's attitude might be pricklier than usual, but something was still off.

Maybe he's sick?

The thought worried Ruth. Mr. Portman was older than Grandma Nan. Getting sick would not be a good thing for him. And knowing the guest, he'd refuse to go to the hospital, even if he desperately needed to.

The bell rang at the front door and Ruth quickened her pace. She opened her mouth to greet whoever came in, but instead came to a screeching halt. Closing her eyes, Ruth shook her head. "Jude?" she whispered hoarsely. What was he doing here? He wasn't supposed to be visiting. They had planned to see each other in a couple weeks, after Christmas was over and the rush of the holidays had slowed down at the motel.

Jude gave her a sheepish smile and stuffed his hands in his pockets. "Hi." A moment passed. "I couldn't wait."

Three words. They weren't *the* three words, but right now they were the sweetest words Ruth had ever heard. With a smile that nearly broke her face, she skipped across the lobby and threw herself into his open arms. "I'm so glad you're here," she whispered into his neck. She felt him kiss the top of her head and for the first time ever, Ruth forced herself not to back up and make sure her wig was in place.

"Me too," he whispered back.

Bringing her head up in order to see him better, Ruth smiled at his bright blue eyes. Suddenly all the turmoil, worry, and heartache of the week was gone. Her worry over Mr. Portman disappeared and all she could see was Jude.

He's here. I can tell him. Just do it. Like a Band-Aid.

Before Ruth could do anything else, Jude brought his head down and kissed her. Something was different about this kiss. It wasn't the playful, I'm having fun with you type of kiss from before he had left. This was more serious. This was I want you...I *need* you.

Ruth couldn't help but answer the call.

Her arms wrapped around his neck and hung on for dear life. She forgot where she was and what she was supposed to tell him. All that mattered was the heat rushing through her as she held Jude. He loved her. He had to. That's why he came back. That's why he was kissing her.

Maybe Grandma was right. Fairy tales really could come true.

Tightening her hold, Ruth gave as good as she got. She had no idea how long he held her, but it was irrelevant. This was exactly where Ruth was supposed to be.

"I'm guessing you need a little time off?" The sarcastic words took a moment to penetrate Ruth's brain.

When they did, she pulled back with a gasp. Her chest heaved as she tried to catch her breath. Even knowing her grandmother was staring at them, Ruth couldn't pull her eyes away from Jude. "Can I go on break?" she asked breathlessly.

"If for no other reason than to keep my guests from being scandalized," Grandma teased. "Get out with ya."

Jude kissed Ruth's forehead, then turned to Grandma Nan. "Thanks, Grandma. I owe you."

"You owe me a lot more than you can repay." Grandma sniffed. She ruined her lofty response with a wink. "Head to the house. It's empty."

Jude led Ruth outside. "Sounds like a perfect plan to me."

JUDE FELT LIKE HE WAS floating on air. All week he had fought with himself. Fought to keep his mind on his work. Fought to not admit he was lonely. Fought to only talk to Ruth once a day. And fought to convince himself he wasn't in love.

None of it worked.

By Saturday he was so miserable that he'd bought a last minute plane ticket and come up, if only to put himself out of his misery. Seeing Ruth had been worth the horrible price of his desperate trip.

He squeezed her fingers while he drove, glancing over every couple of seconds. It was like he couldn't get his fill of her and paying attention to the road just wasn't important at the moment.

"You're going to crash if you don't watch where you're going," Ruth teased.

Jude smiled sheepishly. "I know, but I just...ahhh." He groaned. "I miss you."

Ruth's smile was brighter than the rare sunshine that afternoon. "I missed you too." She frowned. "But what about work? You can't just fly up here every weekend. Neither of us has that kind of money."

Jude blew out a breath and let go of her hand in order to park the car. "I know," he said. "But maybe before I leave tomorrow we can work something else out." He looked at her again. "This long distance stuff sucks."

Ruth laughed. "You don't have to tell me twice." Again, she grew serious. "Jude...now that you're back, there's something I need to tell you."

"Later," Jude said, too happy to listen to something that was obviously sad. "Right now I'm freezing and have a serious craving for Grandma Nan's hot chocolate. Think you can make me some?"

Ruth nodded and got out of the car. She hurried them inside and Jude sighed into the warmth.

"I think rushing down to California and then back up was like jumping into a hot tub, then the snow. My body is going through temperature shock."

Ruth laughed again as she set her coat to the side and headed toward the kitchen.

Before she could get too far, Jude reached out and took her hand, pulling her back into his chest.

"I thought you wanted hot chocolate," she whispered.

He grinned. "I did, but then I realized I have an even stronger craving."

Ruth's face softened and her eyes misted over. "Jude, you're going to turn me into a puddle with all this sweet talk."

He gave her a lingering kiss. "Good. I like puddles." Through her laughter, Jude continued to show her how much she meant to him. He couldn't get enough of her. He couldn't get her close enough. He couldn't fill his lungs with enough of her scent. He couldn't drink in enough of her essence.

As if purchasing the plane ticket hadn't been sign enough, Jude knew he needed to confess all. He needed to forget about Elania and his mother and move on. And if Ruth's kisses were any indication, she was absolutely ready to move on with him.

"Ruth," he whispered against her lips.

"Hmm?" Her eyes remained closed and Jude smirked in triumph at her reaction to him.

"I have a confession to make."

Those baby blues popped right open. "You do?"

Slowly, Jude nodded. "I..." He swallowed the lump in his throat. "I love you, Ruth." His voice had gone hoarse and he was struggling to breathe. The last time he'd said those words to a woman, she had left him without warning, breaking his heart as she married another man. It was terrifying to say them again, but Jude had hope. Ruth wasn't the same as the others. She held no secrets, like boyfriends or engagements or any other secrets.

Still, he held his breath while he waited for her to respond. It felt like his very life hinged on her next actions.

"Jude," Ruth breathed, her misty eyes spilling over. "I love you too," she said with a teary smile. "I wasn't sure you felt the same, but—"

Jude cut off her response. He'd heard enough. She loved him. She. Loved. *Him.* Out of all the men in the world, all the people she crossed paths with every day, every person who enjoyed her smile and her sweet service, Ruth loved him.

He trailed his kisses down her jaw and onto her neck. "You're so amazing," he whispered. "So beautiful. So sweet..."

Ruth's hands were wrapped around his wrists and she let out a hoarse laugh. "I can't believe it," she said. "I...I just never thought..."

"Me either," Jude responded to her. "I thought after Elania, I'd never love again." He pulled back. "But you changed all that. You showed me how to breathe again and now every breath is filled with you." Jude rested his forehead against hers, simply enjoying sharing air with the woman he loved.

The woman he loved.

He wanted to laugh at the words. They seemed so ludicrous, and yet everything about them was just right. The truth of it settled into his heart and he knew there was nothing that would pull it apart.

"I think we'll need to figure out a different plan than our original one," he said. "I can't go a couple of months in between seeing you."

"Me either," Ruth admitted. She wiped at her eyes. "Even this week was too long, but I guess we'll have to get used to at least a little time away, huh?"

Jude sighed and nodded. "I suppose so. After all, I do have to work, and you can't just leave your grandmother in a lurch." He groaned. "But somehow, we'll work it out. The first while might be hard, but we'll find a way to make our visits more frequent." He smirked. "Maybe that relationship with Grayson is going to come in handy. At least I'll have a place to stay every time I visit."

Ruth shook her head, the last of her laughter slowing down. "I suppose that'll help a little."

"Here." Jude took her hand. "Come make me that hot chocolate. I'm starving, and as much as I'd like to fill up on your kisses, I'm afraid my stomach is protesting otherwise."

"Jude." Ruth held him back. "There's something I still need to tell you." Her bottom lip trembled and she pressed it between her teeth as if to stop the movement.

"Okay." He tugged on her again. "But why don't you come tell me in the kitchen? I can eat while you share." A bit of worry slithered down his spine, but Jude shoved it away. This was Ruth. Whatever she was worried about wouldn't be a big deal at all.

He pulled her past the fireplace, but paused when a splash of bright yellow caught his eye. "What's this?" he asked. The couple of times he'd been at the house, he'd been too caught up in Ruth to look at any of the family pictures, but the color of this one was bright enough to have him curious.

"Jude...wait," Ruth began.

He pulled down the frame and studied it. Ruth looked almost the same age, so he assumed it had to be fairly recent. Jude frowned. Except, there were dark bags under her eyes and she was probably twenty pounds lighter than she was now. To the point of looking unhealthy.

She stood behind a bell, pointing to it and smiling widely, surrounded by what looked to be a team of doctors and nurses and some balloons.

Jude glanced up and saw that Ruth's tears were coming in a regular drip down her cheeks now. She was wringing her fingers so hard that Jude almost winced for her.

He went back to the picture. It took him a moment to put it all together, but when his eyes were drawn once again to the bright yellow turban on her head, he felt his heart stop.

When his head came back up, he had no words.

Slowly, Ruth reached up and with a series of tugs and jerks, that glorious hair that he'd never been allowed to touch, slid from her head.

CHAPTER 21

"I was twenty-one when they found the first lump," Ruth said softly. Her eyes had fallen to the carpet. She couldn't bear to look Jude in the eye. Her wig felt like it weighed a thousand pounds as it pulled against the tips of her fingers.

The cool air of the house on her scalp made it itch, but Ruth fisted her free hand and kept it at her side. It was a glaring beacon at the moment, but there was little to be done about it. Ruth had no one to blame this on but herself. She should have told him earlier. She should have given Jude the chance to understand who she truly was.

But no. Instead, she'd hidden and given herself excuses, giving into the fear, and now she stood before him in such a vulnerable way, she might as well have been naked.

"Of course the doctors jumped right into action," Ruth continued when Jude didn't move or respond. "We did surgery, then radiation, but a few months later..." Sighing, Ruth turned and walked to the couch. Her knees were shaking too hard for her to continue standing up. After sitting, she dropped the hair on the floor and rubbed her fuzzy head. "We hadn't gotten it all," she said in a barely audible voice. "In fact, it took us years to get it all."

She dared to glance up, then winced and dropped her gaze again, instantly regretting her decision. The pain and anger blazing in Jude's eyes was enough to make her feel like the world's worst villain.

"A few months ago, after finishing yet another round of chemo, we finally got the news that I was cancer free." She tried for a smile, but it fell flat in the silent room. "The picture is when I had my last treatment." She laughed without humor. "I actually rang that bell more than once during my five-year fight, but..." Ruth shrugged, picking at a loose thread in her jeans. "So I'm officially in remission," she continued, though from the continued lack of response, she didn't know why she bothered. Ruth knew exactly what was coming. Her worst nightmare was coming to life and she had no one to blame but herself. "I came down from Seattle to stay with Grandma as I regained my health. I learned to live in the moment rather than worry about the future. And I'm trying to figure out what exactly I want to do with a life that was almost snuffed out."

Jude turned his back to her and slowly put the picture back on the mantel. His hands gripped the ledge and he hung his head. "Why didn't you tell me?" The words were said through gritted teeth and Ruth felt shame nearly swallow her whole.

"Because I didn't want to be seen as a victim," she responded carefully. "I didn't want you to feel bad for me." She tried to perk her voice up, but her developed skills were failing her. "I'm me. I'm Ruth. Bald-headed, overly friendly front desk clerk, large appetite, mid-twenties me. I...I tried to tell you...so many times, but I just..." Her words meant nothing. It didn't matter if she had *tried* to tell him. The only thing that mattered was that she hadn't. She'd started an avalanche and Ruth knew only pain waited for her when the snow settled.

"And what about the girl I fell in love with?" Jude asked. He spun, the sadness gone and the anger blazing. "Where does she fall into all of this?"

Ruth frowned. "What about her? That's still me."

He shook his head. "No. I fell in love with a Ruth that I trusted. One that I thought would never lie to me. One that saw only good things in the future because the future was bright, not because she was holding back *a secret that SHE NEARLY DIED!*" With each word, Jude's voice had gotten louder and louder until Ruth shrank back in her seat.

"Why does it matter?" she argued. She had to make him see. He had to understand. "I know I should have told you earlier, but can you really blame—"

"Don't turn this on me!" Jude shouted, holding up his hand. "I was honest with you. I told you why I was struggling. I admitted to being foolish and weak and feeling lonely because of what had happened to me."

Ruth held out her hands to the side, but she couldn't hold back the tears cascading down her face. This was a side of Jude she had never seen before and one she hoped never to see again. Mr. Portman was right. She hadn't just lied to him, she had betrayed him.

In that moment, she knew...he would never forgive her.

"I'm sorry," she whispered, her tears coloring her voice. "I don't know what else to say. I'm sorry...and I love you."

Jude's head shook, slow then getting faster. "You don't get to say that to me," he said tightly. "You don't get to say that to me!"

Ruth closed her eyes and hung her head.

"I *trusted* you." He backed up, as if being near her was more than he could stand. As if just being near her would give him the same disease she had once conquered. "I let myself fall in love." He backed up more. "And it didn't matter. You lied. You'll leave me just like all the rest." He worked his jaw. "You're just like them."

Ruth rose to her feet though she felt as if she'd been run through with a pitchfork. She clasped her shaking hands. "I should have told you," she admitted. "I was scared." She took in a shuddering breath. "*This* is exactly why I was afraid. After all, who would want to stay with a cancer survivor?"

Jude jerked back as if he'd been slapped.

"All I can say is I'm sorry." She breathed again, this time a little more steadily. "I won't keep you. Thank you for your time. For your sweet words. For making my life better." She forced her eyes to stay on his face. The tears had stopped for the moment and Ruth felt numb. "I'll never forget you, Jude. But I'm also not going to beg you to stay." She wanted to tell him she loved him one more time, but she held back the words. He didn't want to hear them. They just put salt in the wound she had created when she chose to hide the truth.

Grandma had warned her. Mr. Portman had warned her. Her heart had warned her, but Ruth hadn't listened. She had held tight to that fairy tale she was so desperate for and just as she thought it was coming true, it all fell apart.

Just more proof that life was more fragile than people thought.

"Begging wouldn't help," Jude said harshly. "I can't be with someone I can't trust."

"I understand." Ruth held her face as passive as she could, but it was hard. Her heart felt like it had been torn from her chest. But right now Jude didn't care. She wasn't going to break down in front of him. She'd already shown her remorse. If he didn't want to hear it, she would save it for when he was gone. "Thank you for coming. You're an amazing person."

Jude snorted. "But not good enough for you to be honest with, right?" He laughed harshly. "I must have a sign on my forehead that says *Please, take advantage of me! I'm an easy target!*"

Ruth shook with the work it took not to flinch. "I don't think that at all. You're everything I could ever ask for."

Jude put up his hand. "Please. Save me the speech." His head continued to shake from side to side. "I can't do this. You're just like all the others. You've lied about everything. Why would I believe you now?"

Ruth didn't even try to defend herself this time. Why bother? Jude had every right to feel the way he did, even if she didn't agree with everything he was saying. She started to walk toward the door, but he stopped her.

"Don't bother," he snarled. "I can get it myself." Grabbing his coat from the back of a chair, he stormed to the door and rushed outside.

The slam of the door shook the walls of the house and Ruth's legs finally gave out. She fell to the couch and put a hand to her chest, unable to breathe. The room spun and sweat trickled down the side of her face.

All the emotions she had been holding back for Jude's sake came rushing into her system in an uncontrollable flood, and Ruth wasn't strong enough to handle it. As her vision turned dark, she had a moment's gratitude. Perhaps, by the time she awoke, it would all be okay. If she could just sleep until the pain was gone or until her heart quit beating, then perhaps she'd survive.

JUDE DROVE BACK TO Grayson's as if he were being chased by a hungry lion. The rage burning through his system was almost more than he could handle.

He had trusted her.

HE HAD TRUSTED HER!

She had broken through all the defenses that had built up as other women had taken care of him. She'd taken down his wall brick by sweet brick, and then as soon as he was vulnerable, she had dropped the bomb on him.

Cancer.

Another woman. Another secret. Another person leaving his life.

He slammed on the brakes in Grayson's driveway, his tires squealing just slightly. Normally, Jude would have felt bad about possibly leaving skid marks, but he barely noticed right now. His vision was tinged with red and his mind wouldn't calm down enough for him to think rationally.

Shoving open the door, Jude immediately headed to the staircase.

"Jude! You made it!" Brook called out, walking his way. She skidded to a stop. "Are you okay?"

Jude didn't answer, continuing to storm his way to the bedrooms. "Jude!"

He finally came to a stop, not looking at her, and squished his eyes shut. "What?" he shouted.

"What's going on?"

It was Grayson demanding his attention this time and Jude forced himself to turn around. "You want to know what's going on?" he asked through clenched teeth.

Grayson raised an unimpressed eyebrow. "That's what I asked, wasn't it?"

It was pretty rare that Jude wished he was as big as Grayson. He knew the work that Gray put into staying as bulky as he was and Jude was just fine with his slimmer runner's frame. But right now he wanted to be as big as a house so he could punch his best friend in the face so they would leave him alone.

"Ruth has cancer." The truth tasted like ash. It made Jude want to throw up, but the nauseating sensation wasn't enough to overcome the anger and betrayal he was feeling.

Brook's eyes filled with sorrow. "I know."

Jude froze. "Excuse me?"

Brook shook her head. "Grandma Nan told us about her and at dinner last week, I figured out it was Ruth."

"And you didn't tell me?" Jude shouted.

Grayson put up his hands and stepped in front of his wife. "Hey. Calm down, man."

Jude pushed his hands through his hair and let out a maniacal laugh. "Did everyone know except for me? Am I that much of an idiot?"

"You're not an idiot," Brook shot back. "And I'm pretty sure I'm the only one who had it figured out."

Jude turned to Grayson.

Gray shrugged. "Brook told me, but Ruth said she would tell you, so I let her do that. It's not like it was my secret to tell."

"Maybe not, but I thought you were my friend," Jude growled. A small part of his brain recognized that he was being unreasonable, but Jude didn't care. Even with all the women lying to him, he at least thought he could count on his guy friends. That belief was just as destroyed as his faith in Ruth. It appeared that he was destined to always be alone. He couldn't trust women, and now he couldn't trust his friends.

He pointed a shaking finger at Grayson. "When you got hurt, who stayed with you?"

Grayson stiffened. "You."

"Who ignored your rude attitude and helped smooth over the fact that you tried to bulldoze everyone in your path?"

"You," Gray said softly.

Brook's lips quivered. "Jude," she implored.

"Who put up with you when even Brook wanted to leave because you treated her so horribly?"

"You!" Gray shouted. "Okay? You! You've been the best friend I've ever had."

"And how would you feel if I kept something like this from you?" The question wasn't as loud or as harsh as the other questions, but it had a stronger impact if Gray's wince was anything to go by.

"It wasn't our secret to tell," Brook tried again.

Jude shook his head and backed up. "It shouldn't have been a secret at all," he argued. "I should have been told up front. Ruth knew this would change how I felt about her. She knew I wouldn't want to get involved with someone who was destined to leave, and so she hid it. She lied and abused my trust." Jude turned and walked away.

"Where are you going?" Brook called after him.

"I don't know," Jude shot back. "But you can be sure it's away from Seaside Bay." The ache in his heart grew to an uncontrollable level and Jude had to concentrate on his breathing or it would freeze in his lungs.

"Jude." Grayson's voice was firm, but regretful.

Jude paused at the foot of the stairs but didn't turn around.

"Try to see this from her side."

Jude felt his lip curl in a snarl.

"She loves you," Gray said with conviction. "Don't forget that."

Jude shook as he worked to keep himself from turning around and giving Gray a black eye. He wasn't one for violence, but today Jude was positive it would help him feel better if he could just beat up on something for a while. Unfortunately, odds were that Grayson wouldn't be willing to let Jude vent his anger.

Instead, Jude went upstairs and changed his clothes. He was going to take over Gray's exercise room and he would lock the door. It probably wasn't a good time to be talking with anyone else.

After exhausting himself with cardio weights, Jude would try again to figure out what he was going to do. His plane didn't leave until tomorrow night, but Jude wasn't sure if he could wait that long. Every piece of this town reminded him of Ruth and Jude wanted nothing to do with it.

He couldn't handle seeing the beach or the sweets shop or even Charli's restoration shop. Everywhere he looked would be *her*.

Taking the back staircase, Jude headed straight for the workout room. He stuffed his earbuds in, turned on something harder than normal, and stormed to the weights. One way or another, he was going to get this woman out of his system. And if exercise didn't do it, Jude wouldn't find something else. He just needed to bide his time until his plane left. Then he'd never have to come back.

CHAPTER 22

"Let me know if there's anything I can help you with," Ruth said flatly. "Enjoy your stay." She pasted a smile on her face and waited as the couple nodded, walking away from her.

As soon as they were gone, Ruth let the fake emotion drop from her face. She probably wasn't fooling anyone anyway. Ever since Jude left her yesterday, Ruth had felt numb inside. She probably needed to allow herself time to mourn his loss, but she just didn't have it in her.

She felt like the opposite of Dorothy, going from color to black and white. Every scared little girl hoped for a prince to come save her at some point in her life, but Ruth had gone through her most difficult trial on her own two feet. She wasn't a damsel in distress, she wasn't weak. She had come out conqueror and that was when the prince had left her.

She had no idea that love could hurt so much. It had been terrible when her parents had died. It had been difficult when her only sibling had gone about his life rather than running to her aid.

But nothing hurt like Jude's angry reaction to hearing she had lied to him.

You didn't lie. You simply didn't share everything.

Ruth rolled her eyes at her own stupid thought. "Lying by omission is still a lie," she scolded under her breath.

"Have you eaten today?"

Ruth pinched her lips. She didn't want to worry about things like food. It only reminded her of her last dinner with Jude. Nausea churned in her stomach and Ruth put her hand on it as if she could stop the sensation, but it continued to roil. "I'm not hungry," she stated without looking over her shoulder.

Grandma Nan's frail hand landed on Ruth's shoulder. "You have to take care of yourself," she said.

Ruth shrugged her off. "I'm fine."

"You're not fine," Grandma Nan said sharply. "You haven't smiled since last night and you certainly haven't eaten anything. If you're not careful, you'll end up back in the hospital."

"Maybe that's where I belong," Ruth said, turning finally to look her closest family member in the eye. "Maybe I should have never left."

Tears filled Grandma's eyes and Ruth immediately felt bad. "Don't say that," Grandma Nan said through a clenched jaw. "You've been given another chance at life. Don't you dare waste it by feeling bad for yourself."

Ruth shook her head. "You're right. I'm sorry. I shouldn't have said that. But if this is how it feels to have a second chance at life, I'm not sure I want it." Ruth put her shaking hand on her chest, feeling the consistent beat of the organ. She wondered how it could keep going when every breath still felt like knives in her lungs.

Grandma Nan cupped Ruth's cheek, her skin slightly chilly and soft. "Don't say that. You'll get through this. I still have faith that he'll come around."

Ruth sighed but didn't pull back. "I don't know, Grandma. You didn't see the look on his face. He wasn't just hurt, he was absolutely gutted." She looked up into Grandma's eyes. "He feels like I betrayed him. He'd been hurt before and I made it worse. So much worse." Ruth shook her head. "He'll never forgive me."

"Then it's his loss," Grandma said imperiously. "Nobody is perfect, not even handsome pants Jude. If he can't get over that, then he didn't deserve you in the first place."

Easy for you to say.

Ruth barely kept herself from saying the sarcastic comment out loud. She just couldn't seem to get a good hold on her emotions. All her years of putting on a happy face might as well have never happened. Her smiles felt brittle and her laughter was sharp enough to cut someone. Instead of thinking positive thoughts, she was filled with anger and bitterness, even though she knew that she had no one to blame for her predicament except herself.

She'd been warned. Grandma Nan and Mr. Portman had both told her that she needed to tell him. That Jude deserved to know. Even Brook had figured it out. Grandma Nan had obviously spoken about her to the community and Brook had figured it out at dinner. Luckily, she had been willing to allow Ruth time be the one to tell Jude, though that hadn't turned out quite as Ruth had planned.

He had come with such sweet words, showing up unannounced and admitting that he loved her. Nothing could have been more like that fairy tale Ruth dreamed about. At least until reality had sucker punched her in the gut.

She hadn't thought about him seeing pictures in her house. On one hand, it had kickstarted the conversation. On the other, it had made her seem as if she was never going to tell him.

Ruth put her hand on her sick stomach again. "It's my loss," she said hoarsely. "Jude was the one. I know he was." Her eyes squeezed shut. "And I'll never find another like him."

"Give him time," Grandma Nan said reassuringly. "After he calms down, he'll understand."

Ruth shook her head. "I can't hope for that," she said. "I think it would kill me when it doesn't happen."

Grandma sighed and dropped her hands to her side. "I don't know what to tell you," she said. "But try not to do anything rash."

Ruth settled back onto her stool. "How can I do something rash?" she asked. "I have nowhere to go. No education that makes me a valuable employee. No experience that would allow me to fill out a resume in order to get another job and no money to get out of town with." She shrugged. "I'm stuck."

"Lucky us," Grandma Nan said with a watery smile. "I don't know what I'd do without you."

The front bell rang and Mrs. Swallows slipped inside, her hands gripping a casserole dish. "How's our beautiful survivor?" she asked with a hopeful, but cautious smile.

Ruth held back her sigh. Maybe she was destined to simply spend her life with elderly women who were desperate for someone to dote on. She supposed there were worse things in life, but somehow Ruth knew it wouldn't fill the gaping hole in her heart.

"Down in the dumps," Grandma Nan said, her normal sass making a reappearance.

Mrs. Swallows smiled. "Well, I brought something to make you feel better. My famous peanut butter brownies."

"Famous?" Grandma Nan snorted. "More like infamous. They're guaranteed to make the eater gain ten pounds by simply looking at them."

Mrs. Swallows sniffed. "That's the sign of a good dessert." She turned to Ruth and smiled again. "Go on, honey. Take 'em back and have a piece."

Ruth took the offering, even knowing that she wouldn't be able to keep anything down. "Thank you, Mrs. Swallows. This was really sweet of you."

Mrs. Swallows's cheeks turned pink, obviously pleased with the compliment. "Nothing cures a broken heart like extra dark chocolate and a little sugar."

Ruth gave her a small smile. "I'm sure you're right." She lifted the dish. "I'm just going to take this to the back. Thank you again." Taking a deep breath, Ruth slipped into the break room, leaving the two women to their gossip. She knew she would be the main topic of conversation, but Ruth couldn't bring herself to care.

She plopped down the dish and sat in a chair with a huff. Her energy was gone and all she wanted was to go to sleep. She let her forehead fall to the table. The cool Formica felt icy against her heated skin. Maybe she could close her eyes for just a moment. It wasn't like Ruth had gotten any sleep last night. A few moments wouldn't hurt. Hopefully by the time she woke up, she would find that it had all been a terrible dream. Jude would walk back here and give her a heart stopping kiss and life would be whole again.

She slumped. Yeah...that was worth dreaming about.

BY THE TIME JUDE GOT back to his apartment, it was the middle of the night and he didn't remember anything about the trip. Other than the moment when Ruth pulled his heart out and stomped it into oblivion. His mood had moved from angry to despairing. Never had he felt so hopeless before, not even when Elania had used him.

Without bothering to change his clothes, Jude went into his room and fell face first on the bed.

How could she do this to me?

He felt so disillusioned. He had thought Ruth was different. She was sweet, kind, cared about older people, well...she cared about everyone. Any person, no matter the age, that crossed Ruth's path was taken care of.

"Then why not me?" Jude rolled on onto his back. His misery and hurt were too loud for him to sleep no matter how tired he was. It just didn't make any sense. How could she have lied to him all this time? She claimed she loved him, but had kept something life altering from him. How in the world was he supposed to react to that?

He pointedly ignored Gray's advice to try and see things from her point of view. Jude had been the one hurt in this scenario. Not Ruth. She had chosen to lie to him and he couldn't help but wonder if she would have ever told him if he hadn't seen the picture.

When she'd taken her hair off, Jude had almost fallen to his knees. It was apparent her hair was just starting to grow back. She had maybe a quarter of an inch of hair and unlike the wig, it was fairly dark.

It completely changed her look to see her with what looked like a bad buzz cut. Gone was the girl next door and in her place was...

"A cancer victim."

Jude let the words hang in the air above his head. Cancer. Six letters. How could six letters have such a strong effect on a life? It had stolen Ruth's college years, and now it had stolen the woman he planned to marry.

Jude threw his arm over his eyes and groaned. There was no way he was getting any sleep tonight.

Grumbling, he climbed to his feet and stumbled out to the main area of his apartment. Flicking on a light, he jerked back from the brightness, his eyes having adjusted to the dark.

His first thought was to grab some hot chocolate, but the thought made him want to throw up. Hot chocolate was something he did with Ruth. It was something they enjoyed together. It looked like that might be off the menu forever.

Jude opened the fridge and stood with one arm on the door and the other on the side. Absolutely nothing inside appealed to him. He shut the door with a slam, not even caring that the bottles on top of the fridge shook and threatened to fall.

He turned and put his hand on the counter, staring out the window above the sink. City lights kept him from seeing the stars, but Jude still felt lost. It was like he had been torn away from his best friend. The very soul inside of him was torn between mourning and thrashing everything inside.

He was restless and exhausted.

Angry and sad.

Hurting and remorseful.

How could so many emotions exist within a single body without exploding?

Jude shook himself. He couldn't take this. He *wouldn't* take this. Ruth had lied. The blame lay squarely on her shoulders. He refused to feel sorry for her or have sympathy for her situation.

He wasn't a hard-hearted person by nature, but lying...deceiving...*betraying*... were more than he could handle. He'd had enough of that to last him a lifetime and somehow, every single experience had come at the hand of a woman he had loved.

Jude slapped his cheeks, then scrubbed his face. If he stayed in this apartment much longer, he was going to break down and cry like a baby. No, thank you.

Heading to his room, he grabbed his running shoes out of the closet and tied them on. He didn't even bother to change his jeans. What was the point? This wasn't about exercise; it was about outrunning his life. He didn't need sport shorts to do that. Lifting weights at Gray's had helped in the moment. Hopefully he could do the same now.

Grabbing his key, Jude headed back into the night. His pace picked up before he even reached the ground floor and his body lurched forward into the dark.

At first his pace was erratic, his footsteps uneven as he fought with himself, but a mile or so into the run, he found his rhythm.

Slowly, his mind calmed as his heart rate picked up speed and his breathing grew labored. Good. This was good. Anything that helped numb the pain was good. His skin flushed and he began to sweat, but he continued to push himself onward.

Slap. Slap.

Slap. Slap.

Left, right.

Left, right.

His mind followed his feet, forcing every other worry and thought to dissipate as he concentrated only on the next step.

By mile two, he felt more in control and allowed his mind to wander just a touch. Ruminating lightly over the events of the last forty-eight hours.

By mile five, he was sure of only one thing. It was better this way. There was no way he and Ruth could have worked out anyway, not with the distance and the obstacles between them.

Her desire to help every stray person or animal that crossed her path would have eventually driven him nuts anyway. And if she had thought to try that in Hollywood, she'd have probably ended up mugged in a back alley.

Jude didn't want to spend his life worried his girlfriend or, heaven forbid, wife was constantly in danger. He wanted peace. He wanted ease. He wanted convenient. None of those things came with Ruth Allen.

He unlocked his door as he struggled to calm his breathing back down. "The only way to get those things," he muttered to himself, "is to forget any idea of love and family and friends. When I need to be social, I've got enough people at work to fill that. Otherwise, I'll just stay busy." He took a deep breath. "Nothing else is worth the risk."

CHAPTER 23

"Walk with me."

Ruth's head jerked up at the gravelly voice. "Mr. Portman!" Her smile was more genuine than it had been all week. The elderly visitor had been practically invisible the last several days and Ruth had thought about knocking on his door more than once, but her last greeting kept her from poking her nose into his business. "How have you been feeling? Ready for Christmas?"

The holiday was only a few days away and Ruth found herself as far from the holiday spirit as she had ever been. She couldn't bring herself to enjoy hot chocolate, the beautifully decorated tree in the lobby, or any other activity that reminded her of Jude. Instead, she was constantly being swamped with memories that made her want to weep. She hadn't realized just how much life she and Jude had crammed into just two weeks of December.

Mr. Portman grunted. The dark circles under his eyes weren't any better than they had been before, and now his skin was so pale that Ruth wanted to tease him about becoming a vampire.

"Time is short," he said breathlessly. "Come." Spinning on his heel, he shuffled to the door.

Ruth frowned. "What do you mean?"

Mr. Portman didn't respond, but simply kept going.

Lunging toward the break room, Ruth poked her head inside. "Grandma?"

"Hm?" Grandma Nan pulled her head up from reading a magazine.

"I need to run out. Can you take over the desk?"

Grandma frowned and opened her mouth, but Ruth interrupted.

"I'll explain later. Please?"

Grandma Nan snapped her mouth shut and narrowed her eyes, but nodded. "Fine."

"Thanks!" Ruth almost ran as she worked to catch up with Mr. Portman. "Found you," she said, sucking in a couple of heavy breaths. "You seem like you might be feeling better."

Dark eyes glared at her from under heavy brows. "You need to go after him."

Ruth blinked. "Wait...what?"

"Your man. You need to go after him." Mr. Portman wheezed a little.

Ruth slowed to a stop, torn between going back to the motel or staying with her guest. "I don't want to talk about this."

Mr. Portman also stopped and turned back to her. "You should know how short life is," he said, then cleared his throat. "You know. You've experienced it." He shook his head, nearly knocking his hat off its perch. "You can't let him go."

"I didn't let him go," Ruth argued, then calmed down her tone. "He left."

"Then go get him."

Ruth sighed and hung her head. "Mr. Portman, it isn't that easy. He doesn't want—"

"Men don't just stop loving a woman," Mr. Portman said in a softer tone. "If he loved you before, he loves you now. Use that."

Ruth sighed again and turned around.

"You're scared."

Ruth turned back. "Of course. Can you blame me? I was scared to tell him about the cancer and look what it got me." She splayed her hands to the side. "Fear is self preservation."

"Fear is a lie."

"I think we already went over this once before," Ruth said, re-membering their conversation several days ago when he admitted he knew she was wearing a wig. Her hand floated up to her head, but in-stead of the normal wig, Ruth found the softness of a beanie covering her scalp. She hadn't been able to wear the wig ever since Jude left. It felt too much like she was continuing the lie.

"Then you should have learned," he said gruffly.

Ruth threw her hands to the side. "What do you want from me, Mr. Portman? I'd love to help you, but you're angry about things I have no control over."

He shook his hairy head. "You have control," he said tightly, tak-ing a step in her direction. "You can go to him. You can apologize. You can work it out between you."

Ruth opened her mouth, but Mr. Portman ploughed ahead.

"Do you really think I wouldn't give *everything* to have just one more day with Judy?" he snarled.

Ruth froze.

"One more day. One more hour. One more minute." Mr. Port-man's voice broke, right along with Ruth's heart, for the second time in a week. "Life is fleeting," he said, his tone pleading. "One minute the person you love is there, one minute they're not."

The air between them hung heavy. "Why do you come to Seaside Bay?" Ruth whispered.

Mr. Portman's profile turned toward the ocean. They couldn't see the water from their place on Main Street, but the noise was clear-ly audible. "We were married in Portland," he said softly. "I had no money." He chuckled. "Barely a dime to my name." He shook his head, his eyes dropping to the ground. "It's a wonder she was willing to take a chance on me at all, or that her father didn't shoot me on sight." He took in a quiet breath. "But she was my everything. The very air I breathed." His head came back up. "She used to tell me I was too serious. That I needed to learn to look on the bright side."

Ruth started forward when Mr. Portman coughed and wheezed, struggling for a moment to catch his breath.

He held up his hand to stop her. "Remind you of anyone?" he asked sarcastically, giving Ruth a sideways look.

Ruth gave a rueful smile and shrugged.

He looked at the horizon again. "We camped here. On our honeymoon. It was all I could afford."

"I'll bet she loved it."

He laughed, which broke into coughing before he answered. "She said she did, but I always wanted to give her more." He sighed. "And eventually I did. I worked to give her the very best. I worked through her pregnancies and the kids' early years. I worked through family vacations and holidays." His hand shook as he wiped at his face, sweat beading his hairline. "And by the time I could give her everything...her time was all but gone."

Ruth had no words. Her heart was in her throat. "I'm sorry" felt so inadequate.

"Every year I come back to the memories." He paused. "Because they're all I have left."

Tears filled Ruth's vision and she blinked them back, trying to force the blockage down her throat.

He turned to her slowly and held out a box. "Take it."

Ruth frowned, but obeyed. "What is it?"

He grunted. "If you'd open it, you'd know."

Ruth laughed softly and pulled off the top of the box. Inside was the music box she had helped him rescue from the restoration shop. Someone had sanded it and put a new coat of stain on it. Ruth opened it and a tingy melody began to play. "The Very Thought of You," Ruth breathed. She hadn't recognized it when they'd first picked up the box from Charli's.

Mr. Portman wouldn't look at her. "It was her favorite song."

"I...I can't take this," Ruth said, trying to hand it back.

Mr. Portman only glared. "Don't waste it." Without another word, he turned and walked away.

Ruth watched him go, realizing she had been dismissed. The music box continued the song, the notes floating away on the breeze. She gently closed the lid and the top of the box. Turning back, she headed back to the motel. Was she brave enough to follow Mr. Portman's advice? Ruth wasn't sure, but as she picked up her pace, she realized something...

She wanted to be.

"I THINK THAT'LL DO it," Jude said somberly. "Make sure to ice it when you get home and keep as much weight off of it as possible until the inflammation goes down."

"So, no basketball?" the teenager whined.

Jude shook his head. "No. I'm sorry. You're lucky you didn't tear anything when you fell. If you'll just be patient for a few days, you should be good as new. But if you push it too fast, you could be out for weeks instead."

"Whatever," the teenager said sourly.

Jude looked at the mom, who was scowling at her son. "Maybe next time you'll think twice before trying to skateboard on a porch railing," she scolded.

And that's my sign to get out of here.

Jude backed up to the door. "I'm putting him in your hands, Mom. Keep him in line."

The boy groaned, but the mom gave Jude a grateful smile. "Thanks."

Jude nodded and left, sighing as he got out of the treatment room. He was so ready for this week to be over. It was only a few days before Christmas and he was looking forward to some time off.

Why? Want to sit alone and lick your wounds in private?

Jude scowled at the thoughts. Lately, he had become his own worst enemy. One half of him was still angry about Ruth, and the other half wanted to go crawling back and beg her forgiveness for walking out on her when she'd obviously been through something traumatic.

Gray's words to think of things from Ruth's point of view had been like a sword, slicing through Jude's anger and depression over and over again.

How did Ruth feel?

Jude could only imagine. How would he feel if he spent most of his twenties fighting a life threatening disease? If he'd missed all the college years of being dirt poor and carefree? If he had almost no family support? If he had to lose all his friends because they couldn't handle the drama? If he had lost his hair and his body had been so decimated he barely recognized himself?

If he was being honest with himself, Jude knew he would probably have done the exact same thing as Ruth. He would have tried to put the cancer as far behind him as possible. He would have wanted to be seen for who he was, not who he had once been.

His phone buzzed and Jude pulled it from his pocket.

Got a min?

Jude sighed and glanced at the clock. "Sarah?" he asked, walking up to the front desk.

"Yes, Dr. Lisbon?"

"When's my next patient?"

His front desk manager looked at the computer screen. "You've got twenty minutes." She glanced his way. "Your three-twenty cancelled."

"Thanks. I'll be in my office." He closed the door once he got inside and pressed the call button. "Hey, Car." Jude hadn't spoken to Carson or Gray since he'd gotten back to Hollywood. He'd been too mad. Even now Jude wasn't quite ready to talk, but...

"How's it going?" Carson asked.

Jude grunted. "Did you need something in particular?"

Carson chuckled. "Gray said you were ticked. Guess it's true."

Jude closed his eyes and pinched the bridge of his nose. He didn't trust himself to speak at the moment.

"Tell me what's going on."

Jude jerked. "What?"

"Tell me what's going on." Carson said again. "I've got my own female problems going on over here, so maybe we can commiserate together."

"I'm not having female problems," Jude argued.

"Oh? Then what would you call it?"

Jude looked at the ceiling. "I don't really want to talk, Car."

"Yeah, well, tough luck. Unlike my pansy of a brother, I'm not going to let you get away with walking away. You've got friends. Use them."

"Friends? Really? After what Gray and Brook pulled, you want me to call them friends?"

"Remember that time you dropped punch in my lap?"

Jude slumped in his seat. "Yes."

"It was a thousand-dollar suit."

"I remember." Jude closed his eyes and shook his head.

"I don't recall getting angry because you weren't perfect. In fact, I believe I laughed it off and took care of the dry cleaning bill myself." Carson's tone had a slight bite to it and Jude knew he was headed into lawyer mode.

"I know." Jude's voice was softer.

"And what about the time I offended Elania when I told her her argument was stupid? Remember that?"

"Yes."

"Did you dump me as a friend because I have no class? No, we moved on like normal people and now laugh about it. So, I have to ask...why are you treating Brook and Gray like their choice makes them pariahs?"

"They're not pariahs," Jude defended himself. "But this was serious. I was in love with Ruth and—"

"Are in love with her."

Jude paused. "What?"

"You *are* in love with her," Carson corrected.

"Why do you say that?"

"Because I'm in love too, and as mad as you are, I know you didn't just fall out of love with her." Carson paused and dropped his voice. "Jude, she should have told you. No one's arguing that. But honestly, if you can't get over this, I don't know that you deserve her."

"Hey!"

"That woman went through something where she nearly lost her life. Can you blame her for wanting to be normal for a bit?"

"Can you?" Jude argued. He didn't want to hear this. It didn't matter that it was echoing his own thoughts. He didn't want to hear that he was in the wrong...at least partially.

"Nope," Carson shot back. "In fact, it's the whole reason I ended up meeting Belle. I've always been in Grayson's shadow when all I ever wanted was to be *me*. I don't know if you can understand it, but not being seen is one of the most painful experiences on this earth."

Jude didn't respond. What could he say? He knew Carson was right, but that didn't make it any easier.

"Jude the Dude?"

A snort slipped through Jude's lips. "You're right," he said softly.

"What?" Carson pressed. The humor was easily heard in his voice. "What was that?"

"I'm not repeating it, jerk," Jude said tightly.

Carson laughed. "Once was good enough. Get your butt back up here and let's settle this once and for all."

"I don't think she'll talk to me," Jude admitted.

"Don't be stupid," Carson responded. "You're making excuses. Man up and let's go. I'll even pay for the plane ticket."

Jude took a deep breath. "I can't leave until Saturday, or I'll probably be out of a job."

"Fine. But you're coming and winning the girl back. No if's, ands, or buts."

Jude didn't respond right away.

"Don't make me use nicknames again," Carson threatened.

"Okay," Jude finally answered. "I'll be there."

CHAPTER 24

"Thank you for staying with us," Ruth said politely. "Have a wonderful Christmas."

"We will, thank you," the woman replied with a smile before turning to take her husband's hand.

Ruth watched the couple leave, a melancholy feeling weighing down her chest. The music box Mr. Portman had given her was sitting on the shelf just below the front counter, but even with a wooden counter between them, Ruth could feel it pulling at her. Mr. Portman's story had torn at her heartstrings in a way that Ruth wasn't sure how to handle.

He had shared secrets with her that she felt certain very few other living people knew. How could he stand it? Living so long beyond the woman he loved? Where were his children? Did they never come visit over the holidays? Were they also gone? He had never said how many he had or where they lived.

Ruth sighed and brushed a hand over her head. The texture of the material reminded her that she wasn't wearing her wig and Ruth forced her hand down. Old habits die hard.

She paused.

That was exactly what Mr. Portman had been trying to teach her, wasn't it? He had sunk too far into his habits of believing that time wouldn't run out. That he could make it to the top. That every sacrifice was worth it. That he could give them everything. But in the end, time had slipped away.

Ruth blinked rapidly. The emotion of her little lecture was still gnawing at her. She ached for Mr. Portman. But she also ached for herself. She had found the person she wanted to give the world to, but had lied to them. She was in a mess of her own making, and now the person she loved most was gone.

But it's not too late, a small voice whispered in her mind. "It's not too late." Ruth repeated the words out loud. She needed to hear them. She needed to let them sink in until she figured out what to do with them.

She reached beneath the counter and pulled out the music box, carefully lifting the lid. The melody, sweet and twangy, played through the room. It clashed with the Christmas carols coming from the radio next to the Christmas tree, but Ruth paid it no mind. This was what Mr. Portman had hung onto all those years.

The very thought of you...

Ruth sang along with the few words she knew, choking on the chorus. She didn't want Jude to just be a thought. She didn't want to spend years regretting and wishing things had been different. She wanted him. She wanted a life with him, and she wanted him to want a life with her.

Putting the music box away, Ruth took in a shuddering breath. A slow determination filled her, pushing out her hurt and self loathing. She had made a mistake. There was no getting around that. She wasn't perfect and she had let fear give her advice rather than listening to the people she loved.

But she could fix that. She could change. She could come back to being the woman Jude fell in love with in the first place. Her hand stretched toward her cell phone, determined to start the long journey right this second, but it rang before she could pick it up.

Frowning slightly, Ruth checked the screen.

SBPD

"What in the world?" Ruth answered the call. "Hello?"

"Hello. This is Captain Kenneth Wamsley. Is this Ruth?"

"Yes, it is. Hello, Captain Wamsley. How's that lovely wife and daughter of yours?"

"They're fine, thank you for asking," he said in a brisk tone that was unusual for him.

Ruth had met the captain before and while he was always professional, he had a kind, warm personality. This was not his usual way of speaking.

"Ruth, I'm sorry to do this over the phone, but I felt that I needed to give you a call. I've been told a Mr. Arthur Portman has been staying at the motel. Is that correct?"

Ruth's heart began to hammer against her chest. "Yes," she answered, dread settling into her. Something was wrong. She had only left him an hour ago, but something was definitely wrong. "Why? Did he get lost? Did he yell at someone?"

Captain Wamsley sighed into the line. "There's no easy way to say this, Ruth. But Mr. Portman is dead."

The room spun and Ruth grasped the counter with her free hand, knocking over her stool as she stumbled to the side. "What?" she breathed.

"Is your grandma there? Can you put her on the phone?"

"Oh, dear heavens." Ruth gasped. "He...can't be. That can't be right. I was just with him."

"Ruth? What's going on?" Grandma Nan asked from the break room doorway.

"Ruth. Put Grandma Nan on the phone, please," Captain Wamsley repeated the command.

Ruth held the phone out from her head, unable to speak.

"What in tarnation is going on?" Grandma Nan shouted, coming up behind Ruth. She snatched the phone from her shaking hand. "Who is this?" Grandma Nan paused. "Yes, Ken, it's me. What's going on?"

Ruth closed her eyes, the nausea welling in her stomach to an uncontrollable degree. She was going to be sick. Putting her hand over her mouth, she ran into the break room and then the bathroom. It only took a few moments for her system to be empty. She had barely eaten since Jude had left.

A very familiar sensation of despair crept into Ruth's chest. She had been here before. Kneeling on a bathroom floor, slick with sweat and emotionally spent. Months of her life had consisted of moments just like this, but this time, there would be no possible silver lining. No chance to ring a bell at conquering her treatment. No phone call to tell her family that she had won. This time, no one would ever win. Mr. Portman was gone. Along with his grumpy attitude and sage advice.

The dark bags under his eyes, the sallowness of his skin, the labored breathing, it all came back to Ruth and she felt like an imbecile for not forcing him to see a doctor.

"Are you in there, sweetie?" Grandma Nan asked softly at the door.

It took Ruth a few moments before any words would leave her throat. "Yes," she finally croaked.

The door creaked open and Grandma Nan groaned as she lowered herself to the floor.

"Grandma," Ruth tried to weakly protest.

"Hush, now," Grandma said, wrapping her arms around Ruth. "Comforting is a grandma's job. Don't you dare try to take that away from me."

Realizing she didn't want Grandma to leave, Ruth sank against her relative and closed her eyes. She breathed in the familiar scent of gardenias and dryer sheets before letting the parade of tears flow down her cheeks.

But even as she mourned, Ruth felt that stirring of determination waiting its turn. Mr. Portman's death only made her even more determined to go after Jude. Ruth knew loss. Past and present. She wasn't willing to let Jude go into that category without one final try.

JUDE TOOK A SWIG OF water from his bottle and wiped his mouth on the back of his hand. His run this morning had done little to assuage his stress. He had gone to bat with his boss and managed to get more time off, but if for some reason things didn't work out with Ruth, Jude was going to have a rough next year, since he'd negotiated basically all his future vacation time in order to leave.

Ruth was definitely worth it, but Jude wasn't sure being rejected was.

"She's not going to reject you," Jude assured himself. "She loves you. Ruth is the most forgiving person you know."

While the words were true, Jude wasn't sure he exactly deserved that forgiveness. He'd struck her in her most vulnerable spot. The very thing she had struggled to tell him, the very thing she'd struggled to *trust* him with.

And how had he shown her he was trustworthy? He'd balked, called her names, and walked out. *I'll bet that left a lasting impression.*

Sighing, Jude took another drink of water and headed to the bathroom. He had a plane to catch that afternoon and standing around sulking wasn't going to help anybody.

The airport was busier than normal when Jude disembarked. Christmas was only two days away and people were travelling to family functions all around the world. Navigating the crowds was annoying as well as frustrating.

Now that he was in Portland, Jude just wanted to get down to Seaside Bay and get this over with. He missed Ruth like he'd miss a limb if it had been amputated. He'd helped men and women who had had amputations for various reasons and the phantom ache was real. It had to be similar to the ache that had become a permanent fixture in Jude's chest.

It hurt to think of Ruth. It hurt to think of her dealing with cancer by herself. It hurt to think of her being in pain because of him. It hurt to not hold her. Not kiss her. Not be able to love her.

Jude re-gripped his carry-on. He hadn't bothered to pack a full-size suitcase, not wanting to have to deal with the luggage system. He was staying at Grayson's, so it would be easy to wash clothes as he needed them.

The cold winter wind tugged at his coat as he walked outside.

"Jude the Dude!" Carson waved with a face-splitting grin from the pick up lane.

Jude rolled his eyes, ducked his head, and walked over. "Very nice," he said sarcastically. "You couldn't just wave? Or leave off the nickname?"

"Where's the fun in that?" Carson shot back. He shivered and ducked into the car. "You can put your stuff in the back!"

Jude put his suitcase in, then sat in the passenger seat. "Some chauffeur you are. I thought they're supposed to help with luggage?"

"If I was getting paid, I'd consider it." Carson winked.

"Fair enough," Jude responded. He took a deep breath, letting the heat of the car sink into his muscles. They drove in silence for a few minutes. Jude allowed Carson to get settled on the freeway before asking his questions. "Have you seen her?"

Carson's lips pinched and he shook his head.

"Not once?"

Carson shrugged and shook his head again. "No. Sorry...but there's something you should know."

Dread began to pool in Jude's stomach. "She left, didn't she? Went back to Seattle?"

Carson gave Jude a look. "Do you really think I'd have you come here if your lady love was in Seattle?"

Jude sighed. "Then what is it? I was trying to think of the worst case scenario." He paused. "Crap! It's the cancer, isn't it? She's sick again!"

Carson held up a hand. "Hold on, cowboy. If you'd quit jumping to conclusions, I could get all this out."

"Then just tell me," Jude begged. "I've been dying already, and this is making it worse."

Carson nodded and his eyes glanced sideways before going back to the road. "Do you remember Mr. Portman?"

Jude frowned. "Yeah. He and Ruth were friends." Jude shrugged. "At least as much as anyone was friends with that guy. He wasn't ex- actly what people would call friendly."

Carson chuckled, but it lacked energy. "Yeah, I heard about his fight with Charli." Carson whistled low. "Brave man."

"What's this about?" Jude pressed.

"Mr. Portman passed away two days ago."

Jude froze, his jaw slack. "W-what?" he stuttered.

Carson gave him a sympathetic look. "Apparently, he'd taken a walk, sat down on a bench to watch the water, and just...let go."

Jude blew out a breath and pushed his hand through his hair. "Any word on how Ruth's taking it?"

Carson made a face. "I've talked to Grandma Nan and it sounds like it's been hard on her." He looked sideways again. "I'd imagine she's seen quite a bit of death in her life."

Jude nodded sadly. His heart, which had ached before, felt as if it wanted to fold in on itself. "I'm sure." Jude kept his face forward, though he could feel Carson's questioning eyes on him. Jude should have known the answer to that question, but he'd stormed out too fast to hear it all. Another wave of self loathing ran through him. "I need to get to her," he said hoarsely.

"I'm working on it," Carson assured him. "But I don't think get- ting pulled over by a cop will help our cause."

"Who found him?" Jude asked.

Carson shook his head. "Just a passerby. They called the precinct and Ken had the privilege of speaking to Ruth and Grandma Nan." Carson cleared his throat. "He said Ruth practically fainted on the phone."

Jude groaned and hung his head. What he wouldn't give for wings right now. How many things could happen to the world's sweetest woman before she finally broke for good? He pushed a shaky hand through his hair. If they hit traffic, Jude knew he was going to explode.

"Hey," Carson said softly. "We're going to make it. You'll see her soon."

"The funeral?" Jude choked out.

"Tomorrow." Carson tapped the wheel. "I guess his wife is already buried in Seaside Bay, so the children came into town and planned it here. Apparently, the family has some history there."

Jude nodded. He found himself starting to grow numb. His body wasn't sure how to handle everything he was struggling with right now.

Carson reached across the car and patted Jude's shoulder. "She'll be grateful you're there," he assured Jude.

Jude nodded. "I sure hope so. I let her down when she needed me once before, but I'm not going to do it again."

CHAPTER 25

"I 'll have that sent right over," Ruth assured the man on the other side of the line. "Yes. I understand. Four towels. Not a problem." Ruth nodded. "Okay, now. Thank you. Bye." She hung up and let out a long breath.

With her shoulders slumped and her bald head on full display, Ruth was sure she looked the definition of pitiful and desperate, but right now she just couldn't find it within herself to be anything else.

Her heart was being torn in two different directions and neither one of them was good for her health. The hurt and pain from Jude had temporarily been pushed to the side as Ruth dealt with Mr. Portman and his family. But it was always there...pulsing in the background, waiting for another chance to rob her of her breath and bring her to her knees.

Ruth picked the phone back up and dialed housekeeping. "Hi, Angela. Can we get four towels sent to room two-fourteen?" Ruth listened. "Uh, huh...yep...four...perfect. Thanks!" She set the phone back in the cradle and found herself fighting back tears. With a groan of frustration, she wiped her eyes and roughly grabbed a stack of pamphlets, quickly putting them back in order. "So stupid," she grumbled to herself. "You've cried enough."

The door to the break room opened. "How's it going out here?" Grandma Nan asked cheerfully. She had been working so hard to help lift Ruth's spirits.

The amount of guilt Ruth felt at not responding to Grandma Nan's attempts was heavy, but not heavy enough to outweigh her sorrow.

What had she done in her life to deserve so much heartache?

How about lie to Jude?

"Fine," Ruth assured her grandmother. She sniffed, shook her head, and went back to work organizing the already clean desk. "Mr. Portman's children and their families are both checking out tomorrow morning. They're leaving town right after the funeral in order to be home for Christmas."

"Okay," Grandma said. "They seem like a nice bunch."

Ruth nodded. "Yeah, they've been great." Ruth pictured the three young grandchildren Mr. Portman left behind. They would probably remember very little of their grandpa. The oldest was ten and he would retain some memories, but Ruth knew it wouldn't be enough.

Had Mr. Portman ever shared the stories about his wife? Had they visited Seaside Bay with their parents, or had Mr. Portman kept it a sacred place with he and his wife? Did his kids know about the music box?

A dozen times, Ruth had reached for the box in order to offer it to them, but every time, she held back. Mr. Portman had given the box to her and though she didn't deserve it, Ruth struggled to find the courage to give it away. She wanted something to remember the grumpy old man by, and this had been his gift to her. Surely, it wasn't too selfish to keep such a memento?

The bell on the front door rang and both Grandma and Ruth looked up. The first thing to come through the door was an extra large bundle of flowers, followed by an entire group of women.

"Hello, Ruth," Caro said with a soft smile. Her blue eyes were sympathetic as she waddled farther into the front room.

"Hi," Ruth responded, smiling in kind. She made eye contact with the rest of the women. "Brook, Hadlee, Rose." Ruth frowned. "I don't..."

"I'm Genni," a dark-haired woman with a toddler on her hip said with a smile.

"I'm Melanie, or Mel," a blonde responded.

"You already know me," Charli said with a grin.

"Of course," Ruth responded. "I didn't see you back there. How are you, Charli?"

Charli rubbed her large stomach. "About the same as the rest of the beached whales."

Caro scowled. "Speak for yourself. I'm not a whale. I'm a sea li-on." She sniffed. "Can't you tell the difference?"

"Oh, is that why you haven't shaved your mustache in a while?" Charli teased.

Caro shook her fist in the air. "Come at me, bro."

"Oh my word…" Rose said in exasperation. "Would you two get over yourselves? This isn't about you!"

Caro rolled her eyes and came back around to Ruth before grin-ning. "Someone has to put Charli in her place," she said in a loud whisper.

"I heard that."

"You were meant to!" Caro shot over her shoulder.

Ruth's smile was genuine for the first time in several weeks. These ladies were a fun bunch. If only… She shook her head. Ruth wasn't going to lament what might have been. She and Jude weren't togeth-er anymore and that was that. "Was that for the Portman family sib-lings?" Ruth pointed to the stunning vase of flowers. "I can take you to their rooms."

Rose shook her head. "No. This is for you."

Ruth's jaw dropped and her heart skipped a beat. "What?" she breathed.

"We thought you could use a boost," Caro said, her voice having gone soft again. "We know you've had a rough time lately, and we wanted to let you know that you have friends."

Ruth's eyes immediately filled with tears and she covered her mouth with shaking fingers. "Are you serious?"

They all nodded. "None of us can imagine everything you've been through," Genni said, stepping forward. "We can't really make anything better, but we didn't want you to be alone." She shrugged with a gentle smile. "We all need others sometimes, and even though we haven't known you long, we wanted to make sure you knew that you don't have to be alone from here on out."

"What am I? Chopped liver?" Grandma Nan huffed.

Ruth looked over her shoulder to see Grandma sniffling and wiping at her face.

"Stupid eyes are leaking," Grandma Nan grumbled. She spun around. "You ladies chat. I've got things to do."

Caro cackled. "Grandma Nan never did like to show emotion."

Ruth smiled through her own tears. "Nope. Not even when..." She trailed off, not knowing how much the women knew. Brook had figured everything out, but did all the rest of them know?

Rose smiled. "Not even when you were fighting off cancer?"

Ruth's hand automatically rose up to her head, where she cringed when she realized she had forgotten she wasn't wearing a hat today. "What gave it away?" she tried to joke, but the women didn't laugh.

Rose set the flowers on the desk. "Gladiolas for strength and courage. Iris for hope." She pointed to some yellow/greenish flowers that were set in bundles. "These are lady's mantles and they represent comfort when people want you to know they're there for you." Rose studied the bouquet again. "There're also yellow roses for friendship and red ones..." Rose grinned widely. "Because we know there's another kind of love in your life."

Ruth shook her head, not wanting to ruin their hopes for her. Right now she was just going to revel in the attention. "You all are too much."

"Actually, I'm pretty sure we haven't done enough," Charli said with a sigh. "I can't believe you've been handling this all on your own." She shook her head. "I'm sorry I was such a brat the other day."

Ruth shook her head again. "This is the best thing ever," she assured them all. She held up a finger. "Would you like to see what Mr. Portman did with the music box?"

Charli gasped when Ruth brought it out. "He's a magician."

Ruth nodded. "He was." Now that she had an audience, it was a good time to share everything she had learned about a grumpy old man who couldn't leave his past behind.

JUDE WATCHED THROUGH the front door of the motel as Ruth hugged every woman individually in her foyer. He had no idea that Rose, Caro, Brook, and everyone else would be there. He wasn't even sure if Ruth knew all of them.

She does now.

The tears on everyone's faces would have worried Jude, if they hadn't also been smiling and laughing. An enormous bouquet of flowers sat on the counter and Ruth referred to it several times. Jude could only guess it was a gift from Rose, who was the resident flower arranger.

His heart began to beat against his rib cage as he watched Ruth. She wasn't wearing her wig anymore, something which should have turned him off, but at the moment, she had never looked more lovely.

She looked proud, strong, courageous...and like an angel.

How had he ever doubted her? How could ever convince her to forgive him?

A car door opened behind him. "Are you going in?" Carson shouted.

Jude glanced over his shoulder. "Yeah. Go ahead and go. I'll text when I need a ride."

Carson paused, then nodded. "Good luck."

Jude waved him off, then put his focus back on the motel. Taking a fortifying breath, he grabbed the handle and pulled it open. He was fairly sure the front entry had been filled with voices and chatter only seconds before, but by the time he closed the door behind him, everything was completely silent.

Jude nodded to the women before putting his full focus on Ruth. "Hello, Ruth," he said softly. He immediately wanted to smack himself. Hello, Ruth? That was a brilliant way to break the ice.

Her eyes were wide with trepidation. "Hello," she whispered. The word was barely audible.

Jude took a couple of steps forward, then came to a halt. He didn't have the right to reach out for a hug...yet. "Ruth, can I...?" Jude cut off and stumbled a bit when a slap hit his shoulder.

"You know, I think maybe I need a bit of chocolate," Charli said, obvious innuendo in her voice. "Caro? Think you can help me out?"

Caro nodded with a little smirk on her face. "I should have thought to bring enough for everyone," she said, shaking her head and tsking her tongue. "Come on, ladies, let's get those cravings taken care of."

Jude heard the women greet him, was aware they were walking around him, but he couldn't seem to bring himself to look away from Ruth. She was no longer crying, but she still looked upset.

"Why are you here, Jude?"

Jude held back a wince. She sounded so tired, as if she were ready to collapse at any moment. She probably was, all things considered. "I came to see you."

Ruth's cheeks turned red and she turned away, walking back behind the desk. Once there, she played with a map. "I'm glad you're here."

Hope soared through Jude.

"I need to apologize."

Jude frowned. "What?"

Ruth's tears began again. "I'm so sorry," she choked out, wiping furiously at her face. "I never should have hidden my..." She waved at her head. "I never should have hidden it from you. I just..." Ruth shook her head. "No. It doesn't matter why. I shouldn't have done it. I know I apologized before, but please...I really am sorry. It was a horrible thing to do and I promise not to lie about it again." She put up her hand when he went to speak. "I realize now just how unfair it was for me to hide something so big. I've learned my lesson."

Jude stepped closer. He couldn't help it at this point. He wanted to wipe every tear running down her flushed cheeks, kiss the pink highlighting her cheek bones, and hold her until she no longer shook and shivered with emotion. "Ruth," he said as he arrived at the desk. "Can you ever forgive me?"

"What?" she sniffed, wiping her nose with a tissue. "What are you talking about?"

"I was an idiot," Jude responded. He clenched his hands into fists. "Actually, there are probably better words for it, but I don't like to say them in front of a lady."

That got him the tiniest of smiles. "There's nothing to forgive," Ruth answered. "I'm the one who lied."

"And I'm the one who walked away from the best thing that ever happened to me."

Ruth's eyes widened.

"I love you," Jude blurted out. That wasn't exactly how he had planned to start his little speech, but he supposed it was as good as any. "These last couple of weeks have been miserable. More miserable than when I went home the first time," he admitted. "I've been angry, hurt, depressed, full of guilt, and more lonely than I've ever experienced in my life."

Ruth shook her head. "I'm so—"

"No." Jude shook his head. "You've said that enough."

Ruth snapped her jaw shut.

"I'm sorry," he said sincerely. "I'm sorry I was a coward. I'm sorry I hurt you. I'm sorry I made you feel like you were in the wrong. I'm sorry you finally trusted me with your most difficult trial and I threw it back in your face. I'm sorry I wasn't here when Mr. Portman passed away. I'm sorry I didn't share your burden." Jude leaned in. "And most of all, I'm sorry I made you feel less than worthy." Taking a chance, Jude reached across the counter and cupped Ruth's cheek in his hand. His thumb brushed at her wet skin. "You are the most wonderful, brave, and kindest person I've ever known. I feel like I'm at the bottom of a pedestal looking up into the face of an angel."

"Please don't," Ruth said, covering his hand with hers. Her fingers were cold and clammy. "Please don't put me up there by myself. I don't belong up there."

"What if I were with you?" Jude asked. "What if instead of you being alone, you had someone with you?"

"Do you really love me again?" Ruth asked, her eyes so full of hope that Jude felt a little like weeping himself.

The question was painful. Of all the things he had done, making her feel unloved was the worst. "I never stopped." He scowled. "I just let anger take the lead for a while."

Ruth stepped back from his touch. "I can't ask you to take me on though," she said. "Look at me!" Her voice grew louder. "I'm bald. My skin is still saggy and thin. I'm underweight and have absolutely no curves to my name."

Jude tried to interrupt, but Ruth was caught up in her own rant.

"And there's absolutely no guarantee that I'll remain free of cancer," she said. "I know it's gone right now, but it could come back." She shook her head. "In fact, I have to go to the doctor every six months just to be sure." She took another step back. "I can't ask anyone to take that on." A sob slipped through her lips and she smothered it with her hand, as if realizing she was saying she needed to be alone for the rest of her life.

Jude rushed around the counter and gathered Ruth into his arms. He wanted to sigh at the contact, but other things were more important right now. "You're not asking," he said against her fuzzy scalp. "I'm offering and I refuse to take no for an answer."

She hiccuped a laugh. "Is that so? I have no say in the matter?"

"If you had a valid excuse to keep me away, I would listen." He rubbed her back and grinned when she finally relaxed against his chest. "But sacrificing yourself isn't one. If you were mad at me, or hated me or couldn't forgive me, then I'd understand. But I love you too much to let you continue to go through life alone."

Ruth sighed. "I can't tell you how many times I've dreamed of hearing you say that," she whispered into his shirt.

Jude framed her face and turned it up so he could see her. "Does that mean you forgive me? That you'll date me again?"

"Are you really sure?"

"Would I have come all this way if I wasn't?" Jude pressed.

Her beautifully red lips curled into a cautious smile. "How about we forgive each other?"

"Wipe the slate clean," Jude said, slowly lowering his head. "Start again and move forward...together?"

Ruth nodded. "That sounds perfect."

Jude closed the gap and left the softest of kisses on her lips. "Thank you," he said against her mouth.

"Thank *you*," Ruth responded. "I'm so glad you came back. After the funeral, I was going to try and contact you, but this is much better."

"I shouldn't have waited so long," Jude lamented. "But I was stubborn."

"That makes two of you," Grandma Nan said in her no nonsense way. She bustled past the couple and grabbed the flower vase. "Better put these somewhere else before they get knocked over." She sent a narrow glare to Jude. "Glad you came to your senses."

Jude tucked Ruth under his chin and smiled back. "Me too." He began to walk Ruth backward. "But if I were you, I'd stay out of the break room for a bit." He grinned at Ruth's shocked noise and Grandma's laughter. "We have lost time to make up for."

CHAPTER 26

Ruth squeezed Jude's hand. She was probably about to break his fingers in half, but he only smiled and pulled her slightly closer. Letting go of her hand, he wrapped his arm around her shoulders. Ruth sighed and melted into his side. The funeral had been a bleak activity to look forward to.

It was Christmas Eve morning and Ruth wanted to be anywhere but the little church in downtown Seaside Bay. The sermon was lovely, but it was what it represented that had Ruth so upset.

She'd much rather have Mr. Portman back than listen to how his spirit was free and all the pains and anguish from this life were over.

That's selfish, she reminded herself for the thousandth time. *He's with his wife now. That's what matters.*

"It's going to be okay," Jude whispered in her ear.

"I know," Ruth mumbled back. "But it still hurts."

Jude kissed her temple and settled in to listen to the rest of the sermon. Following the preacher, each of Mr. Portman's two children took the time to share stories of their father and Ruth decided the children must have taken after their mother, because neither of them were nearly as serious or stuffy as their father had been.

The oldest, the son, told stories of how they used to play tricks on their father and how he always scolded them roughly, but had a lingering smile afterwards.

The daughter told how she could often get her father to take out the punishment on her brother, because she looked so much like their mother.

Ruth laughed softly along with the congregation and wiped at her teary eyes. She had shed enough tears to fill the Great Lakes at this point, but somehow they just kept coming. "That sounds about right," she said to Jude.

He nodded, chuckling as well.

Charli leaned forward over the pew back. "He sounds a lot like you, Grandma Nan."

Ruth's jaw dropped and she had to cover her mouth as Grandma glared at Charli. "Better watch it, young lady. That quilt we've been making for you would make a wonderful gift for African children."

Charli grinned unrepentantly and leaned back to rub her stomach. "I'm sure it would."

"That makes sense," Ruth said sagely. "Now I know why the two of you didn't get along."

Rose shushed them all before Grandma Nan could argue back, but even Rose was fighting a smile.

Ruth looked around herself and smiled. In the last twenty-four hours, it had gone from being Ruth, Grandma Nan, and the quilting circle, to a large group of young married couples who seemed to come from every diverse background a person could think of.

They ran a good portion of the business in town, they supported every local activity, and currently half of them were expecting the next generation.

Ruth couldn't have asked for a better group to rally around her broken spirit.

She ducked her head as the final prayer was said, then stood to stretch her stiff limbs.

"Did you want to follow them to the cemetery?" Jude asked.

Ruth watched the family walk out with the casket. "I haven't been invited."

"I need to get back to the motel," Grandma Nan stated. She took Ruth's hand and patted it. "Give the kids my condolences and wish them safe travels."

Ruth nodded, then gave her grandmother a hug. "Thank you. For always being there for me."

Grandma Nan leaned back and waved her off. "Old fuddy duddies like me have to have something to keep 'em young." She hugged Jude and whispered in his ear.

Jude straightened and nodded. "Consider it done."

Grandma Nan patted his cheek, then turned and waved at the group as she walked out.

"I better head out too," Caro said, holding her stomach. "The little one is about to kill me."

Jack put his arm around her back. "I think maybe you should head home and take a nap."

"I thought the babies were supposed to take the naps," Benny said with a grin. He grabbed his wife's hand before she could smack his arm. "Speaking of babies...anyone want to know our Christmas surprise?"

Ruth watched, delighted as the group of women became a flutter of magpies, oohing and aahing over Benny's wife, Allison. The woman was beauty personified, even with her port wine birthmark.

"Wow, that was fast," Jude said under his breath.

"How long have they been married?" Ruth asked.

"A little less than a year, I think." Jude scratched his chin.

"That's not too bad," Ruth said with a shrug. "Lots of people get started right away."

"Is that what you're hoping to do?" Jude asked, his eyes boring into hers. "Do you want to start a family right away when you get married?"

Ruth's shoulders dropped and she found herself jerked into Jude's chest.

"I'm sorry," he said hoarsely. "I didn't think."

"No...it's a fair question," she said, pulling herself together. She wanted to be stronger about telling the truth and this was an opportunity to do that. "If I'm ever blessed to get married, I assume my husband and I will work out what we think is best for us."

"But what would *you* like to do?"

"I'd welcome children into my home any time," Ruth said softly, searching his face. Truth was, she had great hopes that Jude would be the father of those children. But things were still too new between them to ask if he felt that way too. He loved her. He'd come back for her. He'd mended the canyon between them. For now...that was enough.

The future would have to take care of itself for the time being.

"Ms. Allen?"

Ruth turned. It was Mr. Portman's son. "Yes, Mr. Portman. What can I do for you?"

"The family would like to invite you to join us at the gravesite for the family prayer," he said. He looked to Jude. "Your friend is welcome to join us as well."

Ruth put her hands to her chest. "I would love that." She gasped.

He smiled. "Father mentioned to both of us how much you meant to him." His smile widened. "Though he said it through terms that weren't as kind."

Ruth laughed. "Of course. He probably said I was a conniving busybody or something like that."

"Or something," Mr. Portman, Junior agreed. He sobered. "But I think we both know what that really meant."

Ruth's eyes teared up. "I'd be honored to be there," she said thickly. "Your father was an extraordinary man."

"And that's exactly why you're welcome."

THE WALK OUT THE BACK of the church to the cemetery was a short one, but the bitter, wet air made it a miserable five minutes. Jude wanted to take Ruth in his arms and protect her from everything, including the weather, but other than tucking her under his arm, he had little to no power.

He knew she needed to be here. Having the family recognize her relationship with Mr. Portman and invite her along was the best thing that could have happened to her.

"Geez," Ruth said, ducking her head. "I think the weather is just as disagreeable as Mr. Portman was."

Jude snorted. "I thought you liked him."

"I loved him," Ruth said automatically. "But that doesn't mean I didn't know that he was a grump."

Jude marveled at how easy it was for her to give her heart to people. After all she had been through, after being presented with death at such a young age, Ruth continued to simply love. It was such an honor to know that she counted him at the top of the group. "That must be it," Jude said, pointing to the open hole in the ground.

Ruth nodded. She looked up at him. "I guess I should have asked if you minded coming. That wasn't very nice of me. I'm sorry."

Jude shook his head. "I told you. I'm here. I want to be involved in everything you do."

Ruth's pink cheeks darkened and her smile was blinding. "You're amazing," she breathed.

Jude kissed the tip of her cold nose. "Only you think so, but thanks."

Ruth continued to look at him with awe. "Can we do more of that later?"

A slow smile spread across his face. "I think I can accommodate that." He leaned closer. "Will it include a fireplace and specialty hot chocolate?"

"Am I some kind of monster?" Ruth teased. "Of course!"

"Ms. Allen?"

Ruth's face sobered and turned. "Coming." She kept a hold of Jude's hand as she led the way to the edge of the family circle. "Thank you for inviting me."

Mr. Portman's daughter laughed. "There are too few people who would enjoy being part of this group." Her smile faltered and her husband put his arm around her. "He had a heart of gold, but he was really, really good at hiding it."

Ruth nodded and Jude could see the moisture in her eyes. "He was, but I'm completely honored to have seen it."

Jude couldn't help but smile at the way her words had echoed his own thoughts. If his experience with Ruth had taught him anything, it was that some of the best people in life were the ones who could be overlooked the easiest. Mr. Portman's gruff demeanor made others give him a wide berth, where Ruth's soft spoken actions caused her to blend into a crowd. Yet both of them were people that Jude couldn't imagine living his life without knowing.

The family prayer was finished fifteen minutes later and Jude was ready to get out of the weather. Before he could usher Ruth away, however, one of the Portman grandchildren came walking over with a rose.

"For you," the young girl said, before running back to hide her face in her mother's skirt.

Ruth waved at the shy child. "Thank you," she said. "I'll treasure it always."

"Thank you, Ms. Allen," Mr. Portman's daughter said. "We won't forget you."

"I'll come visit him often," Ruth promised.

Mr. Portman, Junior came over to shake Ruth and Jude's hands. "We appreciate it. Have a Merry Christmas."

"You as well." Ruth nodded. "Thank you." She smiled shakily at Jude.

He squeezed her hand to try and give her strength. There had been too many tears during such a happy season. "Ready?"

She nodded, hugging the rose to her chest. "Let's go."

Jude guided her to her car, then held out his hand. "How about I drive?"

Ruth laughed and wiped at her eyes. "Probably a good idea," she admitted. She handed him the keys and he tucked her into her seat.

The trip back to Ruth's house took a little longer than normal, as Main Street was busy with last minute shoppers. Jude cringed. "Um...I have a confession."

Ruth looked his way. "Yes?"

"Since we're being upfront with each other about everything...I don't have a Christmas present for you."

Ruth smiled, then began to laugh.

Jude gave her a look, but it only made Ruth laugh louder.

As she finally caught her breath, she wiped moisture from her eyes. "Thank you," she said between gasps. "I needed that."

"Glad I could help," Jude said wryly, sending Ruth into another round of laughter. "Are you done now?" he asked when it died down again.

"Sorry." Ruth took a deep breath, calming herself, then reached over to put a hand on his thigh. "The best Christmas I could ever have was having you walk back into the motel yesterday. I don't need anything else."

Jude took her hand and brought it up so he could kiss her palm. "You might say you don't want it, but you deserve something."

Ruth shrugged. "I can't say I agree, but I'm so glad you think so."

Jude's mind began to churn as he tried to figure out how he could do something for her this last minute. He knew she meant every word when she said she didn't mind that he didn't have a present, but Jude wasn't willing to accept that. Ruth was an angel and she deserved something special. But what could he do when he only had a few hours left?

"Here we are," Ruth sang as they pulled into the driveway. "Oh my gosh," she breathed, leaning forward. "Is that snow?"

Jude cranked his neck as he waited for the garage door to open. "What? Snow? Here?"

Ruth laughed softly. "It does happen once in a while, you know."

"Huh." Jude pulled in and turned off the car. "I can't remember the last time I had a white Christmas."

"That's because you're a Cali boy," Ruth teased as she stood up. She slammed her door and rushed back out to the driveway, holding out her hand as if to catch a flake.

Jude followed more slowly and nodded. "Yeah...I think you're right. It's not much, but it's trying."

Ruth turned her face up toward the sky. "Grandma would say it's spitting."

Jude choked on laughter. "Spitting?"

She nodded. "Yep. That's what Grandma calls it when it's only doing it a little. It's not a flurry yet, just a few random flakes. Spitting."

Jude took her hand and began to pull her toward the house. "Spitting or blizzard, it's stupid cold out here. Come on, you promised me hot chocolate."

"We're going to have to expose you to the cold weather more," Ruth said as she tripped along behind him.

"Considering how much time I plan to be here, that might actually come to pass," Jude said, grinning over his shoulder. He loved how her cheeks pinkened, even though they were already flushed with cold.

Once inside, Jude pulled her into his chest and gave her a searing kiss.

"What was that for?" Ruth asked breathlessly.

"A warning of what's to come," Jude said in a low tone, letting his eyes caress her lovely face. "If the hot chocolate doesn't work, I've already learned it's a good way to warm up."

Ruth's arms went around his neck and she nuzzled her cold nose just under his jaw. "I think I like this way better than the hot chocolate."

"You know what?" Jude kissed the side of her neck, then nibbled on her ear. "It's probably a good idea for me to practice saying..." He grinned against her skin. "You're right."

"Oooh, I like—" Ruth didn't get a chance to finish her sentence as Jude decided nothing more needed to be said.

But if he had his way, a lot more needed to be done. And it all involved the woman in his arms and staying cozy for the rest of the evening.

CHAPTER 27

Ruth leaned down to smell the pot of hot chocolate, sighing as the sweet, chocolatey goodness entered her lungs.

"Make sure the milk doesn't scald," Grandma Nan called out from the family room. She was putting last minute touches on the tree, which always cracked Ruth up. Grandma never seemed happy to leave it. She was always tweaking the ornaments.

"I am," Ruth called out. "It's not my first rodeo, you know." She grinned when Grandma Nan grunted. Charli was right. Grandma was a lot more like Mr. Portman than she wanted to admit.

Grandma entered the kitchen and made a shooing motion. "He's here. Better get going."

Ruth frowned. "I haven't heard anything." The doorbell rang. She gave Grandma a look. "Spying out the front window again?"

Grandma's eyes rounded in an innocent look. "I don't know what you're talking about."

Ruth laughed. "You're worse than a kid watching for Santa Claus."

Grandma scowled as the doorbell rang again. "Better not keep him waiting."

Ruth wiped her hands on a towel. "I'm on it." Her heart beat a little faster the closer she got to the door. Why was greeting a significant other on a holiday so much more stressful than any other day? She gripped the doorknob, took a deep breath, and opened the door.

"Hello, beautiful," Jude said with a smile. His neck was tucked into his peacoat and white flakes of snow had landed in his hair and his dark scarf.

Ruth loved the contrast of his lighter hair and the dark blue scarf. It helped his eyes pop and she found herself mesmerized by it. How in the world had this gorgeous man decided she was the one he wanted to spend his time with? She felt positively dumpy next to him. "Hello," she said, her hand raising immediately to her head, but it paused at the feel of her beanie. She had chosen not to go bare today. It was Christmas and her loved ones deserved more than her weird, fuzzy bits of hair.

Jude chuckled and shifted his weight. "Think I could be invited in?"

"Oh my gosh." Ruth groaned, stepping back. "I'm so sorry. I was so caught off guard by your handsome face, I forgot you were probably freezing."

Jude snorted a laugh as he stepped inside. He paused as she closed the door and leaned in for a sweet kiss. "You're sure good for a guy's ego."

"And you're good for mine," Ruth said breathlessly. Oh, how she loved Jude's kisses. She would never get enough. The time she had gone without them had been torture and she secretly hoped she would never have to go without them again. Jude was still smiling when Ruth felt a tug on her head. She reached up just as her hat was pulled off. "Hey!"

Jude held the hat above her head, making Ruth jump for it. "Don't hide from me," he said, giving her a quick peck and throwing the hat across the room. "You're perfect the way you are."

"I didn't know we were serving cheese this morning," Grandma Nan called out from farther into the house.

Jude chuckled and Ruth shook her head. "Thank you," she said, her heart nearly bursting from her chest in joy and love.

Jude took her hand and led her away from the door. "Always," he stated firmly.

When they got into the family room, Grandma Nan was snif-fling. She waved a hand through the air. "I can't believe I'm out of tissues," she grumbled, stalking to the hallway. "Might as well never buy it again if it's not here when I need it."

Jude shook his head. "She's a character."

"Good thing we love her," Ruth said wryly.

Jude pulled her closer. "Good thing I love you," he said against her temple.

Ruth had died and gone to heaven. She was sure of it. There was absolutely nothing on this Earth that could be so sweet and so won-derful as Jude and his charming words. It was all so surreal. Snow on the ground, Christmas carols playing softly in the background, the tree lighting up the room, and Jude, holding her tight.

No daydream could have even come close.

"Are we eating or what?" Grandma Nan asked as she walked back out from the bathroom and headed to the kitchen.

"Yes, please," Ruth answered. "I'm starved."

"So...was that an effect of the chemo or something?" Jude whis-pered as they went to the dining nook. "You've mentioned before how much you eat now."

Ruth shook her head. "Nope. It was a result of not being able to eat while I was on chemo. I lost a ton of weight and now that I have my taste buds back, I kinda end up eating everything in sight," she said sheepishly.

"Who wouldn't?" he responded before pulling out her chair.

"Thanks," Ruth said as she slipped into her seat. She looked around the table and sighed in contentment. The table was full of all her favorites. Hot chocolate, waffles, bacon, homemade syrup, whipped cream, and hashbrowns. It was way more than three people could eat, but Ruth was going to give it a valiant try.

"Wow," Jude said, obviously having the same thoughts as Ruth. "I didn't realize I was being treated to a feast."

Grandma Nan huffed. "As if we would serve anything less."

Ruth rolled her eyes. "Grandma…"

Grandma Nan slapped her forehead. "Oh, yeah. I forgot I was supposed to be on my best behavior today." She winked at Jude. "Oops."

Ruth groaned and rested her head in her hands.

"Who's got the motel this morning?" Jude asked.

"A couple of the teenagers who were around while I was in Seattle have asked for holiday hours," Ruth stated, piling her plate high. "Which has worked out well, so that I can have time off once in a while and we don't have to rearrange things too much to get Grandma to her quilting circle meetings."

"Why do I get the feeling that your quilting groups are about much more than quilting?" Jude asked.

Grandma Nan put a finger to her lips. "Shhh…don't give us away."

"Gossip fest is more like it," Ruth said under her breath.

Grandma Nan scowled. "And on that rude behavior, why don't we say grace?"

Ruth felt a blush creep up her cheeks as Jude laughed, but she couldn't fault her grandma. Ruth probably deserved the dig.

After blessing the food, they dug in and all too soon, Ruth leaned back, her hand on her stomach. "Oh my gosh…I'm going to have to be rolled to the family room."

"If I wasn't so full myself, I'd just carry you," Jude said, his head hanging back over his seat.

"Noobs," Grandma Nan said, rising easily from her seat. "By the time you get to be my age, you know exactly how to fill the tank and keep on moving."

Ruth raised her eyebrow. "You ate half of what I did."

"Then perhaps it should be a lesson in self restraint." Grandma grinned, then began to laugh when Ruth stuck her tongue out.

"Come on," Grandma urged. "If you're going to act like a kid, we might as well do it over presents instead of breakfast."

Ruth's heart skipped a beat. For the first time ever, she was going to be giving a boyfriend a Christmas present and she was slightly terrified. She'd gone out on a limb with what she'd chosen, and she was desperate for him to approve.

Jude held out his hand. "Come on," he urged. "I'll help you."

Ruth slipped her hand into his. The warmth of his hold was enough to help calm the anxiety racing through her system. She'd gotten him a gift from her heart and from the way he was looking at her right now, she decided everything would be just fine.

JUDE'S HANDS WERE SLIGHTLY clammy as he joined Ruth on the couch. Late last night, he had finally had an epiphany about what to get Ruth for Christmas, but it was unusual, and he was worried about her reaction.

"Here, Grandma," Ruth said, grabbing a large box from under the tree. "You first."

Grandma Nan took the box with a glare. "I thought we weren't getting each other presents this year."

Ruth grinned unrepentantly, making Jude smile with her. "I don't remember such a promise."

Grandma huffed, but it was easy to see she was eager to open it.

Jude wanted to laugh as the elderly woman tore into the gift as if it were her last act on earth. Eagerness for gifts apparently doesn't die with age.

But when Grandma froze, her eyes wide as she gazed at the inside of the box, Jude became curious. He looked at Ruth, who was waiting patiently for her grandmother to respond.

"Ruth," Grandma Nan said softly. She reached inside the box and pulled out a quilt.

Jude frowned and tilted his head as he tried to figure out the pattern on it. The fabric didn't seem to match and there was no rhyme or reason to the colors or shapes. He was no quilting expert, but something was just a little...off.

Grandma waved her hand in front of her face, but nothing stopped the tears from flowing.

Since nobody offered to let him in on the explanation, he took matters into his own hands. "Tell me about it," he asked, hoping he didn't offend anyone.

Ruth laughed. "It probably looks pretty horrible to you," she said, reading his mind. "But I promise I've learned how to make a proper quilt." She looked over at him. "When I was going through treatments, I was constantly cold. The misty air and overcast skies in Seattle never gave me a chance to warm up."

Jude nodded, completely understanding. He felt the same way about Seaside Bay.

"So, Grandma would send me socks. Funny socks, weird socks, strange socks...you get the idea." Ruth looked back at her relative. "I became known for them in the cancer ward and other patients used to come to my room every Thursday when the mail was delivered to see what my new socks were."

"That quilt is from your socks?" Jude asked, his jaw falling slack.

Ruth nodded. "They were the best hug Grandma could give me at the time and now I'm giving them back."

Grandma Nan stood up and shuffled over to kiss Ruth on the cheek. "I think it's time I went to take a nap," she said thickly. Stepping over slightly, she also left a kiss on Jude's forehead. "Make the most of it."

Jude watched her go, pulling Ruth back into his chest. He kissed the top of her head, smiling slightly at the sharp feeling of her short hair against his lips. "You're a saint."

Ruth shook her head. "No. I just have nothing to my name, so I gave her something sentimental instead."

"Which is exactly what she wanted."

Ruth laughed. "She'd never admit that."

"Of course not." Jude squeezed her just a touch. "Are you ready for my gift?" His heart sped back up at the thought, partly in anticipation and partly in anxiety.

Ruth jerked forward and spun around. "I thought you said you didn't get me anything?"

Jude shrugged, trying to pretend he wasn't worried. "Doesn't mean I was going to leave it that way."

She smiled. "Who did you convince to stay open extra late last night?"

Jude gave her a mock scowl. "Give me a little more credit than that."

Ruth held up her hands. "Sorry." She rose from the couch. "But since I'm already distributing my gifts, I want to give you mine first."

Jude rubbed his hands on his jeans again. What would Ruth give him? She didn't have much, which she'd already admitted to. He didn't like the thought of her spending money on him that she didn't have. "Ruth," he began, but she put up her hand.

Sitting back down, Ruth leaned in to give him a peck. "I wanted to do this," she whispered. "Please don't be mad."

Frowning, Jude took the envelope. It was one of those large yellow ones that held documents and he hefted it. "Did you buy me a house?" he teased.

Ruth just smiled and bit her bottom lip.

Jude removed his arm from the back of the couch, so he could work two-handed and pinched back the tiny metal prongs. Inside, he found what appeared to be a calendar, plus another envelope. This one was smaller, like for a letter.

Setting the calendar in his lap, he opened the envelope, then jerked his head up to Ruth. "Plane tickets?"

Ruth nodded. She took the calendar and opened it, pointing out different weekends that she had highlighted in blue. "I bought tickets for you to see me and for me to come see you." She then showed him a weekend colored in pink. Her cheeks began to turn pink. "I know it was kind of presumptuous of me to assume we'd be together that long, but...I certainly hope we are."

Jude shook his head, looking at the half dozen tickets she had purchased. "Ruth...I love it, but how in the world did you afford all this?"

She made a face.

"I know," Jude said quickly. "I shouldn't ask that, but we'll find a way to make it work without going into debt."

Ruth smiled and ran her fingers over his slight scruff. "I promise, I didn't go into debt."

His brows furrowed.

Ruth blew out a breath. "If it makes you feel any better, I used the last of my inheritance from my parents."

"The last of it?" He choked. "It's gone?"

Ruth looked skyward and shook her head before pinning him with a glare. "Jude Lisbon. I love you. We live hours away from each other and I've already learned the hard way that I *hate* being away from you. The best thing I could think of for Christmas was for us to find a way to keep seeing each other in person." She grabbed the calendar. "But if you don't want it..."

Jude grabbed it back and held it away from her. "Nuh-uh. No take backs." Ruth folded her arms over her chest and Jude chuckled. He kissed her nose. "I'm sorry. I shouldn't have said anything. You being available for me to hold..." He dropped the calendar into his lap and wrapped his arms around her. "To hug..." He pulled her into his chest. "And especially to kiss..." He dropped a lingering kiss on her soft lips. "Is the best Christmas gift I can ever think of." The kiss was a little more intense this time, yet Jude still wasn't ready to pull back. "Thank you."

"You're welcome," she whispered, burying her face in his neck. "I don't think we need the fireplace going," she muttered.

Jude smiled, his masculine pride overly proud at being able to have such an effect on her. "Are you going to open mine now?"

Ruth bounced back and clasped her hands. "Yes!"

He shook his head. The eagerness obviously ran in the family. Shifting so that he could reach into his back pocket, Jude pulled out a card.

Ruth's smile grew. "Awesome that we both went the envelope route."

"Just shows that we're perfect for each other," Jude quipped, enjoying the blush that spread across her face.

Ruth opened the envelope and then the card, taking the time to read it. A moment later, she gasped and put her hand over her mouth, her eyes immediately filling with tears. "Jude...I..." She shook her head, looking up at him. Her blue eyes looked like gems in the Christmas lights and Jude couldn't look away.

"Was it okay?" he asked, his earlier concern mostly gone at her emotional response. "I mean, I know it's not something technically for you, but I thought maybe it would mean something to you."

"Let me get this straight," she said softly. "You donated, in my name, to a charity that provides wigs for cancer patients?" Her breathing was speeding up. "To this girl?" She held up a picture. "This *actual* girl?"

A baldheaded, little girl grinned up at Jude from the picture as he rubbed the back of his neck. "Yeah, but it's a little more than that." He cleared his throat. "This is Tonya." He took the picture and turned it around for Ruth to look at. "She's eight and battling leukemia. Her biggest wish is to be Rapunzel, which is why she was chosen for a wig."

Ruth shook her head, the tears spilling over.

"But we aren't just providing her with a single wig. We're sponsoring her for as long as it takes. Each child gets a new wig every two years or whatever works best for their schedule, until they don't need them anymore or they reach the age of twenty-one."

Ruth continued to not speak and shake her head. Finally, when Jude was worried she actually hated the gift, she let out a loud cry and leapt at him, knocking him backward into the couch.

"You. Are. The. Most. Amazing. Man. I. Have. Ever. Met!" she said, between leaving kisses all over his face.

Jude settled back, letting himself revel in her attentions. He wrapped his arms around her back. "I take it you like it?"

"I love it," she cried. Pausing finally, Ruth looked down at him. "I love *you*."

"And I love you," Jude responded. Cupping the back of her head, he slowly pulled her down, enjoying every bit of anticipation as the distance between them gradually closed.

As he tried to show her with his mouth just how much she meant to him, Jude found his mind shooting forward to something much longer than Ruth's plane tickets, and even longer than sponsoring a cancer patient for the next few years.

This woman had his whole heart and every bit of his soul. Someday soon, when the time was right, he knew that he would make her his for a lifetime. Who would have ever thought that Elania leaving him would have led to Jude to finding the best gift he had ever received.

A beautiful, bald, cancer survivor whose gift for loving others would heal him body and soul. Even with yesterday's heartache, Jude knew, without a doubt, that no other Christmas would ever compare to this one.

CHAPTER 28

"Ruth?"

"Hmm?" She didn't bother to look at her grandmother as she poked her head in the break room door. She was right in the middle of a school assignment as she worked toward a degree in Nonprofit Management. Ruth had decided shortly after Christmas, being inspired by Jude's gift, that she wanted to spend her life trying to help others, and what better way than to help keep charities running smoothly?

That decision had led to Ruth being neck deep in classes, but she was loving every busy minute of it. With the ability to do it all online, she was still able to stay with Grandma and visit Jude on the weekends. It was more than she could have ever dreamed.

"Ruth," Grandma said in exasperation.

Ruth set down her pen and turned to the door. "What?"

"Come out here." Grandma Nan waved. "There's something you need to see."

Ruth frowned. "Okay..." She pushed herself away from the table and began to walk out. "What's going on..." She trailed off as she noticed a little girl waiting in the lobby. Ruth's hand went to her hair, her nervous tick still sticking around despite not wearing a wig anymore. She had gotten her first haircut only a week before and the stylist had done a wonderful job shaping the mass of hair that was working its way in. Shorter on the sides, longer on top, it left Ruth free to do fun spikes, or curls, or just let it swing to the side. It had been a celebratory milestone, but it would more than likely take a while for her to stop worrying about what it looked like to others.

"Hello," Ruth said with a smile. She narrowed her gaze. Something was familiar about...Ruth gasped. "Tonya!" Ruth finally recognized the little girl as the one she and Jude were sponsoring for a wig. And it was a beautiful wig. The long, blonde hair came below the girl's shoulder and truly helped her look like her favorite princess.

The little girl smiled, showing off a smile that was missing a couple of teeth. "Hi, Ruth!"

Ruth's heart was in her throat. "H-how in the world did you get here?" Ruth looked around. "And where's your mother, or father?"

Tonya's smile grew. She pulled a hand from behind her back and held out a card. "This is for you."

Ruth walked forward and took the card. She dropped to her knees. "How do you know who I am?" she asked.

Tonya laughed. "I know everything." She pumped her eyebrows.

Ruth laughed with her. "Of course! What was I thinking?" She looked at the card, then came back to Tonya. "Do you live around here?"

Tonya clasped her hands behind her back and shook her head.

Ruth looked back at Grandma. "What's going on?"

Grandma Nan rolled her eyes. "Why don't you open the card and find out?"

"Okay, okay," Ruth muttered. She put her attention back on the card and finally began to tear at the envelope. She glanced sideways and smiled at Tonya. "Do you know what this is?" She was beginning to assume it was a thank you note, but how sweet was it that Tonya had come to deliver it in person? Ruth had no idea where the young girl lived, but it was a special treat to have her here. Now if she could just figure out where Tonya's parents were. It seemed odd that they weren't around.

Ruth pulled the card out of the envelope and opened it. Inside the card was a piece of paper. In fact, it was a small calendar, but only for the month of August. One day in August was highlighted and

Ruth read the words, then fell from her knees to her backside, bare-ly noticing the sting on her tailbone. She looked over at Tonya. "Is this..." Her eyes went to the door where Jude was striding inside.

He came straight over and knelt down next to Tonya. Pulling out a velvet box, he opened it, showing off a brilliant diamond soli-taire. "Ruth Lindsay Allen," he said with a smile. "I have a question for you."

Ruth dropped the card and her hands went to cover her mouth. She could barely breathe, but she couldn't look away.

"You snuck into my life at a time when I thought I would never be happy again," he said with a rueful smile. "And not only did you help me find that happiness again, you helped me find myself. But now that I've found myself, I've discovered that I don't enjoy my own company nearly as much as I enjoy yours."

A bubble of laughter broke through Ruth's lips. Jude wasn't due to come visit for several more days. She was so utterly and completely caught off guard, but it would be a bold-faced lie if Ruth said she hadn't been dreaming about this exact moment for months.

"And I happen to know that I'm not the only one who feels that way," Jude said, his smile widening. "Every person who crosses your path adores you. They can't help it. You're kind and giving, and you never fail to leave us all with smiles on our faces." He glanced at Tonya. "And I know that Tonya will feel the exact same way, which is why my proposal comes with a caveat."

Ruth's head tilted and her smile fell just a little. This, she had not expected.

"I'm asking you to be my wife," Jude said. "But...I'm asking you to marry me on August twenty-eighth."

Jude was looking at her expectantly and Ruth was holding herself back from tackling him in joy, but she had to ask, "Why August twenty-eighth?"

Jude turned to Tonya.

"Because that's the weekend after I finish chemotherapy," she said in her young, high pitched voice.

"Which makes her available to be our flower girl," Jude clarified.

It was too much. Ruth buried her face in her hands and bawled. She felt Jude gather her into his arms on the floor and Ruth melted into his hold.

"Will you marry me, Ruth?" he whispered against her ear. "Please?"

Laughing through her tears, Ruth pulled her head up and turned so she could wrap her arms around his neck. "It would be the most amazing thing ever to be your wife," she said. "But there's only one problem."

Jude's smile fell. "What?"

Ruth put a hand in her hair. "I always wanted to look like Rapunzel when I got married." She turned to Tonya. "Would you mind playing that role for me instead? It looks like my hair will be a little more like Rapunzel *after* her haircut."

Tonya giggled and nodded. Now that Ruth was closer, she could see the shadows under the girl's eyes and the extra pale skin. It was a look Ruth knew well, and for the first time, she finally understood why Jude had still thought her beautiful. Tonya was the prettiest thing Ruth had ever seen. And having her as a flower girl would be a cherry on the top of the world's best sundae.

She turned back to Jude. "I suppose that settles it," she said, leaning in until they were resting their foreheads against each other. Oh, how she wanted to kiss him until she couldn't breathe. Unfortunately, they had too big of an audience at the moment, but later...Ruth was going to do everything she could to make him understand just how much she loved him. "On August twenty-eighth, I'll become Mrs. Ruth Lisbon."

Jude gave her a soft, lingering kiss, pulling back before it grew too heated. "It sounds perfect." He leaned back just enough to pull the ring out of the box and put it on her finger.

Ruth held it out and watched it sparkle. "I think this is my favorite gift ever," she whispered.

He kissed her cheek. "You're my favorite gift ever."

"I'm on a cheese diet," Grandma Nan said from behind the desk. "Come on, Tonya. Your mama's waiting in the back." She held out her hand and waited until Tonya had skipped over to take it. "Let's go find her." Grandma Nan glared at Ruth and Jude. "Don't you dare scare off my guests, you hear? If I'm paying for a wedding, I need as many of them as I can get."

Ruth just shook her head while Jude chuckled.

"No promises," Jude hollered just as the other two disappeared through the break room door. His eyes came back to Ruth once the door closed. "I warned her," he said with a shrug. He resettled his arms around her. "Now...where were we?"

Ruth tapped his lips. "You were taking my breath away."

"Oh? Was that all?" Jude gave her several soft kisses. "Well, let me finish the job..."

EPILOGUE

Aspen Harrison wiped her brow with the back of her hand. Her hand was shaking, and she clenched it into a fist. "Okay," she breathed, observing the wedding cake and dessert set up. "I think that does it."

Estelle, her older sister, wrapped an arm around Aspen's shoulders. "You're amazing," she cooed. "Mom and Dad are going to be so proud." Letting go of Aspen, Estelle pulled her phone out of her back pocket. "In fact, I need to get a bunch of pictures so we can show them." She began to click away, then paused and looked back to Aspen. "And also so we can put them up for the new owner of the Harrison Bakery."

"You mean The Three Sisters Cafe," Aspen corrected. As happened every time that she said the new name of the business she and her sisters were inheriting from their parents, Aspen's mouth moved into a wide smile, only to fall a second later.

Her parents, Antony and Emory Harrison, had been running a bakery in Seagull Cove, Oregon for almost thirty years. In fact, it was on the thirtieth anniversary of the shop that they were planning to hand the reins over to Aspen, Estelle, and their younger sister, Maeve. The only child not involved was their brother who was currently away on a military tour.

It was a bittersweet moment, and came with an extreme amount of pressure. Their father, Antony, hadn't been ready to retire just yet, but his diagnosis with Parkinson's disease had brought his career to a screeching halt. Aspen had always hoped to inherit the bakery, but not under these circumstances. She wanted to make her father proud, to prove she had the chops to follow in his footsteps, but she hated that her inheritance was one of necessity, rather than a show of trust. And none of those feelings addressed the despair the entire Harrison clan was struggling with at their father's diagnosis. Aspen couldn't even imagine what her mother was going through.

She took a deep breath. She couldn't change anything. She couldn't stop her father's shaking. She couldn't cure him. She also couldn't stand by and watch his beloved shop disappear, not after everything he and Aspen's mother had accomplished. No...the best thing Aspen could do was carry on his tradition, but she would do it her way.

The sisters had decided that in order to truly get a fresh start out from under the shadow of their parents, they wanted to rename and revamp the whole shop. It would still be a bakery, but they wanted it to be just a little bit more.

Maeve, who was an accountant, would be running the books. Estelle, who had majored in marketing, would run the front and work on building the business from the advertising side while Aspen, who had followed in her parents' footsteps and gone to culinary school, would be baking and creating the masterpieces in the back.

And it all started with the wedding cake display in front of them right now.

Aspen knew she had more than likely gotten the gig for Jude and Ruth Lisbon's wedding because she had underbid every other cake decorator, but right now she needed to build her catalog if she was ever going to really show her parents that she could carry on the family tradition of excellence.

It was intimidating to be the daughter of two acclaimed bakers. They had chosen to stay in small town Oregon in order to raise their family, but their names and creations were well known throughout the world, thanks to the magic of social media.

Their father's chocolate creations were internationally award-winning and it was an honor to be his daughter.

But more than anything, Aspen wanted to be known for herself, not for her lineage. Taking over the cafe was her chance to do that, even if it had come under sad circumstances. Her parents had taken off to tour Europe and visit family, in order to enjoy what time they had together, leaving their girls to either sink or swim.

Swim, she assured herself. "We're definitely going to swim."

"Who's swimming?" Maeve asked, coming up to Aspen's side. She tucked a curl behind her ear and studied the display. "It's perfect." She smiled at Aspen. "You're a miracle worker."

Aspen turned and hugged Maeve tightly, ignoring her less exuberant sister's complaints. "We're going to do this!" she cried.

"I'm sure we will," Maeve said primly, backing up from any further touching. "But we're not going to do it by assaulting each other in full view of our customers."

Aspen laughed and bounced on her toes. "I can feel it," she whispered. "This is just the beginning." She pushed her sadness over her dad away. She wouldn't dwell on the negative or it would show in her baking. Her concern right now was to prove herself and make her dad proud.

Estelle came back their way. "This is a great start," she agreed. "But I have something even better lined up."

Aspen frowned. "What're you talking about?"

Estelle looked around to make sure they were alone before leaning in and dropping her voice. "Who can make or break a restaurant just by posting a picture online?"

Maeve groaned. "Who cares?"

Aspen's eyes grew wide. "Oh my gosh, you're talking about Eat It Austin, aren't you?"

Estelle nodded, a small smirk on her face. "And guess who managed to get ahold of his boss and finagle an actual review?"

"You didn't," Aspen said flatly.

Estelle pumped her eyebrows. "I did."

"Estelle! He could ruin us!" Aspen scolded.

"Or…" Estelle said firmly, giving Aspen a look. "He could send us racing right out of the gate."

Maeve shook her head. "That guy seems like a jerk."

"That guy is the biggest food critic in the US," Estelle pointed out. "And he's based out of Portland. With his endorsement, we're a sure thing."

Aspen felt as if she might faint. She could barely breathe and her vision was dimming.

"Aspen!" Estelle gave her sister a shake. "Breathe!"

Aspen sucked in a breath, her mind clearing and quickly working through everything Estelle had just revealed. "He's going to have to like my stuff before he'd give us an endorsement," she said hoarsely.

Maeve sighed and made a face. "If that's all, then I don't see what you're freaking out about. No one can eat your desserts without raving that heaven fell onto their plate."

Aspen shook her head. "That won't be enough. He's tough."

Estelle put her hand on Aspen's shoulders. "And so are you." She tilted her chin and gave Aspen a motherly look. How did older sisters always manage to pull that off so well? "You're the best baker I know. It's time everyone knew it." She winked. "Just don't tell Dad and Mom I said that."

"You're just trying to make me feel better," Aspen said, shaking her head. She had never been so terrified in her life. Eat It Austin was the creme de la creme of food critics. He was young, handsome, and knew how to pose for a camera, which meant his female followers gobbled up everything he said as if it were pure gold. But he was also manly, well educated, and knew how to throw down an insult if something didn't live up to his expectations, making men enjoy a good laugh while following him as well.

"OH MY GOSH!"

All three sisters spun to see Ruth, the bride rushing into the banquet room. She put her hands over her mouth, her short hair standing up in darling spikes on top of her head. Not many people could pull off such a bold look, but Ruth did it with unexpected elegance.

Ruth turned from the table and stared straight at Aspen. "It's perfect," she breathed. With her hair and makeup done, the woman was beautiful, but she had yet to change into her wedding dress, and the button-up shirt paired with athletic pants was an interesting look.

Before Aspen could absorb the compliment, Ruth spun and grabbed one of the cheesecake bites from a tray, downing it in one bite.

"Oh my gosh," Ruth said again, this time with her mouth full. She closed her eyes as if in bliss and didn't open them for a few moments. When she finally looked at Aspen again, Ruth was smiling wide enough to give the Columbia River a run for its money.

Ruth walked over and took Aspen's hands. "Thank you so much," she gushed. "For making my reception perfect. I'll be recommending your bakery until the day I die. My guests are going to be so happy! And the cake is everything I asked for."

Aspen couldn't help the smile that tugged at her lips. Ruth was a little on the dramatic side, but it was easy to see she was completely sincere.

Estelle elbowed Aspen's side and gave her an *I told you so* look.

"Thank you," Aspen said to Ruth. "It was such an honor to be a part of this." She squeezed Ruth's hands. "You have an open table at our cafe any time."

Because they *would* have a cafe. This was exactly what Aspen lived for. Making people happy with food. Food critic or not, sick father notwithstanding, Aspen was determined to succeed. She didn't come from a family of quitters. She came from a family of achievers, and now it was her turn.

Eat it Austin could come take a bite of anything he wanted. Aspen knew what she was doing and she wouldn't let his fame intimidate her.

The Three Sisters Cafe was going to officially open for business in two months, and when it did, it would dazzle even the toughest of critics.

Keep Reading Aspen's Journey to Love in
"The Sweetest Words"

NEWSLETTER

You can get a FREE book by joining my Reading Family!
Every week we share stories, sales and good old fashioned fun.
Join us at lauraannbooks.com

www.ingramcontent.com/pod-product-compliance
Lightning Source LLC
Chambersburg PA
CBHW071755190726
48292CB00003B/989